Sherr'
Th
...
Fudg... ...
paths ... with ...
Helen
x

ARIANA

EMMA NICHOLS

Britain's Next
BESTSELLER

First published in 2018 by:

Britain's Next Bestseller
An imprint of Live It Publishing
27 Old Gloucester Road
London, United Kingdom.
WC1N 3AX

www.bnbsbooks.co.uk

Lyrics from 'Time After Time' © 1984 Cyndi Lauper

Also available in paperback - ISBN: 9781983251061

Other books by Emma Nichols

To keep in touch with the latest news from Emma Nichols
and her writing please visit:

www.emmanicholsauthor.com
www.facebook.com/EmmaNicholsAuthor
www.twitter.com/ENichols_Author

Thanks

Without the assistance, advice and support and love of the following people, this book would not have been possible.

Bev the Copper - thank you for the burnt salt,
and so much more.

Valden - thank you for your comments, as always.
I'm glad you loved this one so much.

Mu - for your on-going patience and support, thank you.

To my wonderful readers, thank you for continuing to support my endeavours. You are always in my mind when I write and I can only hope that you love reading this sunny summer romance as much as I did writing it.

With love, Emma x

Dedication

To the healing power of love.

1.

Chrissy leaned against the wooden door frame of the semi-open workshop, squinting into the bright sun, her shades perched on her head, keeping her long, dark hair from falling into her eyes. 'The Sophia II's moored up, in the east-cove,' she said, casually.

Nikki barely flinched, but the increase in tension in her neck caused her hand to tighten around the wood-plane in her hand, the pressure taking a chunk out of the side of the boat. 'Damn it,' she cursed, under her breath, standing and rubbing fiercely at her bare forearm to remove the itchy shavings that clung to her skin.

Chrissy eyed her quizzically.

Nikki rubbed her index finger gingerly over the indentation she had created, sighed, and rested the plane gently against the boat, easing it over the damage to smooth out the surface. Her hands failed to deliver the light touch she needed, and she abandoned the plane to the workbench, disgusted with her sudden incompetence. 'Damn it,' she muttered again.

'They didn't say they were coming?' Chrissy asked, trying to pin Nikki's stressed response to the fact that she hadn't expected The Sophia's arrival.

Even though there was no designated port on the small Ionian island of Sakros, and boats moored up where their owners resided, it was still common courtesy to notify Nikki, the harbour master, of a visit.

Nikki stared into the space behind Chrissy, brushing absentmindedly at the tiny particles of wood-dust that had stuck to her hands. *Two years too late!* An image of old Sophia's cremation service darted into her awareness, the room filled to the rafters with mourning locals, and the distinct absence of Sophia's family. 'Want a beer?' Nikki asked softly, her tone holding more remorse than frustration.

'They should've told you,' Chrissy protested.

Nikki smiled graciously at the display of passion. 'It's okay,' she said. *When did the Carter-Cruz' ever announce their visits? That said; when did they last visit? Not once in the previous twenty years!* She walked through to the bar, pulled out two bottles of Volkan Grey and handed one over.

'Thanks,' Chrissy said, taking the beer and following Nikki through the covered bar to the beach at the front of the taverna, pulling her shades down to protect her eyes as she moved into the bright afternoon sunlight.

'The Sophia II's moored up,' Manos said, hurriedly passing them on his way into the bar, beads of sweat twinkling like stars on his forehead.

Nikki rolled her eyes. 'I heard,' she said.

Sitting on the large driftwood bench and leaning against the rock-face, staring out to sea, she sipped from the bottle. *She's back!* The thought churned her insides as her eyes settled on the large, white house on the hill that separated the east-from the west-cove. She took in a deep breath and sipped from the bottle. The cabin cruiser would be moored beyond the rocks separating the coves, and out of view. She could feel the tightness in her chest increasing; the injustice; the betrayal, and desertion, tangling in a knot. The Carter-Cruz' had undoubtedly played a big part in her life, at least Teresa had, and for the most part leaving an unpleasant taste that had lingered.

Chrissy assessed her boss closely. She seemed distant and distracted. 'You okay?' she asked with genuine concern.

'Yeah,' Nikki responded in a timbre that lacked conviction. She turned her attention to the calm, clear-blue water that darkened at the point on the horizon where it joined the lighter-blue skyline, the soft swish of the waves lapping at the shore, competing with the chirping of crickets, the near-deafening cicadas and the occasional clattering sound from the kitchen. Her eyes scanned the west-cove in front of her, and further west, where the Kefalas ferry sat, moored to the jetty, and the leisure boats beyond, idling on the beach.

She glanced over her shoulder at the bar, the taverna, and the workshop to the rear, next to her apartment. This place was the only home she had known, and she had been happy. She pondered. Was she happy? She toyed with the necklace that tracked the line of her collarbone, her thumb and forefinger delicately caressing the rainbow-patterned shell at its centre-point. *Ariana had been a lifetime ago.*

Chrissy stood and meandered back to the bar. In the three years she had worked with Nikki and Manos, it was the first time she had seen her like this. She seemed uncharacteristically pensive, agitated even. Something was bothering her about the arrival of the Sophia, but it was abundantly clear that it wasn't anything she wanted to discuss.

'She okay?' Manos asked as Chrissy approached, his keen eyes monitoring Nikki from a distance. The wrinkles on his forehead and something in his whispered tone said that he expected Nikki to react badly to the news. His hands were livelier than his normal relaxed pace of working; he was worried.

Nikki leaned her head against the rock, presented her face to the warm sun and closed her eyes, hoping to release the tension that seemed to have overtaken her normal functioning, and sighed. The comforting heat failed to penetrate her awareness, her mind instantly consumed by the movie of her last moments with Ariana, just before Teresa took her daughter off the island; the image just as clear as it had been back then, the hurt as excruciatingly painful.

'Please don't go. I can't bear it if you leave. I love you!' she pleaded, shaking Ariana by the arms, trying to hold her faltering gaze. Ariana tensed, shifted her eyes, and wouldn't look at her.

'They're making me go,' Ariana whispered, eventually.

It was then she noticed that the whites of Ariana's dark-brown eyes were red and her face was puffy. She had been crying. She did care.

'Please, stay with Sophia,' she begged, naively.

'I can't,' Ariana responded, weakly.

At that moment, she realised Ariana was going to leave the island. For all the dreams they had shared and their plans of being together, it would never happen. It could never happen. 'You have a choice,' she spat angrily, regretting the words immediately.

'I don't!' Ariana retorted sharply.

She had never felt another's rage before, not as she did then. Ariana's glare had the quality of marble-stone, her body of steel, and she pulled out of the hold with urgency. The sense of finality that passed between them at that moment rendered her immobile. She stood, speechless, just watching the back of the ash-blonde head until her eyes couldn't focus through the tears.

Nikki shuddered, her eyes opened, and she bolted upright, her fingers instantly reaching to suppress the pressure at the back of her eyes.

Manos approached, sipping his beer. 'You okay?' he asked, his voice quiet, his face etched with concern.

Nikki jolted, swallowed, blinked, and, reorienting herself, dragged her thoughts into the present moment. 'Humm,' she replied. No, she wasn't okay, but she needed to be. She needed to get to grips with the fact that the Carter-Cruz' had returned.

He nodded, placed a steadying hand on her shoulder and stared out to sea. He had come to understand Nikki well over the years; in many respects, she was much like him. She had lived an isolated life as a young child and matured into an independent, confident woman. She didn't seek counsel very

4

often, preferring the privacy of her mind, and rarely got stressed about anything. He turned to her, studied her. She would talk eventually but in her own time.

Nikki stared up at the man who had been the nearest thing to a father to her since her parents had died and tried to smile. His gaze was kind, warm, understanding, and his love soothed her, as it had done the time he had explained to her that her mum and dad were in heaven. She had been four years old and cried for a while, and he had cried with her. He wore the pain of her life as well as his own, in the fissures that wrinkled his stubbly beard, but his dark-brown eyes still sparkled with the excitement of a child. He had always had the power to draw her out of her moods back then, to help her to see the good in life in spite of the bad things that happened. He had been there the day Ariana deserted her, and every day since. He had been her family now for thirty-two years.

'What do you think?' she asked, hoping her voice hadn't betrayed her uneasiness.

'The Sophia II,' he said, rhetorically. 'I don't know. Hasn't been around these shores since...' He paused trying to recall the time lapsed.

'Twenty years,' she answered, her voice thick with tension.

'Aye,' he said, scratching at his stubbly chin and chewing on the toothpick dancing between his teeth. 'Two years since old Sophia passed on,' he added ruefully through a sigh. 'Thought they would've shown up before now,' he continued, a whistling sound accompanying another intake of breath through his clamped teeth.

'Two years and two months,' Nikki corrected him. She picked at the loose corner of the label on the bottle in her hand, sipped, winced at the now warm liquid, and placed the beer on the sand at her feet. She cracked her knuckles and rubbed her hands up and down her thighs anxiously. She released a long breath, leaned her head back against the firm rock and closed her eyes again, trying to release the pressure in her head and the tightness in her chest; hoping to appear nonchalant, and failing. Anger bubbled at the surface, tormenting her, and her hands closed into a tight ball. The white blotches appearing across her knuckles, contrasting with her tanned skin, she screamed silently.

'Curious, eh!' he said, interrupting her thoughts.

'No,' she said, more abruptly than she intended, her eyelids flickering but remaining closed, her stomach reacting to the lie slipping effortlessly from her lips.

'Aye!' Manos responded knowingly. 'We'll find out soon enough,' he said, turning and heading back towards the bar.

'Hmm,' Nikki responded, her tone marginally softer.

He stopped after a couple of paces. 'You never know,' he added; three words that only Nikki would understand.

'That ship sailed a long time ago Pops,' she said, her eyes remaining closed, fighting the rage building inside her chest again.

His beard twitched, and he tilted his head to the side, but she couldn't see him. 'Hmmm!' he mumbled to himself.

Nikki forced her eyes to open and squinted towards the hilly boundary of the cove, the rocky outcrop below joining the cliff to the sea and linking the beaches. Reminded of times she and Ariana had spent playing on the rocks as children; a warm feeling diffused the anger slightly. She smiled at the memory of the two of them scrambling between the coves to escape the wrath of Ariana's mother. It had been their safe territory, directly below the white house and out of sight, and maybe for the same reason, it was still her favourite place to fish. Her eyes tracked the cliff face to the top, the grassy verge leading back to the rose garden and the obscured south facing aspect of the side of the house.

The large, white house had once been highly regarded by locals. Constructed over three levels, and Sophia had insisted on using local materials, to blend into the natural terrain. Sophia had painted the Mediterranean-blue shuttered windows and white walls herself over the years, and her husband had laid the original terracotta-tiled roof more than half a century ago.

Nikki had seen the breath-taking views over both coves, from the dual-aspect master bedroom on the top level. She had also sat on the kitchen-balcony, overlooking the west-cove and the taverna on many occasions, drinking wine, and occasionally ouzo, chatting with Manos and Sophia after harvesting the olives. Sophia had been like family to her then, too. She wiped at her damp eyes.

Sophia had spent many an evening in the taverna talking through her plans for the development of the estate over the years. Firstly, the expansion of the olive grove to include the production plant that would enable them to export some of the olive oil. And then, the citrus orchards, producing lemons, limes and oranges, and then eggs from the free-range chickens, and a range of vegetables to sell to local inhabitants, the Kefalas' bar, and *The Ionian* restaurant based on the northern side of the island. Now, the estate covered most of the southern half of Sakros and was a major employer, as well as supporting the small tourist trade that passed through during the holiday season. Nikki had learned a great deal about the successful development and management of a business, but more than that, she had realised the importance of enjoying life. Sophia had loved life, right up to the end, and even after two years and two months, Nikki still felt her absence.

She hadn't been inside the house since Sophia's death, but it was certainly looking weary and in need of tender loving care and a little renovation. *Perhaps that's why they're back?* She huffed at the cynical thought. Teresa Carter-Cruz held no love for either the estate or the island. But, thankfully, at least the house hadn't been left to her; it was Ariana's. But, that said, in the Carter-Cruz household that would mean very little. *Teresa's influence was bound to be alive and well! Teresa always had the upper hand.* Nikki huffed again at the caustic thoughts, her head shaking from side to side. Maybe Ariana had escaped her mother's clutches by now? She smiled a more hopeful smile. Wishful thinking!

She drew in a deep breath and released it slowly. Yes, she was curious... and, she was also frustrated, and the more she dredged up the past, and Teresa, the stronger that frustration was growing. 'Aarrgghh,' she moaned out loud. *Why now? Why not when Sophia needed you?* Nikki stood and paced onto the beach, glaring towards the white house, secretly hoping for a glimpse of Ariana, and feeling anxious as to how she might respond if she did catch sight of her.

She wandered down to the jetty and checked the ferry's mooring lines, for no other reason than to occupy herself. She couldn't see any movement at the house, and continuing to look was causing her to feel more anxious, so she stopped, stepped aboard the ferry and started sweeping the deck with more vigour than the relatively clean space warranted.

A shimmer of light caught her eye, the sun reflecting on a bedroom window, and her heart skipped a beat. Regaining her breath, she continued to watch, hoping, as she had hoped every day in the months after Ariana left, that she would be there, staring back at her, and smiling. Nothing.

'Ferry tomorrow.' Manos said approaching her with a half-smile.

'Aye,' she said, standing and jolting herself from her concerns. They ran the ferry to Ithaka every Friday. She forced a smile. He was trying to distract her, and she knew it. 'Come on Pops, I've got a boat to restore, and you've got a menu to prep for tonight,' she said.

8

Manos nodded. 'Kitchen's ready,' he said, as they sauntered up the beach.

She glanced at the powder-puff clouds forming over the western edge of the cove. 'Think I'll go fishing later,' she said, the thought bringing a warm glow to her tanned cheeks.

'What you don't catch, you buy,' he said, with a chuckle.

She laughed. She didn't care what she caught. Just being out there in the silence of the night was good enough, and it would give her time to get to grips with her confused thoughts. She increased her pace across the sand, with renewed determination, stepped through the bar and out the back, picked up the sanding tool and studied the old fishing boat with deep affection.

'Right little lady, what're we going to do with you?' she mumbled, her hand sweeping slowly across the peeling blue-paint on the vessel's bow. She sucked through her teeth and set the sander carefully down on the wood. The buzzing noise drawing her concentration, the dust floating away on the light warm-breeze, she worked diligently until she had revealed the bare wood beneath the flaking paint. Standing, assessing, her hands caressing the smooth surface, she rubbed her forearm across her face, sticky with sweat and dust, and smiled.

'Looks good,' Manos remarked, smiling warmly.

'Coming along,' she said, stretching and pressing her thumbs into her lower back. Boat restoration was as much a hobby as it was a part of their business, and she was in no rush to finish this particular project.

'Beer?' he asked.

She nodded, noting the sun was hiding behind the rocks. She'd lost track of time, and that was a good thing. Working on the boat had taken her away, revived her, refreshed her, and, rekindled old feelings; warm feelings that reminded her of the times she and Ariana had fished together as children. The raw anger that had surfaced earlier had already been chipped away, leaving an altogether different feeling.

'You eating?' Manos asked, handing her the cold bottle.

'I'll take something out with me.'

He nodded and handed her a paper bag. 'Thought you'd say that,' he said.

'I'm going to get a shower,' she said, taking a long slug of the chilled drink. 'Ahhh, that's good!' she remarked.

'The shopping list is behind the bar, in case I don't see you in the morning,' he added.

She smirked. 'You'll see me,' she said.

He had teased her for a long time now about not being around another day. He was only sixty-five and as fit as a fiddle, but it had become a habit and one which sometimes irritated her.

'I put your fishing gear out front,' he said.

She winked, leant in and placed a kiss on his stubbly cheek. 'Thanks Pops,' she said. 'You sure you can cope here?' she asked with a wry smile, scanning the five bench-tables that made up the restaurant, three of which were empty. It was still early though, and the place would soon be buzzing, and she would hear the laughter from the rocks, and she would know, Pops would be coping just fine without her.

'Away with you,' he admonished, moving to clip her around the ear. 'You're not too old for disciplining,' he teased.

She chuckled, ducked under his arm, leaned in and planted another kiss on his cheek. 'I'll be back after midnight,' she said, heading for the shower.

'Aye,' he said. He would be waiting.

2.

Ariana gazed out from The Sophia II's highly polished deck, at the empty, isolated beach. Her shoulders slumped, her face drawn, looking closer to gaunt, she closed her eyes and breathed in the salty-warm air. The last few months had taken every ounce of energy she possessed, but she had done it. Free at last, she could concentrate on providing a future for her daughter, for them both. She released a long breath and opened her eyes.

'This it?' Soph asked, scanning the small barren cove bounded by rocks and what appeared to be a series of sandy pathways, leading to where she didn't know.

'Yes,' Ariana replied, her voice weary, her tone tinged with something between concern and relief.

There was a noticeable absence of the refreshing breeze that had accompanied them on the cabin cruiser. 'It's hot,' Soph remarked, checking the deep-blue sky and rubbing at the beads of sweat clustering above her lip. 'I like it,' she added before her mum could comment.

She hadn't known about the island until recently, and even then it hadn't meant anything to her, having never met or heard anything about her great-grandmother. Sakros was suddenly looking like the best-kept secret in the Carter-Cruz household if ever there was, and there had been a few of those that had come out of the woodwork recently, she mused. Even though she had kicked against leaving London, and the trip to get here via Italy where they had picked up The Sophia II had been hideous, she wasn't averse to a holiday in the sun.

Scanning the isolated beach, tuning into the birdsong and the crickets chirping loudly, and the soft hush of the waves lapping the shore, she grinned. She gazed over at the rock face and the vast array of shrubs bordering the beach and gracing the steep pathways to the cliff-top, with the sweet-salty aroma drifting in the warm air. This place was awesome.

She stepped off the boat excitedly and wandered down the short jetty. Reaching the beach, she threw off her deck shoes and wiggled her toes in the soft, warm sand, stopping when she touched the cold bit beneath the surface. 'Cool,' she mumbled, with a chuckle. A couple of paces up the beach, she stopped suddenly, faced into the sun, and lay down.

Ariana sighed. Her features softened as she watched Soph settling herself on the beach and basking in the warm sea air. Heartened by Soph's obvious delight, going some way to containing the concerns that had given her so many sleepless nights, she started the short trek up the sandy slope to the white house.

She stopped just past halfway to gain her breath and perched on the familiar ledge, overlooking the cove and The Sophia II. The crew were busying themselves. She inhaled the heady scent of sage and smiled, fond memories of years past creating a soothing feeling she hadn't felt in as long as she could remember. Her eyes quickly absorbed the array of colours provided by the wildflowers: mauve geraniums, yellow chamomile, and the delicate star-shape of blue borage, and then there was the olive grove to her left with dark green leaves scattered across the southern tip of the island, row after row, stretching for what seemed like forever. Each plant would be laden with young developing fruit. Twenty years, and yet it was as if time had stood still. Nothing had changed. Except, of course, grandma Sophia was no longer here. She sighed at the thought, feasted on the beautiful landscape in front of her, and then Soph, still laid out on the sandy beach below.

Rising slowly to her feet, she continued up the dusty path, puffing as she reached the flatter, wider area at the top of the incline, leading directly to the house. She stood, settled her breathing again, wiped the sweat from her eyes, and gazed at the whitewashed walls. The house looked in better condition from the beach, where the sun seemed to accentuate what little white paint still clung to the rendered walls. The shutters were fixed open, airing their insides, and even here the blue colour was flaking from the wood. Even though this was the more exposed aspect of the house, she sighed, suddenly feeling the weight of the task ahead. As she approached the door, it opened.

'Hello Mrs Carter-Cruz,' the beaming smile greeted her, the dark-brown eyes assessing her with interest.

Ariana didn't recognise the young girl, though her features resonated, her tanned skin and dark curls, native to the island. 'Hello…' she responded, her tone seeking a name.

'I'm Gianna,' the girl said, her white teeth shining with her expanding grin. She stepped back from the door, for Ariana to enter the house. 'Maria and Nikos' daughter,' she added.

'Ah, yes, how are your mother and father?' she asked, her smile forced. Knowing the impact the message she was just about to deliver to the Papadopoulos family, a wave of guilt passed through her and anxiety flared in her gut.

'They're good,' Gianna said, excitedly. 'Papa's in the garden and Mama's in the kitchen. They're expecting you.'

'Yes,' Ariana said reservedly, observing the young girl with mild curiosity. She looked over her shoulder at the puffing and panting noises heading towards them.

'Wow, that's steep,' Soph said, with a beaming smile. She rubbed her forearm across her brow to gather the sweat, scanned the house briefly and settled her gaze on the smiling dark-eyes that were fixed intently on her.

'Gianna, this is my daughter Soph.'

'Hi,' Soph said, her grin widening. She studied Gianna through squinted eyes, her head tilting at the young woman who stood a couple of inches shorter than her five-feet-eight-inches. She looked a bit older than Soph, almost eighteen years, maybe nineteen, or twenty even. Her eyes wandered down the slender body, small breasts, and slim tanned legs. She looked fit. *Cute!*

'Hi,' Gianna said, staring at the scruffy looking mousy-brown haired girl, her eyes drawn to the sparkling piercing in her nose. She could feel the heat rising to her cheeks, Soph's eyes lingering on her, asking questions, finding answers.

Soph smiled mischievously, her gaze flicking from the girl staring at her to her mother and back again. She stepped past a still-staring Gianna and into the house. Ariana followed her into the cool space. 'Why's it so cold in here?' Soph complained.

'The house is designed to keep out the heat,' Ariana said, taking in the décor. This part of the house was always colder than the other side, but the chill that passed through her had a quality unrelated to the temperature.

'Where's my room?' Soph asked.

Gianna looked flustered.

'Downstairs, take your pick of the two rooms on the right. The second one will be warmer,' Ariana answered, casually. Soph dived down the stairs. 'Gianna, we have luggage to...'

'I'll get it,' Gianna responded enthusiastically, bolting out the door and down the slope to the moored cruiser.

'Hello Ariana.'

The familiar voice turned Ariana's head, and she opened her arms. 'Hello Maria,' she said, taking the woman into her embrace.

'It's been a long time,' Maria said, pulling back and regarding Ariana affectionately. 'You look well,' she added.

'Yes.' Ariana held her gaze and released a deep sigh. She didn't feel well, she felt tired and in need of a long break, but the chances of achieving that during their brief stay would be slim. 'How have you been?' she asked.

Maria had started working for her grandmother when Ariana was a young child and had been with her until the end. Ariana stared with fondness at the woman eleven years her senior; reminded of the times Maria had baked cookies for her as a young child. Then, there was the time she had cried because her mother wouldn't allow her to play with the other children on the beach and Maria had sat in the garden with her and made a picnic of the cookies and juice. When Ariana reached her teens, Maria had covered for her so she could explore beyond the confines of the estate. Since Sophia's passing, Maria had helped with the maintenance of the grounds and supplying food to the workers. Ariana's heart pained, weighed down by the blow she was about to deliver.

Maria lowered her gaze a fraction. 'We're well,' she said, in a tone that held sorrow. 'It's been difficult since your grandmother...'

'Yes,' Ariana interrupted. 'I'm sure.' She strained a smile, wanting to move the conversation along.

She hadn't had the time to give any thought to Sophia's death, consumed by the depression that had taken over her life in the last few years, her husband's philandering ways and her mother's persistent need to control her, and now it almost seemed as though it was too late to grieve. She didn't even know how she felt about her deceased grandmother. She hadn't heard from her since shortly after the birth of Soph and had never understood why the letters had stopped suddenly.

Teresa had been infuriated that the estate had been left to her, and hadn't held back telling her she was unworthy of it, even though Teresa had estranged herself from Sophia since leaving the island. The vitriolic abuse her mother had launched at her had been the last straw. Now, she had no choice. She was here to sell up and move on, and that would have consequences for both Maria and Nikos, and Gianna too. She sighed, mustering the courage to speak.

Maria smiled. Focusing her attention back to their newly arrived guest, she cleared her throat. 'You must be thirsty,' she stated. 'I'll make coffee,' she added, hurrying towards the kitchen.

'Thank you.' Ariana said, softly. She glanced around the foyer and peeked into the reception room. The white-marble fireplace still looked spectacular, but the walls needed a lick of paint. Something was comforting about the scent of the lightly polished wood and the sweet smell of fresh roses that filled the space. She stood, staring, gathering her thoughts. This wasn't going to be easy!

'Ariana!' The deep resonance jolted her, and she turned.

'Nikos!' She exclaimed, smiling as the man bounded towards her. He hadn't changed much over the years either. Twelve years her senior, he had always been like an older brother. He had been kind and had taken the time to talk to her and teach her about the plants and farming the land as she had wandered around the estate as a child. He had worked for her grandmother since leaving school at fifteen and finally taken over management of the estate when his father retired ten years ago. Her stomach lurched.

'You look as lovely as ever,' he said, his soft-brown eyes sparkling. He pulled her into his arms and placed a kiss on her cheek. 'How have you been? It's been such a long time.' The words spilt excitedly from his lips, his eyes holding hers with a mix of warmth and fascination.

'I'm good, thank you,' she said, averting his gaze. 'I think Maria is making coffee,' she added. 'Join us won't you? There's something I need to say to you both.' With her heart pounding in her chest and her hands beginning to sweat, she walked through to the kitchen.

'There's so much we need to catch up on,' Nikos was saying, his arm hanging around her shoulder.

She didn't respond. She felt sick. What she had to say would change everything, after which he most likely wouldn't want to catch up with her about anything. She tried to breathe deeply, to tame the thumping in her chest, but it was making her light-headed and anxiety was squeezing at her gut. Coming here after so long, she hadn't imagined she would feel any warmth towards the old place. It should have been a simple exercise. But already, the smells, the sounds, and seeing the house again: the comforting familiarity of it all, reminded of something she had felt years ago. Happy. Regret struck her unexpectedly, and she started shaking, finding it impossible to speak. She tried to smile but a strained expression appeared, and her heart felt as if it were about to implode.

The aroma of garlic and herbs drifted in the kitchen air from a pot bubbling away on the stove. It didn't help. 'I need to talk to you both,' she said, her voice broken, facing two pairs of questioning eyes and encouraging smiles. She swallowed hard, but her mouth was dry. She couldn't face them, and her eyes wandered to the sea beyond the kitchen-balcony. Small, young grapes hung from vines that spanned the trellised roof. They weren't ripe yet, she noted distractedly. 'I'm selling the house,' she said. The calmness in her voice surprised her, but when she looked back at the wide-eyes staring at her, her insides crumbled. Nikos' open-mouthed glare, and Maria's paling face, frozen and confused, released the trembling in her stomach. She fought back the acid that rose in her throat and the heavy feeling pressing down on her shoulders that was causing her legs to want to give way.

Nikos turned away and walked out of the kitchen in silence. Maria continued to stare. 'Tell me this isn't true,' she said, her voice cold, accusatory.

'I'm so sorry,' Ariana said. She turned swiftly, exited the kitchen, and dashed out the front door, a sharp prod of guilt causing her head to spin. *Aarrgghh!* She hated herself, hated her life; hated everything!

Teresa had arranged for Nikos and Maria not to tell anyone about her visit and they had honoured the request, and now this was how she repaid them for their loyalty. She felt ashamed. She had had no choice, she told herself repeatedly. There was no other way. She was selling the house. And, if there was one thing she had learned from her mother it was to deal with bad news swiftly and concisely. *People will get over the pain quickly enough.* Her mother's words rattled around her head while her feet carried her through the rose garden and onto the ragged cliff top, overlooking the adjoining coves. She stood, breathing deeply, fighting an internal battle; one she felt as if she had been fighting all her life.

She could see the ferry on the far side of the west-cove; the paddleboats, kayaks and windsurfers laid out on the beach just beyond the jetty, and the rocky route bordering the beach, and then across the sand to Kefalas. The taverna looked as it always had done, its big bright red and blue sign, the bench tables on the sand, and the loungers set out along the beach with red and white parasols, looking like lollipops from a distance. Laughter from the bar echoed around the cove, and she smiled, momentarily lost in that other world. *Nikki!* The thought jolted her. Her eyes desperately wanted to seek Nikki out, her mind curious, her heart unsure. Her pulse racing, she changed direction and headed for the lower ridge, overlooking the isolated, abandoned, east-cove, and the moored Sophia II.

By the time she stopped at the ledge her legs were trembling and her mind was a blur, a physiological response for which she could find no legitimate and logical explanation. *Nikki Kefalas. Surely not!* She slumped heavily on the sandy ridge and supported her back against the grassy bank. Even the cheerful music emanating from the large cabin cruiser didn't raise a smile. She studied the vessel with its chrome rails glistening in the sun, the white of its bows blinding-bright, the British flag hanging limply in the absence of any breeze.

Twenty years. She had convinced herself Nikki would have moved on, and maybe she had. Seeing the taverna though, the leisure crafts, the ferry, and hearing the laughter, she hadn't expected those feelings to come flooding back, and she was suddenly less sure. With all the years that had passed and the fact that they had never spoken since she left, it hadn't seriously occurred to her that Nikki would be here. Yes, she had briefly considered it of course but dismissed the idea as highly unlikely. Nikki had always been the stronger of the two of them; she was talented, stunningly beautiful and would surely have made a life for herself off the island, somewhere more... cosmopolitan, and with a woman who loved her.

Her stomach lurched at the thought, and a burst of anxiety rattled her. She recoiled into the grassy bank, clasped her knees to her chest, a voice screaming noooo in her head. She wanted to go back to the cliff top, continue to scan the beach, watch from a distance, not getting too close, in case she should have to face the truth, but she couldn't move. *What if Nikki was still here?* She sat, shaking her head, unable to process the thought. Did she still feel something for Nikki?

She stared at her shaking hands, tears flooding the back of her eyes and a steady flow starting to trickle down her cheeks. She wiped them away, with a hint of irritation. One thing was for sure; if it hadn't been for her grandmother, she wouldn't be here now. Inheriting the property had given her a lifeline, and she was going to be able to create a future for her and Soph with the proceeds. The thought should have provided more comfort than it did, instead of leaving her with a strange feeling of uncertainty.

Ariana wiped at her damp eyes. Everything she either owned in her own right or cared about now sat in the white house behind her. Tomorrow, the Sophia II would return to

British waters and be reunited with her parents. She sighed, closed her eyes momentarily, leaned back into the bank, and soaked up the warmth of the sun, her mind drifting to the quiet hush of the waves against the rocks below, the gentle aroma of wild chamomile going some way to easing the tension in her shoulders. She was mentally and emotionally exhausted. She had been for too long now. Just one last step, a few weeks, and she could start living her life.

*

Ariana stirred. She rubbed at her hot cheeks, although the sun had shifted and she was now sat partly in the shade. She must have fallen asleep. *Soph!* She sat bolt upright, an automatic response, remembered that her daughter was almost eighteen-years-old and perfectly capable of looking after herself, and then relaxed her shoulders a fraction. Nikki's image came to mind, and a warm fuzzy feeling settled in her chest. She eased herself to stand, rubbed at her eyes and started the short climb up the ridge, music and laughter from the moored cruiser following her up the slope.

'Where are you going?' Ariana asked Soph, dashing past her as she exited the house.

'For a walk.' Soph shrugged like her mum had asked the stupidest question in the universe.

'Have you eaten?' Ariana asked.

Soph rolled her eyes. 'Yeah. There's some stuff on the stove,' she added, her eyes indicating towards the kitchen.

'Where's Maria?'

'Dunno. I think they left.' Soph answered, shrugging again, scuffing her feet and kicking up the dust. 'I'm gonna wander,' she added, turning away from her mother.

'Okay... stay safe,' Ariana called after her. If she could have seen Soph's face, she felt sure she would be wincing at the unwarranted concerns. She sighed, watched her daughter disappear down the dirt track and turned into the empty house.

3.

Nikki swept back the rod and cast it out into the shadows, the last flicker of the sun rippling on the surface of the sea. She observed the water, sighting the float as it bobbed to the surface and danced gracefully. The beach had cleared now but chatter from the tavern filtered across the sand, the place providing a sense of seclusion without loneliness. The rocks and descending sun easily obscured her from view, one of the reasons she liked to fish from this vantage point, directly below the white house on the hill. She gazed out to sea, drawn into a meditative trance, her thoughts settling with the constant whoosh and gentle movement of the water below her.

She slowly wound in the line, the reel clicking as it turned. She spotted the slim figure, head bowed, eyes glued to the phone in her hand, strolling bare-foot down the shoreline, long before the girl noticed her. She cast the line effortlessly again, the soft whistle of the reel lasting a full four seconds, and rested the rod in the crook of her arm.

The girl approached lazily, her deck shoes tied together, resting over her shoulder, her feet flicking at the shallow water. 'Hi,' she said, loitering a few feet away, staring out to the darkening sea.

'Hi,' Nikki responded, her eyes on the float to avoid the contact that might send her heart thumping in her chest. She knew exactly who the girl was.

'Fishing?' the girl asked.

It was a dumb question. 'Yes,' she said, glancing over at the girl, holding back a chuckle.

The girl shrugged. 'Is there anything more interesting to do here?' she asked, gazing down at the beach she had just walked.

'I guess that depends?' Nikki responded. 'It's a small place, but there's always Ithaka four miles that way or Lefkada about twelve miles over there if you're looking for something else. Ferry goes on a Friday to Ithaka and as and when to Lefkada.'

The girl huffed. 'Can't,' she said.

'There's no phone signal on the beach, and it's sporadic in the bar,' Nikki added, nodding her head towards the taverna at the other side of the beach.

The girl huffed again.

Nikki glanced across at the scruffy hair. It was difficult to see the colour of her eyes, but she resembled her mother well enough. 'You're Ariana's daughter, aren't you?' she asked, turning her attention back to the water, the float still dancing softly with the gentle waves.

The girl turned sharply to face her. 'How did you know?' she asked.

Nikki smiled warmly. 'I said, it's a small place.'

'Oh!' Soph averted her gaze.

'Sophie, right.' Nikki stated.

'Soph,' she corrected.

Nikki nodded. 'Ah, okay. Hi Soph, I'm Nikki.' She smiled, drawing a smile from Soph. 'You must be what? Eighteen now.'

'You know a lot, don't you?' Soph tilted her head and stared at Nikki.

'I knew your great-grandmother, Sophia.'

Soph shrugged. 'Never met her,' she said, her eyes darting to the water tickling at her feet.

Nikki remained silent.

Soph kicked gently at the shallow waves as they approached and fell away again.

'What do you like to do?' Nikki asked, eventually.

'Huh?'

'For kicks. You asked about something interesting to do. What interests you?'

'Music, I guess,' Soph shrugged.

Nikki reeled the line in, checked the bait and cast it out again; every movement watched quizzically by the young stranger. Four seconds again before the reel stopped. 'Do you play?' Nikki asked her eyes on the float.

'Guitar.'

Nikki looked at her more intently and smiled. 'Bass or acoustic?' she asked, with genuine interest, noting Soph's dark-blue eyes staring back at her.

'Acoustic. I used to play for a band,' Soph said, with increasing enthusiasm.

'What happened?' Nikki asked.

'We came here, and I quit.' Soph sucked through her teeth and kicked at the water with more vigour than she had previously.

'That's a bitch.'

'Yeah, is.'

'How long you here for?' Nikki asked.

A whizzing sound interrupted any response; the reel was spinning. Nikki grabbed the lever, halting the line and the rod bent violently. She started turning the reel, slowly drawing in the line. 'Think we caught a fish,' she said with a grin.

'Really,' Soph said excitedly, moving closer to the rocks.

'Grab that net,' Nikki said, pointing to a pole resting in the water. 'You can help me land it.'

Soph baulked. She'd never even seen a fish caught, let alone assisted in the process. 'I...'

'It's okay. I'll guide you.' Nikki said. 'Just hold on to the pole and keep the net under the water. I'm going to ease the fish into the net. When you see it, close to the surface, slide the net under the fish and lift it out.'

Soph lifted the pole, her heart racing in her chest. Nikki was calmly winding the lever; the fishing rod bending, straightening a fraction and then bending again, the ripples growing as the fish thrashed just under the surface. She held the net under the water as instructed, her eyes eagerly seeking out the fish. 'There,' she squealed, a glistening of silver skimming the surface then ducking away again. She moved the net to a position underneath the activity as Nikki slowly clicked the reel, edging the fish closer.

Soph's eyes widened as she followed Nikki's movements, locating the fish, just underneath the surface now, she could see it clearly. Swiftly, she pulled up the net. It was heavier than she had expected, with the water's resistance, causing her to fight for her balance on the rock's slippery surface. 'Shiiiittt!' Her feet lost their grip, and she slipped into the water, losing control of the net.

Nikki locked the reel and reached out a hand. She was trying not to laugh, but with the sight of the flapping teenager, and her screaming about being in the water with a live fish, she couldn't help herself. 'Here,' she said. 'You're fine; it's not that deep.'

Soph grabbed the offered hand, clambered quickly out of the water and sat, knees pressed to her chest, staring wide-eyed. 'I think it bit me,' she said.

Nikki chuckled loudly. 'Maybe,' she said, winding in the reel. Nothing appeared at the end of the line.

'Where is it?' Soph asked, glaring at the bare hook with worry.

'I think it got away.' Nikki said, with a broad grin. 'You okay?' she asked.

Soph was shivering. 'I'm really sorry,' she said, staring vacantly.

'Hey, no worries, there's plenty more fish in the sea!' Nikki said with a chuckle.

Soph smiled weakly.

Nikki reached into the water, pulled out the net and rested it back against the rocks. 'You want to try again?' she asked.

'Maybe another time,' Soph said, rising to stand. 'I need to get back,' she added, her arms wrapped around her chest, comforting herself from the shock. 'It's getting dark,' she said.

'Yes.' Nikki watched Soph make her way gingerly down from the rocks, onto the sand and quickly put on her deck shoes. She smiled ruefully at the young girl's fastidiousness. Sophie Carter-Cruz had lived a precious life; she pondered with a shake of her head.

'See you around,' Soph said, heading for the sandy track back up the hill.

'It was good to meet you, Soph,' Nikki replied, but the girl was already out of earshot. She cast the line into the water, perched on a flat piece of rock and searched through her food bag. The float swaying lightly on the sea's surface and the soft whoosh of the waves capturing her attention, protecting her from her thoughts, she savoured the calamari and potato salad Pops had prepared.

*

'You're back early,' Manos remarked, a contented smile lingering on his lips.

He looked comfortable, resting on the lounger on the beach out the front of the bar, a strong aniseed smell emanating from the glass in his hand. The bottle and a second glass sat on the sand as if he had been waiting for her. 'Fish weren't biting,' she said.

'Aye,' he said.

'Ariana's daughter showed up,' Nikki said.

'Drink?' he asked. He sucked through his teeth as he reached for the bottle and poured a large shot of the clear liquid into the glass.

'Thanks.' She dropped her gear to the sand, took the glass and sat on the lounger next to his. 'Good night?' she asked, referring to the restaurant.

'Every night's a good night,' he said, with humility, and it was.

The Kefalas family had worked the restaurant now for three generations, and there was no shortage of guests, no matter what the time of year or the time of day. Locals made up their largest client group and ate regularly, and then there were the seasonal visitors who would seek out the place based on a recommendation. They didn't advertise. Everyone knew Kefalas', and there wasn't one person on the island who hadn't eaten there, or partied there, at some point in time.

She sipped at the ouzo, winced as the burn hit her throat and the aniseed cleared her nose. She coughed lightly. 'God, that's strong,' she said, her words getting stuck on their way out.

'She's selling,' Manos said, his tone unchanging.

Nikki took a moment to process the two words and work out to whom he was referring, and then the penny dropped. 'What!' she shouted then skulked down in the lounger at her own raised voice, hoping she hadn't disturbed anyone, and working hard to control the anger that had flared. 'Teresa!' she spat, rising to her feet and beginning to pace across the sand.

'No, Ariana! Nikos came in earlier. Ariana gave them the news. No sign of Teresa.' He was shaking his head as he spoke. 'You know, they knew she was coming, but Teresa swore them to secrecy,' he said. 'I'm surprised,' he added, with more than a hint of remorse. He sucked through his teeth and sipped at the drink in his hand.

Nikki's head was spinning and the only sounds bouncing around her mind were her confused thoughts. She hadn't heard a word Pops had said. The anger had started a fire in her chest, and now her eyes were burning too. She pressed her finger and thumb firmly into her tear ducts to prevent the rage from spilling. *Ariana won't sell the house, Nikki.* Sophia's words ran

27

like a movie script on repeat; Sophia sat in the wicker chair on the kitchen-balcony, shaking her head, the china cup in her hand rattling against the saucer as she rested her coffee cup. It hadn't occurred to her, or to Sophia, that her granddaughter would want to sell the place. Teresa, Sophia's daughter, on the other hand, the money grabbing… Yes, she would sell without a second thought, but that's why Sophia had left the house to Ariana and not to Teresa. Sophia had tried to secure the future of the place for the local community, but apparently failed.

Nikki continued to stamp out her frustration across the sand, flicking her fingers urgently through her hair, trying to make sense of the truth. The last thing Sophia wanted was to sell the estate. 'She can't sell,' she said.

Manos sipped at his drink. 'If she owns the house she can do as she pleases,' he said, his tone more matter-of-fact than Nikki might have expected.

'Shit!' Nikki cursed.

His eyes turned to her as he swallowed. 'What will you do?' he asked.

Nikki stopped pacing and stared at him. His eyes were soft, and his wrinkled skin held the wisdom of his years. There was no urgency, no angst, just an acceptance of the way things were. And right now, his relaxed demeanour irritated her. 'Stop her,' she said, with determination.

'Aye,' he responded, his smile offering compassion, his eyes sparkling in the moonlight.

'Uurrgghh,' she huffed. Picking up her fishing gear, she marched through the empty restaurant to the rear door. Dropping her gear at the workshop as she passed, she took the few short paces and entered her adjoining apartment. Fuelled with rage, she slammed the door behind her. *Why now? Why? Why?* She paced around her living room, trying to loosen the tension in her body; it wouldn't shift. She stepped through to her bedroom and stopped at the window, staring into the dark, night sky, anger building. The white house was obscured from view by the taverna, but the thought of it belonging to someone else! *You can't do that Ariana; you can't sell.* Years of repressed pain, the hurt, the disappointment, and the sadness, converged in her mind and transformed into the rage that now blinded her. Fists clenched, jaw clamped, she wanted to scream but couldn't. She wanted to yell out to the world, but the words wouldn't come. She wanted to go up to the house and shake some sense into Ariana. Ariana who had never been able to stick up for herself; Ariana who had lived under the control of her mother, Ariana who had broken her heart, and would now break Sophia's trust. No! She would do everything in her power to stop Ariana from selling the house.

With fury driving her, she marched out of her apartment, across the beach ignoring Pops, and started to climb the sandy path. Reaching the top, the lights from the house guided her to the front door. Her eyes fixed on the blue wooden door, her fist thumped down repeatedly, until it opened.

'Nikki!' Ariana gasped, her hand swiftly covering her mouth, her eyes wide.

Nikki froze, the wind knocked out of her sails. Her mouth tried to move, but the words she had wanted to scream out were stuck, and she couldn't swallow. Ariana's dark-brown eyes, peeking over the hand clamped to her mouth, had locked onto hers and taken her breath away. The ash-blonde hair, resting lightly on narrow shoulders looked a little better coiffured than she remembered. Nikki's racing heart surprised her too. She hesitated, trying to gain some sense of composure, a jelly-like feeling starting to challenge the muscles in her legs.

Ariana released her hand from her mouth and tried to stand taller than her five-feet-six-inches. It took all her resolve, and she still felt small, weak, and strangely confused.

The momentary distraction, which had thrown Nikki off course, lifted. 'You're selling,' Nikki asserted, her hands finding their way to her hips and resting there, the tone in her voice a surprise. The anger that had driven her to stand at the blue door this late at night had shifted to something less intense, something far more vulnerable than she would have liked to admit.

'I err… Umm.' Ariana stood, dumbfounded, avoiding direct eye contact. Guilt warred with her desire to pull Nikki into her arms. Her hands were trembling. Her whole body was shaking. Guilt was winning.

'You're selling?' This time it was a question and the tone more determined. Nikki stood her ground, her hands remaining steadfast on her hips, her eyes seeking the answer.

'Yes.' The response was timid, remorseful even. Ariana's eyes lowered, and her hand lifted and rubbed at the back of her neck.

'Why?' Nikki asked.

The resonance in Nikki's voice caused Ariana to flinch. It wasn't just that she never justified her decisions to others, except perhaps her mother, and then, of course, there was her ex-husband. There was something else though, something more profound and hauntingly pure in the tone, that touched her. She gulped. She moved to speak but was interrupted.

'Hey Nikki,' Soph said, a broad grin on her face, rubbing at her hair with a towel, her presence instantly defusing the tension between the two women.

'Hi,' Nikki responded, more curtly than she intended.

'Mum, this is Nikki from fishing.'

'Yes.' Ariana said, trying to smile with her daughter, heat flushing her cheeks. She had known who Soph was referring to when she arrived home wet from her walk babbling about being bitten by a fish, but she hadn't expected Nikki to turn up on their doorstep tonight and neither was she willing to engage in a conversation with her about the sale of the house in front of Soph.

'Did you catch any more fish?' Soph asked, enthusiastically.

Nikki smiled weakly. 'No, I think you shocked them more than they shocked you,' she teased. She started to chuckle as the image of Soph sliding into the water and her response to being up close and personal with nature softened the atmosphere. Ariana was smiling, and the soft lines accentuating the almond shape of her dark-brown eyes caused Nikki's breath to hitch.

'Would you like to come in?' Ariana asked, against her better judgement.

'Umm, no. It's late. I umm, shouldn't have come,' she added, starting to babble again. The conversation they needed to have could wait.

'Maybe we can catch up tomorrow?' Ariana offered, politely.

'I've got the ferry run,' Nikki said.

'Ah, right.'

With Ariana's intense gaze on her, Nikki was feeling exposed. The years of absence between them hadn't changed a thing; her feelings for the woman she now faced were it seemed as strong as ever. She cleared her throat. 'Do you need anything from Ithaka?' she asked.

'No, I think we're fine, thanks. Maria...'

'Ah, yes, of course.' Her brain had stopped working. Of course, Maria would make sure they were well stocked; she always had done. What would happen when Ariana sold the place? The whole Papadopoulos family and the other casual staff would all be out of work, and work on the island wasn't that easy to find. Nikki turned towards the dusty track and started to walk.

'Nikki!' Ariana called.

Nikki stopped, turned, and locked onto Ariana's eyes. 'Yes.'

31

Ariana faltered. 'You look well,' she said, her broken voice betraying her inner thoughts.

Nikki nodded, her lips pursed. 'You've caught the sun already,' she replied, pointing at Ariana's red face. 'You need to get some cream on that,' she added, turned, and continued down the path.

4.

Soph leaned back in the wicker chair on the kitchen-balcony, her hand resting lightly on the strings of her guitar. 'Have you always lived here?' she asked.

Gianna nodded, her eyes fixed on the sparkling diamond in Soph's nose, shifting in colour with the sunlight as she moved her head. She placed a bowl of chopped fresh-fruit on the table, next to the yoghurt. 'Is that real?' she asked, pointing.

Soph grinned. 'Diamond, yeah.' Soph studied Gianna's dark-brown eyes, her tanned skin and short curly hair, darker than her own. She had the most amazing eyelashes that had the effect of painted eyeliner, highlighting her eyes. She was pretty. Hot even. She smiled, eliciting a grin from Gianna that revealed perfectly white teeth. 'You're pretty,' she said, her eyes never leaving Gianna's, enjoying the impact of her compliment in the darkening of Gianna's skin.

Gianna's smile broadened, the heat in her cheeks and the tingling down her spine challenging her concentration, and her mouth. Something was intriguing about Ariana's daughter, something wild, and exciting. She exuded calm confidence that was alluring.

'Gianna!' shouted her mother.

Gianna pointed her finger over her shoulder towards the voice and smirked. 'I have to go,' she said.

'Sure.' Soph's eyes dropped to the guitar, and her fingers started to pluck at the strings.

Gianna's grin spanned her face, as she approached the kitchen, excited by the rise in adrenalin that had caused her to feel weirdly self-conscious in Soph's presence. She picked up the coffee pot and a jug of milk and headed hastily out to the table. She stopped, suddenly deflated by the empty chair. Soph had gone. She gazed down the steps leading to the garden below. Nothing.

'Gianna!' her mum called again, jolting her out of her trance. She turned slowly and meandered back into the kitchen, feeling both subdued and warm inside at the same time. She huffed to herself. She couldn't see the point of laying out a load of food for two people anyway, and now the interesting one had disappeared. She had an overwhelming desire to run, track down Soph, and spend the rest of the day talking to her. Soph was fascinating.

'Morning Maria, Gianna.' Ariana said, entering the kitchen in a hurry.

'Morning,' Maria responded, her tone detached, formal and with a hint of residual anger from the unfinished conversation of the previous afternoon. How could she drop a bombshell like that and then leave them without any information? They needed answers. The uncertainty they now faced had kept both her and Nikos awake for most of the night. Neither had wanted to come into work today, and they had only done so out of loyalty to Sophia's memory. She missed Sophia deeply, but now, she was also confused and angry.

Gianna mumbled, 'Morning,' slipped out the door and headed out to the garden. She would see if her Papa wanted any help in the olive grove. Her parents had only briefly mentioned the house sale, and it didn't mean that much to her, but they were both peeved as hell. She liked Ariana though; she had a kind smile. And, she wanted to spend time with Soph. She grinned at the thought.

Ariana walked through the kitchen to the balcony table and filled a cup with coffee, added a large quantity of milk and sipped the drink. 'I'm sorry I threw the sale at you yesterday,' she said, softly. She too had spent a sleepless night, tossing and turning. Seeing Nikki had been like a shot across the bow; it had hit her harder than she could have anticipated and the damage had been more devastating. It was as if her heart had awoken instantly and yet it lay in pieces, each crying out to be reconnected to the other, to become whole again.

'Is there a plan?' Maria asked, sternly.

'I have a few things I need to do,' Ariana responded, sipping at her drink, eyeing Maria's reaction over the top of the cup. 'The place needs renovating,' she said tentatively, not wishing to assert that they hadn't looked after the property.

Maria nodded. Her eyes were watering, and her hands were beginning to toy with the cloth in her hand.

'I'm planning to be here for a few weeks,' Ariana added, hoping that her presence might provide some reassurance, though about what she couldn't articulate because the proposition was so feeble.

Maria didn't so much as flinch at Ariana's words. 'Do you want anything cooked for breakfast?' she asked.

'No, fruit is fine, thank you.' She placed her cup on the table and stepped towards Maria with open arms. 'I'm sorry,' she said. She moved in and hugged the unresponsive body for a few seconds before letting go.

Maria stood stiffly. 'It's been a big shock,' she said, unsure of how to respond to Ariana's physical contact. *Did she care, or was it guilt?*

Ariana nodded, her face tense, her lips pursed. 'I know, I am truly sorry,' she said, her eyes pleading for Maria to believe her.

Maria nodded, turned towards the sink and rinsed her hands under the cold tap.

'Maria?' Ariana said, quietly.

Maria turned to face her, holding her gaze, curious as to what bombshell was going to be dropped next and fighting the insecurity that pounded in her chest and had her stomach turning.

Ariana held the worried gaze. 'I want you to take time off, while I'm here,' she said eventually, the words hanging in the painful silence that lingered between them.

Maria's mouth fell open, and she lost all sense of balance. She slumped against the sink, her hands clamping the sides of her head.

'You'll be paid in advance, of course,' Ariana said quickly. 'I just need some time, together, with Soph,' she added. It was partly the truth.

Maria's back tensed. She couldn't imagine having guests at the house and not cooking for them. She had cooked for Sophia until the day she died. What was she going to do with time off? This was the start of the end. She shook her head, trying to process the last few hours, willing it all to be a dream; a nightmare from which she would wake up. She was unable to speak. Old Sophia would be turning in her grave.

'I'm going to take the ferry today,' Ariana said, changing the subject. 'Do we need anything?' she asked.

Maria tightened the grip around her head, fighting the tears that pressed at the back of her eyes, pride keeping her head in her hands. She wouldn't let Ariana see her cry. She shook her head.

Ariana stood for a moment in the discomfort before turning away. She breathed deeply as she stepped out of the house and into the early morning sun. She wanted to scream, what about me? What about my life? But that wasn't Maria's concern and now wasn't the time or place. She needed to speak to Nikki, and sooner rather than later.

*

'Hello Ariana,' Manos greeted with a warm smile, the dimples on his stubbly cheeks deepening and curling the short hairs on his face. He held out his hand to help her onto the ferry.

'Hello Manos, you look well,' she responded. He still had a sparkle in his dark eyes, even though the years, and the sea-air, had aged his naturally rugged skin and the stubble on his face had turned whiter than snow. She glanced around the small foot-ferry. Two men, looking like locals with their dark hair and bronzed faces, were leaning against the starboard bow railings, their heads shifting back and forth, the cigarette smoke drifting with their words.

He closed the gate behind her and released the rope holding the boat tightly to the jetty. 'I didn't know you were coming today,' he said, with a wry smile.

'No...' she replied, distractedly.

'Well, it's good to see you. It's been a long time,' he added, his heart glowing with warmth, his eyes studying her skittish behaviour with curiosity. She had turned into a pretty woman, a little skinnier than he might have deemed healthy, and overly consumed by whatever seemed to be troubling her. Her hurried nature reminded him of Teresa though, even if her looks didn't. Teresa's features were sharper, finer, and she was noticeably taller than Ariana. He'd always thought of Teresa as a beautiful woman, but Ariana had a softness to her that had been absent in Teresa. Ariana was far more like her grandmother than she was her mother. He hoped the same was true for Ariana's character too, but from what he was seeing in her edgy behaviours and the way she had heartlessly announced that she was selling the house, he had good reason for concern. He sucked through his teeth, averted his gaze and wandered to the cabin.

Ariana wandered around the boat, feeling flustered. She couldn't see Nikki anywhere and didn't have time for chitchat with Manos. Maybe Nikki was below deck? The whirring sound increased and water gushed out the back of the ferry. They were moving. *Where is Nikki?* She wandered around the deck again, felt the breeze through her hair and the light-spray from the sea tickle her face. She peered into the cabin as she passed. Manos smiled. Nikki must be in the hold.

*

Gianna ambled down the dirt path to the boundary by the cliff, seduced by the gentle strumming of a guitar. Her stomach was doing something strangely fuzzy, her pulse increasing with every pace closer to the source of the music. She stopped, crouched down, and watched.

Soph was sat facing out to sea, her feet hanging over the edge of the rocks, her body swaying with the rhythm of the haunting music she was creating with her fingers.

Entranced, Gianna closed her eyes. She'd never heard such sounds from an instrument before. She could feel the music caressing her, and her mind drifted to the hands that were having that effect on the strings. She had already noted the short nails, well groomed, on long, strong fingers, and then there was the way Soph looked at her, smiled at her, and teased her. She hadn't needed to wonder; Soph was definitely into her. She opened her eyes abruptly at the impact her thoughts were having on her body. It was kind of cool, a warm feeling, exciting too! Biting down on her lip, another sound hit her ears, and the music stopped suddenly.

'Hey!' Soph's voice called out.

Had she really groaned out loud? She had two choices: hide, or stand up and fess up. She stood. 'Hi.'

Soph smiled. *Cute!* Gianna was rubbing her hands together in front of her body, looking decidedly uncomfortable. *Adorable.* 'You like music?' she asked, resuming her playing.

Gianna cleared her throat. 'Umm, yes.'

'Me too,' Soph said, facing out to sea again. 'Do you play?' she asked, continuing to sway as she strummed.

Gianna giggled. 'No,' she said, shrinking with embarrassment at her nervous response to Soph's genuine interest. 'How long have you played?'

Soph's head rose as she considered the question, her hands continuing to make the strings dance. 'About five years,' she said.

'Wow! You're brilliant,' Gianna said.

Soph stopped playing and put down the guitar, ignoring the compliment. 'Do you like it here?' she asked.

Gianna twitched. She hadn't expected the question, and the sudden shift in the energy between them, without the music, confused her. 'Umm,' she stuttered. 'I have plans,' she said.

Soph turned to face her. She looked serious. 'Yeah!' she said, her tone probing for more information.

'I want to do something with my life,' Gianna responded, tilting her head to the side as she spoke, her gaze fixed on a point over Soph's shoulder, to where her vision of 'that life' existed.

Soph nodded and turned back to the sea. 'Good for you,' she said. She didn't know why she had asked the question. She didn't know what she would do with her life, or whether she had ambition anymore, but having had it drilled into her she should have, she valued ambition in others, sometimes.

'What about you?' Gianna asked, tentatively.

'I like it here,' she said.

'What do you want to do with your life?' Gianna asked again.

Soph tensed. It was an involuntary response, but one that she had developed. Her ideas about what she wanted to do with her life being repeatedly quashed over the years. 'Dunno,' she said, curtly.

Gianna turned towards the path.

'Wait.' Soph said, standing quickly and stepping towards Gianna, her eyes flitting towards the olive trees to avoid direct contact. 'Sorry, I didn't mean to...'

'It's okay,' Gianna interrupted, bruised by the sadness in Soph's gaze. She smiled at Soph's ruffled appearance, easing the tension. 'You want to do something?' she asked, her eyes drawn to the glistening diamond, the tingling down her spine causing her to shudder.

Soph held Gianna's gaze, a warm feeling infusing her chest, a smile forming slowly. 'Want to see my other piercings?' she teased.

Gianna gulped, and her cheeks flushed. 'Maybe,' she said, her lips curling seductively.

Soph chuckled.

'Want me to show you around a bit?'

Soph tilted her head, her eyebrows rising suggestively. 'Okay,' she said, picking up her guitar. 'Lead on.'

'I'll need to let Papa know,' Gianna said.

'I'll dump this,' Soph said, holding up the guitar. 'Meet you out front,' she suggested.

'Okay.' Gianna grinned.

Soph smiled. She was enjoying the light-headed feeling that came with talking to Gianna, and the subtle, aching sensation in her groin at the sight of the dark, alluring eyes. *Definitely cute, and hot!*

*

Nikki looked up from the pole she was ramming into the sand, at the front of the taverna. She studied the two young women approaching and smiled.

'Need a hand?' Soph asked.

Nikki stood and stretched. 'Sure. Can you hook the net over the other pole and hold onto it, while I sort this end out?'

Soph shrugged matter-of-factly and reached for the roped end of the net. Looping it over the top of the pole, she stood watching Nikki attach the guide rope to a weight on the sand. 'Want me to attach this one?' she asked, pointing to the weight at her side of the net.

'I'll help,' Gianna offered, pulling the string taut while Soph attached it to the weight. 'Do you play volleyball?' she asked, smiling at Soph.

'At school, yeah, not on a beach though.'

'We have a tournament tomorrow, and a BBQ party in the evening, if you fancy it?' Nikki said, her eyes directed towards Soph.

'You have to come, it will be fun,' Gianna added, her eyes twinkling with excitement.

Soph sucked through her teeth and tilted her head, 'Maybe,' she replied.

'Your mum's invited too,' Nikki added.

Soph rolled her eyes. 'Right,' she mumbled.

Nikki tilted her head and her smile held compassion. 'Everything okay?' she asked.

Soph shrugged. 'She's...' Soph stopped. This wasn't the right time to articulate her irritations with her mother. She was on holiday, and that meant having fun.

'Where is Ariana?' Nikki asked. 'Pull on the rope when I do,' she instructed.

'Dunno, she went on the ferry this morning,' Soph said, pulling on the guide rope to create tension in the net.

Nikki's eyes widened and her lips pursed. 'Oh!'

'Do you want to practise?' Gianna asked Soph.

'Sure.'

'Do you girls want a drink, soda, beer?' Nikki asked, heading into the bar. 'I'll get a ball,' she added, distracted by curiosity and mild amusement that Ariana had taken the ferry when she hadn't wanted anything from Ithaka.

41

'Beer,' both girls responded enthusiastically. Their eyes locked onto each other briefly, smiling, drawing them closer.

'She's cool,' Soph said, watching Nikki's back as it disappeared inside the taverna.

'She is,' Gianna nodded.

'And hot,' Soph added, watching Gianna's response.

Gianna flushed, swallowed, and tried to speak. 'Hmmm,' was all she could say, her words deserting her, her body reacting to Soph's clear revelation.

Soph laughed. 'She is.'

The thump of a ball landing at her feet shifted Gianna's attention. 'Practise,' she said, grateful for the diversion.

Soph dived to the other side of the net and glared as Gianna prepared to hit the ball into the air.

'This is practise, not competitive, right!' Gianna said, knocking the ball up high over the net.

Soph didn't have to move much to get to it, put her arms out, hands clasped, and sent the ball back to the other side with perfect precision.

'You can play,' Gianna remarked, sending the ball higher.

Soph stepped in, jumped, and smashed the ball down over the net, a mischievous smile creeping across her face as the ball thudded into the sand.

Gianna flung her arms in the air. 'Hey, that's cheating!'

'I was just getting warmed up,' Soph shrugged, starting to chuckle.

Nikki approached with the two beers. 'How's the game going?'

'One, love,' Soph responded with a beaming grin.

'We're just practising,' Gianna retorted with a half-grimace, unable to stop the smile forming as her eyes lingered on the ruffled brown hair and deep-blue eyes glaring at her.

42

'Aye,' Nikki said, smiling at the obvious attraction between the two young women. 'I'll be in the kitchen if you need anything,' she added. 'Ferry will be back shortly,' she said, heading towards the bar, pointing to the boat on the horizon heading in their direction.

Soph's eyes lost their shine as she gazed out to sea. She was having fun and didn't want it to end. But it would stop because the fun always did.

'Soph!' Nikki called over her shoulder. Soph looked towards her and nodded. 'I was wondering, do you want to play guitar here tomorrow, after the volleyball?'

Soph frowned.

'She's really good,' Gianna added excitedly. 'Go on Soph, say you'll do it.'

'I can pay you,' Nikki offered, with an encouraging smile.

Soph was sipping at the chilled beer, her ears failing to register Nikki's words fully. She shrugged, her heart racing at the idea. She'd never performed solo before, but there was something about this place, already, and about Nikki, and Gianna. She'd felt it as she stepped onto the beach yesterday, as she had mooched around the house in the early hours and watched the sunrise, then wandered through the gardens and sat on the cliff top looking out to the dark-blue sea, the warm breeze against her face, the sun on her skin. It made her feel good, confident, and for the first time in a long time, she had enjoyed strumming. If she dared to think about it for long enough, she might even begin to write music again. She wouldn't make herself any promises though. A smile slowly formed. 'Okay,' she said. Gianna was leaping towards her, raising her hand for a high-five. She responded, but instead of slapping palms she found herself holding Gianna's hand, their eyes connecting, the touch sending an unexpected wave of fire through her fingers and down her arm. 'Your serve,' she said through a croaky voice, releasing the hold.

'Practise, right!' Gianna reminded her, collecting up the ball and running to the back of the court.

Soph smiled, Gianna's cheeks were darker than usual. 'Sure,' she said, taking her position on the sand, a mischievous-smile gracing her lips again.

5.

Nikki leaned back in the driftwood seat, sipped at her coffee and watched the ferry docking. She had enjoyed watching the girls having fun. She liked Soph; she reminded her of Ariana all those years ago, and yet Soph was also a lot like her great-grandmother. She missed Sophia, and she knew Pops did too. They all did! She stood, suddenly alerted. Ariana was marching across the beach, directly towards her, at a pace, and judging by her posture; she wasn't happy. Nikki felt like laughing at the peacock display, but something suppressed the rising chuckle. Compassion, concern, pity?

'Why weren't you on the ferry?' The words flew at Nikki like a sniper's bullet, picking off its target directly and with ease.

Nikki flinched, an instinctive reaction to the assault, but didn't respond. This wasn't Ariana; she reminded herself.

'Where were you? I've wasted a whole day,' the assault continued.

Nikki frowned. *Such passion!*

'Ithaka is a beautiful island, there's lots to see,' Nikki said, calmly.

'I didn't go to see the island. I went to talk to you,' Ariana retorted, her arms straightening down her side, her fists clenched in frustration.

'Hmm!' Nikki responded. She couldn't think of anything to say. She hadn't known Ariana was going to take the ferry to speak to her, how could she have known? 'I asked Pops to take the run today, so I could...'

'That's pretty damn clear,' Ariana spat, her vision starting to blur through the tears that were forming.

Nikki gazed at the lost woman, seeing clearly, the little girl inside fighting to survive, overshadowed by the life she had lived. She sighed. 'Would you like a drink?' she asked softly.

Ariana's shoulders dropped, her hands unclenched, and she rubbed at her sore eyes. She held Nikki's compassionate gaze, momentarily letting her guard down and feeling the sadness escape in an instant. She swallowed it down, restored her defences and nodded, but not before a tear slipped onto her cheek.

'It's okay. Come on,' Nikki said softly, taking a small step towards Ariana. She wanted to hold her and comfort her, but Ariana didn't give off any vibes that would suggest that was either wanted or would be well received. 'What would you like to drink?' she asked, turning quickly and heading into the bar.

Ariana followed her, rubbing her hands through her hair, confused by the conflicting emotions that seemed to be competing for her attention. 'Wine please,' she replied.

'White? Red?'

'White.'

Nikki poured two glasses and wandered back to the driftwood seat, followed by Ariana. She smiled at Pops as he passed with a crate of supplies. 'Good day?' she asked him.

'Aye,' he responded, his coy smile and the glint in his eye revealing all she needed to know. It was always a good day in Pops' world.

Ariana sat, still rubbing her hands through her hair, still processing her thoughts, and wrestling with her feelings, overwhelmed, and tired. She squeezed a tight smile at the old man as he passed. 'Thanks,' she said, taking the offered glass from Nikki, her tone tense. She sipped at the drink, staring into space. Eventually her breathing softened, her eyes scanned the cove, and she smiled. 'I'd forgotten how beautiful it is here,' she said, easing her back into the seat.

Nikki didn't respond. She watched Ariana, perplexed, wanting to ask questions but sensing Ariana wasn't in any place to have a conversation let alone answer them. She'd never seen anyone as out-of-place as Ariana looked. Lost, confused, and so uptight. Ariana may have only arrived yesterday, but she was indeed giving off some strange vibes.

She had fleetingly sensed something else last night, as she held Ariana's gaze, and she had known Ariana well enough to realise she had felt something too, but in an instant that connection had disappeared. She swallowed, turned, and stared out to sea. The sun had started its descent, although still providing light and warmth and highlighting the white house on the hill. Her eyes drifted to the beautiful building and her distant memories.

'What can you see?' Pops asked her.

She squealed with delight, looking through the binoculars he had just given her for her eighth birthday. 'The white house, there's a girl up there,' she responded.

'Are you spying?' he asked, teasing her.

She turned to him with a serious gaze. 'Do you think I can be a real spy one day?' she asked.

He chuckled. 'Of course you can. You can be whatever you choose to be.' He kissed her on the forehead.

'Why doesn't she come down and play with us?' she asked.

He took in a deep breath, gazed towards the white house. 'I don't know, Nikki.' He ruffled her hair. 'Have you seen any new ships?' he asked.

She hadn't realised that he was deliberately trying to distract her, but when he had gone back to the bar, she redirected the binoculars towards the white house with increased fascination.

'I'm sorry Nikki.'

Ariana's voice grabbed her attention from the fleeting memory, and she sipped at the wine in her hand. 'You seem tense,' Nikki replied.

Ariana twisted the stem of the glass in her hand, her thumb rubbing the light condensation that had formed on the outside. 'Yes,' she said, through a deep sigh, her tone marginally calmer than moments earlier. Pops passed them again, heading for the ferry. 'Do you need to help Manos?' she asked.

Nikki shook her head. 'Nah, he enjoys the exercise,' she said with a wry smile.

Ariana smiled, watching the old man go about his work. Guilt pricked her, and she wriggled in the seat. She hadn't taken the news that Nikki wasn't on board the ferry too well and had been quite rude, insisting that he bring her back. Even as she had been asserting herself she had known her request was unreasonable, but she had been outraged. She had thrashed all night, building up the courage to speak to Nikki, and the ferry trip had seemed the perfect opportunity. Now, she was struggling to speak, furious with herself for behaving like an emotional adolescent.

'What did you want to talk about?' Nikki asked.

Ariana sipped at the chilled drink, savoured the light, zesty sensation on the back of her tongue. 'Nice wine,' she said, avoiding the question.

'Yes, it is.' Nikki turned to face her and smiled. 'It's locally produced,' she added softly.

Ariana's breath hitched. Nikki's light-hazel eyes seemed to penetrate her, expose her. She couldn't deny the warmth in her core, melting the frustration and stress. It was also disconcerting, messing with her mental plans, confusing her logic. And, the feeling was unexpected. But, it felt so good. Better than anything she had experienced in a long time. One look. One smile. One slither of her shattered heart bonding with another! That's all it had taken, and the woman sat next to her, on a bench so familiar, as if they had perched here every day of their lives, together; Nikki was the source of that feeling. She leaned back into the seat, her proximity to Nikki instantly

48

deepening her sense of comfort and security, sucking her into a world in which she did not belong. The intensity caused her to flinch, and she sat stiffly again.

Nikki studied Ariana carefully, her heart burning with the pain she could see her struggling with, but they needed to talk. 'Your grandmother didn't want the house sold,' she said calmly.

Ariana tensed.

'That's why she left it to you and not your mother,' Nikki continued. She didn't want to cause any more distress than Ariana was already suffering, but Ariana needed to know the truth. 'Sophia knew your mother would sell it in a heartbeat for the money, but you...'

Ariana stood abruptly, the glass in her hand shaking. 'I need to go,' she said. Placing the drink on the rock that backed the driftwood seat, she turned swiftly and set off across the beach.

'That went well,' Manos remarked, passing with another box of groceries.

Nikki's eyebrows rose in response. 'I'll give you a hand,' she said.

'There's one more box,' he said.

'Do you think she'll go through with it?' Nikki asked, watching the back of the ash-blonde head as it bobbed towards the path leading up to the white house.

Manos shrugged, flicked the toothpick from one side of his mouth to the other. He moved to speak but remained silent.

'She's so...' Nikki started in a whisper, unable to articulate the aura Ariana had thrust upon their small island.

'Scared,' Manos muttered, his tone etched with remorse. Ariana reminded him of a baby bird, waking up, before it realised it had wings and could fly, floundering in a nest built by its mother, too frightened to leap out, take off, and soar.

Gianna sat on Soph's bed watching with fascination, Soph's hands flitting between the strings of her guitar and the pencil and paper in front of her. There was something about the intensity as she worked that was having a strange effect on Gianna. Giddy and excited, Gianna didn't want the feeling to end.

Soph looked up and smiled.

Gianna stared intently. 'Did you study music at college?' she asked, her heart racing.

Soph shook her head, tinkered with a few notes and made some comments on the paper. 'No,' she replied, tinkered again, scribbled over the previous comments and wrote something else.

Gianna flushed. She'd interrupted. 'Sorry,' she said, interrupting again, adjusting her position on the edge of the bed.

'I didn't go to college, and we came here,' Soph clarified, her eyes avoiding Gianna's troubled gaze as she worked.

'Oh, sorry!' Gianna frowned.

Soph silenced the strings with her hand and looked up. 'It's cool here,' she said, with an approving smile.

Gianna tilted her head, assessing the musician. Soph seemed to have missed out on a lot, and yet, it didn't appear to bother her. She was the most laid back person she'd ever met, except for Nikki maybe, and Pops of course.

'Hey, you want to try?' Soph asked, standing and holding out the guitar. 'Come on; I'll show you.'

Gianna giggled, stood reluctantly, crossed the space, and sat in the chair. Soph rested the guitar in Gianna's lap, cupped Gianna's hand around the neck and positioned her fingers on the strings.

'Aww!' Gianna moaned. 'That hurts,' she said.

'You need to press down hard. Look,' she said, showing her hand to Gianna.

Gianna rubbed her thumb tenderly across the callused skin at the tips of each finger. 'Wow!' she remarked, her mouth dry with the impact of the touch.

A wave of heat targeted Soph's cheeks, and she pulled back sharply. 'It'll take years to get them like that,' she said, reassuringly. 'And it'll hurt in the meantime,' she added with a coy grin, her eyes indicating for Gianna to press down on the strings. She moved around the back of Gianna, leaned over her shoulder and reached for her free hand, guiding her through the strumming movement. The subtle sweet scent of Gianna's skin stole her attention and she paused before swiftly releasing the hand.

Gianna turned her head towards Soph. 'Is this right?' she asked, allowing her thumb to brush softly over the strings.

The warm feel of Gianna's breath so tantalisingly close, her dark eyes so alluring, and so innocent, caused Soph to jolt and she stepped back. 'You sure you haven't done this before?' she asked, shaking herself off and re-establishing a physical distance between them.

Gianna giggled and continued to play. Soph tried to wince at the noise, but she was smiling too broadly. Gianna stopped strumming, stood and handed back the guitar. 'I'll never be as good as you,' she said.

'Practise, remember,' Soph teased. 'You'll thrash me at volleyball,' she added with a beaming grin and a shrug.

'I need to go,' Gianna said.

Soph felt her stomach drop. It was still early, but then again, they had spent the whole day together, and Gianna did have her family to be with too. 'Sure,' she said, placing the guitar on her bed and leading them up the stairs.

'Tomorrow?' Gianna asked.

'Volleyball party, you bet,' Soph said with a chuckle.

Gianna smiled.

'Hey!' Soph said as she opened the front door for Gianna to leave. Gianna held her gaze. 'Thanks for showing me around, it's been a fun day,' she said. Gianna's eyes sparkled at her.

'It has,' Gianna responded, her tone reflective.

'Come round early tomorrow, and we can do something before the volleyball,' Soph said, hunger in her voice.

Gianna beamed a broad smile, her white teeth contrasting beautifully with her tanned skin. 'Okay.'

Soph watched as Gianna sauntered down the dirt path.

'Did you have a good day?' Ariana's voice interrupted Soph's reverie.

Soph turned into the house and faced her mum. 'Yeah, you?' she asked, still with Gianna's warmth.

'Packing boxes are arriving on Monday, so we'll need to start clearing grandma's stuff,' Ariana said, ignoring her daughter's question. 'And then I need to write a list of the things we need, to get the place renovated.'

Soph's sly grin went unnoticed. Soph had seen the state of the house and delighted in the fact that the renovations were going to take a while to complete. And in any event, she wasn't the one in a rush, and she wasn't inclined to jump in and help. If she did anything, it would be at her own pace and not dictated by her mother. She was enjoying herself, and she wasn't going to let her mother get in the way of her having fun either. 'There's something going on at the beach tomorrow. I'm going with Gianna; you're invited too,' Soph said.

'I'm not sure I'll have time,' Ariana said. 'There's too much to do here,' she added.

Soph shrugged and rolled her eyes. There was always too much to do and too little time, in her mother's world. For as long as she could remember, when not depressed, her mother had been stressed, and always seemed to need to be doing something, or achieving something, or changing something. She was exhausting to be around, and Soph was sick of chasing whatever it was her mother was seeking.

No wonder her parent's divorced, she mused. That said; her father hadn't been there for her either. He had always been busy, travelling; a Director in the Carter-Cruz family business, he seemed to relish his work and had never shown any interest in her or her music, or her mother come to think of it. In fact, he had sided with Teresa against Ariana when they had talked about whether she should be allowed to study music. Her grandmother Teresa was crazy, and, controlled everyone. She didn't quite get the dynamics within her family, and she didn't care to try to work it out. There were far more exciting things to be doing with her life. Being here for one! The welcome thought caused her face to soften momentarily. 'Why are you always in such a hurry?' she asked.

'I'm not,' Ariana argued defensively, turning towards the kitchen. 'Food's on the table,' she said, walking speedily away.

Soph held back the laugh, bubbling in her throat, at the apparent contradiction her mother had just demonstrated. 'I'm not hungry,' Soph said, shaking her head and meandering down the stairs. She refused to get drawn into Ariana's mad world. She couldn't wait for tomorrow to come and the chance to spend time with Gianna. Gianna made her feel good.

6.

Ariana gazed out from the ground floor bedroom terrace overlooking the west-cove. She could see the taverna, the volleyball net, the bench-tables set out on the golden sandy beach around a large steel bowl, suspended and filled with wooden logs. The warm feeling in her chest expanded as she watched, and yet the strange sensation also caused her to jolt.

'You do not go down to that beach,' her mother said, her tone angry for no apparent reason, other than Ariana wanting to play with the dark-haired girl in the white shorts, who kept looking up at the house through the binoculars. Had her mother seen her waving at the girl? Her heart had raced with excitement until the point her mother had spoken. Then, it was as if a balloon inside her had popped in an instant. She daren't ask why she shouldn't go and play on the beach.

'Go and see if Nikos can show you how to tend the grove,' she said.

Ariana released a deep breath, her chin dropping to her chest with the weight of the disappointment in her heart. Nikos had shown her how to tend the grove already. She was eight years old and wanted to grow up, so she could make her own decisions. 'I hate you,' she mumbled inaudibly.

'Off you go,' her mother said, smiling sweetly.

Ariana glanced to her left in the direction of the rocky outcrop at the base of the cliff, her thoughts drifting to a more pleasant memory, and she smiled.

She had watched, the sun setting behind the west-cove, as Nikki ambled across the sand, a small bag resting over her shoulder, fishing rod in hand. She had seen her trek across the beach to the rocks below the white house on many occasions, but tonight would be different. Tonight, she would go and sit with her while she fished. Her father had returned from a business trip, which was great if only because he made her mother smile in a way that nothing or no one else ever seemed to do. He had taken Teresa out on the boat, for dinner in Lefkada. They wouldn't be back until late-morning.

'Will you be okay on your own this evening?' Sophia asked. She smiled kindly, and Ariana could have sworn her grandmother winked at her. Something about the tone in her voice had given her permission to explore freely.

Ariana tried to control the bursting sensation in her chest. 'Yes,' she said, her voice struggling to pronounce the word, the 'Y' unheard. She cleared her throat, heat rising to her cheeks.

'Good, I need an early night,' Sophia announced, apparently ignoring Ariana's embarrassment, promptly filling a glass of water and heading for the stairs up to her room on the second floor. 'Good night,' she said.

'Night grandma.' Ariana said, heading for the front door. She stood for a moment, taking in the sense of freedom the night offered, the lightness in her chest, the joy in her heart. With a grin that spanned her face and a skip in her step, she headed for the rocks on the beach.

Her heart thumped as she approached Nikki. 'Hey,' she said, excitedly.

Nikki turned to face her, a warm smile appearing slowly, her hazel eyes, dark, widening, causing her smile to deepen. 'Hey,' she responded.

Ariana nodded, her heart still racing, her eyes lowered.

'Do you want to fish?' Nikki asked.

Ariana shrugged. She'd never tried it.

'You have to watch the float,' Nikki said, pointing to the small, orange stick bobbing on the water's surface.

'Ah huh,' Ariana said, studying the water. She moved closer, sat down next to Nikki's feet and pulled her knees into her chest. 'You fish a lot,' she said.

'It's fun,' Nikki responded.

Ariana gazed up at the warm smile. She liked Nikki. Nikki was always kind, pretty, and her only friend, even though they didn't get to play together very often because of Ariana's mother. 'Can I have a go?' she asked, enthusiastically.

'Stand up.'

Ariana stood.

Nikki held out the rod so that Ariana could see the position of her hand on the handle and reel. 'Hold it like this,' she demonstrated. 'You wind in the line turning this handle,' she demonstrated.

Ariana could feel her mouth drying, her heart fluttering and her hands beginning to shake. She didn't know if she would be able to hold the rod properly and suddenly felt very self-conscious. She flustered.

'Here, take it,' Nikki insisted.

Ariana was about to object, when Nikki thrust the rod into her hand, Nikki guiding Ariana's hands into the right position. The touch was confident, warm, reassuring.

'It's okay,' you won't drop it,' Nikki insisted with a chuckle, abandoning Ariana with the rod. She dived into her bag and pulled out a sandwich. 'You want some?' she asked.

Ariana shook her head. The buzzing in her stomach had stolen her appetite. This was so exciting.

Ariana watched Nikki's movements on the beach now, from the kitchen balcony; she was a stunningly attractive woman, of that there was no doubt. Even at this distance the sight of Nikki, wavy hair dancing as she worked and her muscular, lean body, wreaked havoc with her. It had her insides doing summersaults, her heart racing, her mind playing tricks, presenting possibilities that could never exist. *Urrgghh!* She couldn't allow herself the luxury of feeling any connection to this place, nor to this woman, not again. She needed to stay focused, clear the house, sell, and create a new life for her and Soph. She needed to provide Soph with opportunities that the prolonged, messy divorce, depression, and Teresa, had stolen from her over the years. She owed Soph that much.

She turned her attention away from Nikki's activities. At least the climate was pleasantly warm. The deep blue skies, the odd wispy cloud failing to make its presence felt, the soft ebb and flow of the sea, the light breeze that rustled through the olive groves. There was something quite; she couldn't think of the word that fell somewhere between, haunting and relaxing, about being here. The pace of life was a lot slower, frustratingly so in fact. And yet, the familiarity of it left her feeling quite, surprisingly, comforted.

She turned, suddenly alerted, her grandmother's room calling to her. She had to start clearing the house, which remained untouched since Sophia's death. She sighed deeply. Sorting through Sophia's belongings wasn't a task she looked forward to, but she needed to do it. And then, she would move onto the list of repairs and redecoration. The thought weighed heavily, her feet slowed, and she climbed the stairs to the master bedroom on the second floor.

She opened the door tentatively. The homely scent of lemon and rose drifted into her awareness and she stopped, reminded of her grandmother, sadness suddenly overwhelming her senses. Her eyes welled up in an instant and tears flooded onto her cheeks. She wiped at them frantically, but they wouldn't stop. She started to sob loudly, stopped herself to avoid being heard, and closed the door behind her. Her knees refused to carry her, and she slumped to the wooden floor, leaned against the door and allowed her eyes to explore the room, silent tears caressing her face.

The white dressing table sat underneath the east-facing window, affording a stunning view over the olive groves, the bulk of the estate and the east-cove. The white crocheted cloth, upon which rested an ornate jewellery box, a hairbrush and a small hand mirror, were all perfectly positioned. The pictures, of the wildflowers, probably growing somewhere on the surrounding land, adorning the whitewashed walls. The Mediterranean-blue throw over the bed, matching perfectly with the window frames and shutters. The west-facing window, with its view over the taverna, the same aspect as from her bedroom and the kitchen terrace. There was never a shortage of sunlight in the room. Sophia always loved the sun, and the warmth, she mused. For the first time, she could feel her heart aching, yearning. She hadn't had the time to feel two years ago, or even two days ago. Hell, two years ago she couldn't feel anything! She drew in a breath, released it slowly and stood.

Approaching the dressing table, she could see down to the east-cove to the jetty, in the direction the ledge where she had dozed. The beach was desolate; the Sophia II had departed. The sand lay undisturbed, but for the trail of footsteps leading from the jetty to the path up to the house. She wrapped her arms around her body, not that the weather was cold, the chill of isolation causing her to shiver. Where to start?

*

'Where's your Dad?' Gianna asked.

'Dunno,' Soph responded with a shrug, pulling her t-shirt over her head.

Gianna gulped.

'Come on,' Soph said, dropping her top to the ground and loosening her shorts.

Gianna stared at the small, blue stone sitting just above Soph's belly button.

'It's a sapphire,' Soph said with a coy smile. 'You swimming or what?' she asked, dropping her shorts, revealing a bikini that in itself revealed a tattoo that climbed from Soph's upper thigh and across the outside of her belly.

Gianna's eyes widened. 'Wow, that's.' She gulped. 'Amazing.'

Soph smiled. 'It's a dragon,' she said.

Gianna scanned the image, her mouth agape.

Soph shoved her in the arm and ran towards the water, laughing. Gianna stripped down to her bathing suit and followed her in.

'Ahhhh!' Soph wailed as she surfaced. She ducked under the water again, swam ferociously to nowhere, and then back towards Gianna.

Gianna laughed. 'It's not that cold,' she said, standing with the water to her waist, her arms wrapped across her chest.

Soph's brows rose, and her lips curled, immediately before she thrashed her hands in the water, dousing Gianna, and laughing hysterically at Gianna's squeals.

'You...' Gianna glared with a mischievous grin. She dived under the water and upended Soph. Both sank, bounced off the sandy floor, and then emerged spluttering with laughter. 'Have you seen the fish?' Gianna said, with a twinkle in her eye.

Soph's eyes widened, and she tried to move swiftly. Held back by the water's resistance she screamed, her arms flapping until she reached the dry sand.

Gianna bent over, laughing loudly. 'Really, you're that scared of fish?' she asked, through the tears.

Soph grumped. 'Only since one bit me,' she harrumphed, her lips beginning to curl at the irrational response.

'They don't bite, Soph,' Gianna said, wading towards her.

'You sure?' Soph asked, absorbed by the compassion in Gianna's sparkling eyes.

'Sure. Have you ever been snorkelling?' she asked with a tilt of her head.

Soph shook her head.

'We can do that one day,' Gianna said. 'Come on; the water will feel warmer this time.' She tilted her head towards the sea, grabbed Soph's hand and ran them into the water.

Soph didn't resist, but it didn't stop her heart thumping in her chest either. She dived beneath the surface and headed for deeper water. With her feet off the ground, she reasoned there would be less chance of being bitten. And, at least there was the distraction of Gianna gliding effortlessly through the water in front of her.

She watched, droplets glistening on Gianna's tanned skin, her hands pressing calmly against the resistance as she trod water, her legs working tirelessly to keep her afloat. 'You swim a lot?' Soph asked.

'There's a lot of water here,' Gianna responded, with an adorable smile.

Soph held her gaze, her feet paddling like a swan's, her hands steadying her. 'My mum and dad got divorced,' she said.

Gianna's eyes squinted. 'Sorry,' she said.

Soph made as if to shrug, but the motion took her face below the water, and she spluttered. Gianna was laughing when she surfaced. It helped. 'Come on,' she said, indicating towards the rocks jutting out from below the white house. 'Let's go hunt,' she said, with no idea about what she might catch.

'We haven't got a net,' Gianna said.

'We can practise,' she laughed.

Gianna frowned.

'You know, do like, a recce, and you can teach me,' she said.

'Race you?' Gianna said, her arms working the water effortlessly, her body propelling her forward at a pace.

Soph got off to a slow start, her eyes consumed by the body moving through the water. She didn't care.

By the time Soph reached the rocks, Gianna was sat on one waiting for her, smiling. Soph looked up and grinned.

*

Ariana wandered down the dirt path leading to the west-cove. She had at least sorted out her grandmother's clothes. She had made up a bag for throwing away, and the best stuff she would offer to a local shop. Even though tempted to peak, she had stacked the photo albums and diaries without sneaking a look inside. It wouldn't have done to drag out the process, and she knew if she had started going through them she would still be there now. Then she had walked around the outside of the house taking notes; though not sure what materials she needed to repair the walls or the shutters, other than white and blue paint, which she had found in the garage. Some of the worst affected shutters looked as if they were in need of complete replacement, but she was clueless as to how to even start and didn't have the wood. She had searched through the double garage and found various tools, most of which she didn't have a name for or know what to do with them, but she hadn't found anything that looked like it could be used to repair the rendered walls. She was going to need some help to source the materials, and that would mean asking Nikki. She drew in a deep breath and released it slowly, trying to control the pounding in her chest.

With Sophia's ashes to collect from Manos, Ariana paced across the beach towards the taverna. Music drifted into her awareness distracting her from her thoughts, and her pulse quickened the closer she got. The beads of sweat glistening on

Nikki's tanned shoulder grabbed her attention, and she cleared her throat, puffing to catch her breath. She raised the sunglasses from her eyes and perched them on her head, clipping her hair back with the move.

Nikki looked up from the table and smiled ruefully at the woman who seemed to do everything at a rate of knots. 'Hi,' she said, continuing to set out the cutlery. Resting a napkin under a small coloured stone on the side-plate; Ariana's soapy scent drifted into her awareness, and the stone leapt from her hand, landing with a thud on the plate. 'Oops!' she remarked, her cheeks darkening instantly.

Ariana twitched uncomfortably, too consumed by her agenda to notice Nikki's awkwardness. The one thing that should have been at the forefront of her mind when she arrived on the island had slipped down her to-do list in her haste to get the house ready for sale, and she was feeling ashamed. 'I need to collect grandma's ashes,' she said, sheepishly.

The smile on Nikki's face shifted to something more sombre. 'Ah, yes, of course,' she said, stopping what she was doing. She left the cutlery in a pile on the table and stepped towards the bar.

Ariana stared, entranced by the view; her eyes tracking the bare shoulders, the exposed back and resting for a moment on the trim waist and the light-blue denim shorts hugging the narrow hips and the firm arse. She gulped, fighting for the words that deserted her. 'Umm, it doesn't need to be right now,' she said, suddenly backtracking as a wave of anxiety hit her in the stomach. 'I, umm, just mean... I mean I hadn't mentioned before... I erm...'

Nikki stopped, turned, and gazed at the flustered woman. Her heart slowed a fraction, and she swallowed down the sadness that still clung at the back of her throat at the mention of Sophia. 'Is there anything I can do to help?' she asked with genuine concern.

Ariana stood, her eyes locked onto Nikki's. She didn't know whether the electric feeling passing down her spine was preferable to the tension and stress that had become her constant companion. At least she seemed to be able to control the latter. The tingling warmth that she experienced around Nikki scared the shit out of her. 'I... umm. Can you bring the ashes to the house, maybe tomorrow?' she asked. Her eyes dropped to the sand at her feet. 'Please?' she added.

Nikki could feel the ache in her heart growing with the torment of seeing Ariana, of having loved her all these years, and yet feeling so estranged from her. Ariana being here now was even more painful than the years of absence and longing had created. She seemed to have changed beyond all recognition. The woman who stood before her now appeared detached and strangely aloof, just like the woman who had made her leave the island twenty years ago. Teresa. Had Ariana become the very person she had despised back then? 'Of course,' she said, answering Ariana's question. 'Can I get you a drink?' she asked. 'Since you are here,' she added.

Ariana glanced around as if looking for a reason to reject the offer. There was so much to do and so little time, the mantra started.

'Please?' Nikki insisted.

'Thank you,' Ariana nodded, a tight smile containing the desire that niggled just below the surface; a longing that would have her racing back across the sand, up the hill and locked behind the walls of the white house for fear of the consequences of acting on her feelings.

'Coffee?' Nikki asked, studying Ariana curiously. She was even more beautiful, she mused.

'Yes, thanks.' Ariana replied, averting the quizzical hazel-eyes resting on her, causing her to flush. Settling her gaze on the driftwood bench, her feet responding to her thoughts, she strolled towards it.

Nikki smiled at the apparent slowing of Ariana's pace.

Ariana sat, sighed, and eased back against the rock. Closing her eyes, the sun on her face felt good, comforting and relaxing. Her heart slowed, her shoulders softened; she could breathe.

Nikki watched from the bar as she poured them both a cup of coffee. She almost didn't want to disturb Ariana in her brief moment of peace. Compassion drove the smile that appeared as she approached the closed eyes. Reminded of the woman she once knew, her stomach flipped. Controlling herself, she sat on the seat next to Ariana and sipped from her cup.

Ariana's eyelids fluttered. 'I forgot how peaceful it is here,' she said.

Nikki remained silent.

Ariana opened her eyes and eased herself up, returned her sunglasses to her nose and took the offered drink from Nikki's hand. 'How have you been?' she asked tenderly, briefly holding Nikki's gaze from behind the dark lens, before turning her attention to the sea, and the horizon.

Nikki frowned. She hadn't even thought how she might answer that question. 'Fine… I guess.'

'This place looks amazing,' Ariana added with genuine fondness.

Nikki nodded. 'We still have the workshop out back,' she said.

'Perhaps I can take a look, before I…' she didn't finish the sentence.

'Please don't sell the house,' Nikki said, softly. She hadn't meant to raise the subject and berated herself as the words aired. Her shoulders tensed, she placed her cup on the rock to her right, and her head lowered to watch her fingers trying to massage away the tension in her palms.

Ariana shook her head, but the words wouldn't come. She took a sip of the coffee and found it hard to swallow.

Clearing her throat, summoning courage from a place she didn't realise existed, 'I have no choice,' she said. There was no tension in her voice, just resignation.

Nikki baulked at the words that triggered her memory of the conversation they had had just before Ariana had left the island twenty years earlier. *I have no choice.* 'Is Martin behind this, or your mother?' Nikki asked in a curt tone, before she could stop herself. She stared across the short distance between them, examining the subtle movements in the fine lines that shaped Ariana's mouth as she processed the question.

Ariana sighed deeply and turned towards Nikki. 'Martin… I, we got divorced,' she said finally. Her mouth tried to form a smile, and her eyes refused to comply.

She looked older than her thirty-six years, worn down, consumed by something that didn't make her happy. Nikki considered the shadows, peaking from under Ariana's sunglasses, the faint lines that seemed ever-present on her forehead, the absence of the dimple in her right cheek that would always appear when she smiled. 'I'm sorry,' she said, even though she wasn't. She wanted to reach out and touch Ariana, hold her, and caress her. She clasped the front edge of the bench seat and leaned forward, taking her weight onto her arms, and gazed out to sea. 'Sophia didn't know, did she?' she asked, certain she knew the answer. If Sophia had known about Ariana's divorce, she would surely have mentioned it to Nikki.

Ariana held her gaze. 'No,' she said. She paused, as if gathering her thoughts, her eyes never lifting from Nikki's mouth.

Nikki nodded.

'Grandma…' Ariana stopped speaking, her eyes dropped to the cup shaking in her hand, and she placed it on the sand before continuing. 'Sophia, we lost contact. I don't know how it happened. Soph was ten, and I was in a bad place.' She paused. 'Things weren't going well with Martin.' She paused again as if

65

wanting to say more. 'Anyway, long story short, I left him, and we moved in with my mother, and I started treatment for depression. The letters stopped coming, and I didn't have the energy to write either.'

Nikki frowned. Sophia had written to Ariana regularly; she had seen the letters. The words were trying to leap from her mouth, but she thought better of it and bit her tongue.

'Martin was a womaniser, but he was also addicted to the lifestyle working for my mother's business had afforded him: the fast cars, the partying, drinking, gambling; the free flow of money was a bigger lure than being with his wife and daughter. It meant so much to him, he couldn't stop, and he lost it all. He bankrupt us.'

Nikki pursed her lips as she absorbed Ariana's every word.

'My mother didn't agree with the divorce and did her damnedest to try to stop me, asserting that I wasn't mentally fit to decide for myself. No matter what had happened to us as a family, he was still good for the business.' Ariana continued, shaking her head, the pain clearly visible in the tension locked into her jaw.

Nikki wanted to ask questions. What about Teresa? Where was she? Was she coming back to the island? That thought caused her to shudder. She tried to reach out, comfort Ariana but stopped. 'I'm so sorry,' she whispered.

'So,' Ariana started again, her tone suddenly more upbeat. 'So, I couldn't get here before Sophia died and if she hadn't left the estate to me I wouldn't be here at all,' she said, wincing at the truth. 'When I found out about the will I was still too unwell. Martin tried to claim the inheritance, and then my mother cut me off. Her last gesture of goodwill was for the Sophia II to bring us here, and she only did that to save face with Soph. Soph doesn't know most of this by the way,' she added.

'Shit!' Nikki said, the word slipping out, barely audible.

'Now, it's down to me.' Ariana shrugged. She released a deep breath.

Nikki studied the smiling eyes that seemed softer than they had been before Ariana had talked. She smiled in return, a sad smile, the pain of Ariana's revelation still sitting heavily in her chest. She could feel the anger rising, blinding her mind; the years lost, years that Sophia would have loved with her granddaughter. The years, she too had missed. She pressed at the corners of her eyes, trying to shift her focus from the rising negative emotions.

Ariana drifted to Nikki's toned muscles; her tanned arms; her broad shoulders, her muscular back. With her heart pounding and her mind throwing distracting thoughts at her, she reached out and placed her hand on Nikki's arm.

Nikki flinched, the movement instantly causing her to release the bridge of her nose. She watched in mute fascination, the trail of goosebumps flaring up her arm.

Ariana jolted her hand away. 'Sorry!' she said. When Nikki lifted her gaze and looked at her, her hazel eyes were darker. Ariana started to shake. She stood suddenly compelled by the need to flee.

Nikki stood quickly and pulled her into her arms. Ariana's initial stiffness melted and she fell into the embrace. 'I'm sorry, Ariana. I have no idea what you've been through,' she whispered, holding her close.

Ariana reclaimed the breath that had been stolen from her with the unexpected embrace and leaned into Nikki's warm shoulder. Captivated by the flowery, slightly spicy scent, and her soft skin, finding it hard to resist, she snuggled closer. 'It has been difficult,' she said, taking a deep breath, and releasing it slowly. Her eyes wandered from Nikki in the direction of the increase in noise, customers arriving at the bar, laughing and chattering. She pulled out of the warmth. 'You need to work,' she stated.

Nikki nodded, reached up and swept Ariana's hair behind her ear, her fingers lingering, her thumb tracing the side of Ariana's neck as she moved her hand away. 'I'm so sorry,' she said.

'I have nothing Nikki,' Ariana said. 'The estate is Soph's and my future. I have no job, no home, and no family.'

Nikki wiped at the tear that had slipped onto Ariana's cheek, then held both her arms and squeezed. 'When did you last take a break?' she asked, upping the tempo in her voice.

Ariana released a chuckle through the tears. She couldn't remember. She shrugged.

'Exactly,' Nikki said, with renewed enthusiasm. 'So, why don't you take a break for a few weeks, while you're here?' She could feel Ariana's resistance to the idea through the increase in tension in her jaw. 'You're only waiting for a sale, the least you can do is chill out while you're here. Soph's enjoying herself,' she added, hoping to press home the point.

Ariana nodded, allowing a tiny smile to form at the edges of her mouth.

Nikki watched the corner of Ariana's lips lift a little, and smiled. 'Good, that's settled then.' Nikki's eyes wandered to the increasing numbers around the bar. 'I'd better go and help,' she said.

Ariana glanced across at the party and smiled. 'Yes, looks like it's going to be busy.'

'You going to have a glass of wine before or after we play volleyball?' Nikki asked. She wasn't going to take no for an answer.

Ariana squirmed.

'You and I are going to take on the girls,' she added.

Ariana frowned.

'Soph and Gianna,' Nikki clarified.

Ariana laughed. 'I haven't played in years,' she said.

Nikki shrugged and beamed a grin. 'Who cares?' she said, heading towards the bar.

7.

Ariana sat back on the driftwood seat feeling strangely lighter. She smiled to herself at the tingling warmth that lingered in her muscles, stifled a giggle at the sense of freedom that overwhelmed her. She felt like a child, and yet she felt more grown up than she ever had.

She wanted to shout out and tell everyone. It had been the first time she had talked openly about her life, except for the time she had spent with the therapist. Even though she hadn't mentioned all the sordid details to Nikki; about catching her husband with the other women, her mother's vicious verbal assaults on her, ordering her to stay married, threats of revealing how fucked up she was to Soph. She had shared her past with Nikki. And, for some strange and inexplicable reason, that mattered.

Maybe it was the way Nikki had stared at her with compassion, and a sense of shared pain as she bared her soul, and the display of protectiveness that Nikki had shown. Then there was the touch. She hadn't remembered how good Nikki felt, her strength, and the heat from her body, amalgamating to form something quite intoxicating. For the first time in a very long time, she felt truly safe. Protected, cared for, loved even.

A small woman with long dark hair approached, singing, and held out a large glass of wine. 'Thank you,' Ariana said, her glance unhurried, observing the woman with curiosity.

'Hi, I'm Chrissy. I work here. Nikki said I need to look after you,' she said.

She must have been in her early thirties, Ariana thought. She looked happy, easy-going and had a warm, friendly smile. 'Thank you,' she said softly, suddenly wondering about the woman's relationship to Nikki. The idea stirred something in her, something she couldn't name.

'Let me know if you need anything,' Chrissy said. 'Volleyball will be on all afternoon and the fire pit's for food later. I can get you a snack if you're hungry now,' she offered.

'I'm fine, thanks,' Ariana replied, mirroring Chrissy's smile.

She glanced over the woman's shoulder, back to the bar. Nikki was laughing, pouring drinks, and chatting with the locals. It suited her; she looked younger than her thirty-six years and so full of life. Ariana sipped at the chilled drink and placed the glass on the flat rock. *Maybe a break was a good idea?* She could still get the house refurbished. It might even be fun, she mused, with a wry smile.

She sat back in the seat, slipped off her sandals and wriggled her feet into the sand. She groaned softly at the cold feeling against the balls of her hot feet and sipped at the wine. The soothing effect caused her mind to still, and her ears to tune into the ambience of the cove: the voices emanating from the bar, the low whooshing of the waves, and the intermittent buzzing of the insects busying in the bushes and shrubs that bordered the sand and rock. There was something very familiar about nature here. There had been birdsong in London of course, and the other cities to which she had travelled, but nothing quite like the incessant, rhythmical hum, and rustling that seemed to blend effortlessly with the aroma of the burnt salt from the slowly ripening olives, the delicate scent of fresh fish and the sweet smell of the wildflowers and herbs. She gazed at the shades of blue dancing on a wave of heat at the horizon. Drawing closer, the water shifted in colour from dark-blue to light blue and then to the softest green she had ever seen. It almost looked clear. Her eyes eventually found themselves staring at the house on the hill, and then the white foam forming on the gentle waves brushing against the rocks below and then back to the white house. She sighed. Even in its imperfect state, it still looked majestic.

'Sea snails,' Gianna said, pointing into the shallow water as they slowly edged their way around the slippery rocks.

'You eat them?' Soph scrunched up her face. 'Yuk!'

'Well, I mean, you can eat sea snails, but not these, they're too small,' she said, chuckling at Soph's wide-eyed frown.

'Look, is that a crab?' Soph asked, pointing at the pincers on a small, shelled creature, wriggling its way quickly across the bottom of the rock-pool.

Gianna stared into the water. 'Yes,' she said, reaching in and pulling the tiny creature from its home, taking care not to squash it.

Soph jolted back, her foot slipping. She tried to correct her balance without putting her hand down but failed, making contact with barnacled shells firmly fixed to the rugged rocks. She squealed at the sharp contact and pulled her hand away. 'Awww.'

Gianna laughed, reached out, and grabbed Soph by the arm. 'They won't bite,' she said, maintaining a firm grip to support her and losing the tiny crab out of her other hand, back into the water. She took Soph's hand and studied the grazed palm. Soph's eyes had narrowed, and she puffed out a slow deep breath. Gianna stopped laughing. 'You really scared?' she asked, her voice soft, laced with concern.

Soph nodded, though Gianna's touch was heightening the nerves initiated by the threat of being bitten, and adding something else. She held Gianna's concerned gaze, willing for Gianna to keep her safe. Soph had tried hard not to be afraid of the things that might be lurking in the water, and while they had been in the deeper sea, swimming, and unable to touch the seabed, it hadn't been too bad. But, as soon as her feet touched the surface of a rock or the sand under the water, no matter how shallow, she worried that the sea creatures were going to attack her. Her hands were shaking, and her legs had quickly taken on the consistency of jelly when she had made contact with the sharp shells.

'Shall we go back?' Gianna asked, tenderly caressing Soph's injured hand.

Soph nodded. She couldn't help but enjoy the comfort of Gianna's hand in hers. But, when their fingers interlinked and the tingling sensations filtered down her spine, an altogether different feeling struck her.

Gianna slowly tracked her way back to the edge of the rocks, Soph following her every move, squeezing the life out of the supportive hand. 'You okay to swim now?' she asked, with a kind smile, encouraging Soph to let go so the blood could find its way back to her, now white, fingers.

'Sure,' Soph replied, instantly missing the reassuring touch.

Gianna smiled knowingly, turned and dived into the deep water. She emerged a few yards from the rocks. 'Come on,' she called. 'Race you to the shore.' She leant into the water and started to swim.

Soph grinned; her courage restored by the challenge, she dived into the water and swam with all her strength. By the time she reached the shallow water and stepped up the beach to where they had dropped their clothes Gianna had dressed. The water from her bathing suit was seeping through her shorts and t-shirt, causing the clothes to cling around the shape of her body. Soph shuddered, picked up her clothes and stepped into her deck shoes. 'I'll carry these,' she said, her voice broken.

Gianna's sparkling eyes deepened the smile on her lips. 'Volleyball!' she said.

Soph chuckled, that hadn't been the thought occupying her mind. 'Right,' she said, following Gianna up the path towards the house.

'I need to go home and get changed,' Gianna said as they strolled. 'I can meet you at the beach.'

Soph didn't need to eye her up for size. 'I've got shorts and a top if you want?' she offered.

Gianna didn't need to think twice about the question. She had no desire to create any distance between them. 'Okay,' she said, trying to sound casual and feeling anything but. She had known from the time she set eyes on Sophie Carter-Cruz that there was something extraordinary about her, and the more time she spent with her, the more she learned about her, the more she liked; and the more she wanted. Descending the external steps to the ground floor, and Soph's bedroom, her legs weakened by her lustful thoughts, her heart pounded, and her hands felt clammy.

'I'm going to grab a shower,' Soph said, searching the chest-of-drawers for clothes. She handed Gianna a pair of long cotton beach-shorts and a sleeveless t-shirt. 'These any good?' she asked.

Gianna laughed out loud. She would never have expected Soph to wear shorts with pineapples and bananas printed on them. 'Thanks,' she said, with a hint of sarcasm. She grinned at the clothes in her hand, the sight instantly dampening the desire that had coursed through her body just moments ago.

Soph was laughing. 'My grandmother gave them to me. I've never worn them,' she said, rolling her eyes.

'Hmmm,' Gianna responded, staring at the pants. 'Wonder why?' she said, laughing hysterically. 'They don't even match,' she added, holding the bright pink top up, against the orange tones in the shorts.

Soph doubled over with laughter, reached into the drawer, pulled out a white vest and threw it to Gianna. 'There's another shower next door,' she said, indicating with her eyes to the right of the bedroom door. 'You can leave your clothes in there too,' she added, still fighting the giggles, locking onto

Gianna's wide-eyed happy face. She looked so pretty, and so, hot!

'Thanks,' Gianna nodded. Still chuckling, she exited the bedroom and entered the family bathroom.

Soph dived into the en-suite shower and dived out. Within five minutes she was washed and dressed, her scraggly, wet hair dripping down the back of her neck. She stepped into the corridor and didn't have to wait long before the fresh scent of shower-gel, drifting down the short hallway, aroused her senses. 'You smell great,' Soph said before she could censor her thoughts.

Gianna smiled, closed the gap between them and placed a brief kiss on Soph's cheek. 'You smell good too,' she said.

The touch was fleeting, but it seared Soph's skin and sent a bolt of lightning straight down her spine. Floored, she struggled for words, tried to swallow and couldn't.

'Come on,' Gianna said, jolting Soph out of the trance. She stepped past her, out the door, and headed up the steps.

Soph couldn't see the smile of contentment on Gianna's face, or her flushed cheeks as she bit down on her lip, or the long breath she blew out as she reached the path leading down to the taverna's beach. She could see the nape of the tanned neck that she wanted to kiss though, and she could feel her heart pounding in her chest, and she wondered if Gianna's heart was racing as much as hers. Soph's smile broadened with every step. She ran a couple of paces to catch up with Gianna. 'Volleyball huh!' She reached out and brushed her fingers against Gianna's then broke into a run. 'Race you,' she yelled, but Gianna was already on the chase.

Soph stopped. Twenty paces into the soft sand had her legs screaming and her lungs bursting. She bent over double, puffing hard, trying not to laugh and failing. 'Hang on,' she shouted.

Gianna had overtaken her before they reached the beach. Looking over her shoulder at the command to stop, she ground to a halt. 'I win?' she asked.

'Sure,' Soph puffed.

Gianna punched into the air. 'Yes!'

'I forgot my guitar,' Soph added.

'Want me to go back for it?'

'Nah,' I'll go,' Soph said, raising her hand. 'I'll see you over there.'

'Okay.'

Soph turned, trudged back to the track and started the climb. By the time she reached the top she was sweating, still puffing, and her lungs felt as if they were about to explode. For the first time in her life, she felt happy.

'You two get on well,' the male voice said.

Soph jumped. Lost in her reverie, she hadn't seen Nikos approaching. Her smile reflected her cheery disposition. Nikos wasn't smiling though, and his disapproving gaze steamrollered her thoughts instantly. 'Hi Nikos,' she said, reservedly. 'Are you coming to the party?' she asked, tilting her head towards the beach.

'No,' he replied. 'I have work to do.' He was courteous enough, but something in the way he looked at her sent the message that he wasn't happy with her for some reason.

She nodded. Nikos was probably pissed with her because of her mother. She shrugged. 'Oh!' she said, with a tight smile. She wasn't going to let Gianna's Papa take her fun away. She'd had enough of that with her father.

He forced a smile, but his eyes remained dark, sullen. He nodded politely and darted down between two rows of olive trees.

Soph stood for a moment adjusting to the effect of Nikos' apparent dislike of her, a sudden weight dropping from her chest into her gut. A hollow space that appeared, then suddenly filled with wave after wave of vibrations, gentle at first then increasing in intensity. She could hardly breathe, and within seconds her hands were shaking. Slowly she made her way back to her room, fighting to stop the tears spilling from her eyes. *Why did everyone try to ruin her happiness?*

*

'Hey Gianna, come and play.' Giorgos shouted as she approached the locals mingling around the bar and the volleyball court.

'Sure.' She jogged the last few paces, and he threw her the ball.

Gianna stepped up to the service line, eyed the opposing team of two, tossed the ball in the air and hit it high over the net. The ball remained in the air, passing to and fro, the two teams vying for an opportunity to finish the point. Giorgos blocked, drawing their opponents into the net. They scrambled the ball back, and Gianna sent the ball to the back of the court, taking advantage of the space that had opened up. One man dived to the ground, but couldn't get to the ball before it hit the sand.

Ariana watched the game playing out. Gianna was athletic, with a keen eye for the ball, and a good pair of hands. Suddenly reminded of the earlier-promised match, knowing her volleyball skills were more than a little rusty, she observed her more closely, with admiration. Gianna reminded her of Nikki; slightly too scrawny maybe, but fit, adventurous, and a little flirtatious even. Ariana shifted her gaze to the bar area, Nikki's intense eyes smiling back at her, she flushed. Nikki was holding up a glass, asking the question. Ariana nodded. Pulling her attention from Nikki and back to the game, she caught sight of Soph meandering across the sand, guitar pinned to her back.

She started to smile then stopped as the concern on Soph's face registered in her mind.

'How are you doing?' Nikki asked, interrupting her worried thoughts and handing out a fresh glass of wine.

'Oh, good,' Ariana responded, though still distracted by her daughter.

'You ready for a game?' Nikki asked.

A loud crack from the fire-pit caused Ariana to jump, bringing her attention back to Nikki and the aroma of smoking wood that was beginning to drift intermittently on the light breeze. 'Whenever you are,' she responded, raising a smile.

'Give me five,' Nikki said. 'You can get warmed up if you like,' she added, with a chuckle.

Ariana broadened her smile, her eyes on Soph, whose demeanour seemed to have shifted. Soph was smiling at Gianna. Ariana released a long breath. *Good!* She sipped at her drink and approached the court and the cheering spectators.

Gianna smiled cheekily and dragged a protesting but chuckling Soph reluctantly onto the court. 'Stand there,' she said. You cover the front, I cover the back, got it?'

Soph grinned. 'Got it,' she said, giving her attention to the other side of the net.

Ariana smiled. 'Go girls,' she cheered, retracting with embarrassment as her conditioning kicked in, admonishing her frivolous behaviour, even though her voice didn't reach above the other screams and shouts.

'Go girls,' Nikki yelled, almost into Ariana's right ear.

Ariana chuckled, rubbed at her ear and yelled again, 'Go girls! Woop, Woop!'

Nikki wrapped an arm around Ariana's shoulder and squeezed. 'They look like they're having fun,' she said, releasing the hold and sipping at her wine.

Ariana turned to face her, staring intently. 'Thank you,' she said, with sincerity.

Nikki shrugged. 'Any time.' Her smile lingered, her hazel eyes sparkled, and there was no lack of depth to the gaze that had shattered Ariana's defences in the short time she had been back on the island. 'Come on, we're on next, against those two,' she said, with a wink. Her eyes narrowed, assessing; her game face firmly affixed.

Ariana burst out laughing. 'Ha, ha, ha! You know how long it's been?' she asked.

'Too long,' Nikki responded.

Ariana's jaw dropped a fraction as she processed the undertone behind the words. Nikki stepped onto the court and toyed with the ball in her hands. Ariana followed her and faced her daughter on the other side of the net. Both women glared, then smiled.

'Game on,' Gianna shouted.

The locals cheered.

*

Ariana flopped onto the sand, gasping for breath. 'That was fun,' she said.

Nikki handed her a glass of water. 'Wine?' she asked. 'I assume you'll stay for the party now,' she said.

Ariana gazed at Soph and Gianna on the court again. They hadn't lost a game yet. She smiled. 'Okay.'

'Good,' Nikki said, heading for the bar.

Ariana finished the glass of water, leaned back on the sand and closed her eyes. She drifted, with the crackling of the wood fire and the smell of roasting meat, lamb, and spices, for company, and with the gentle ebb and flow of the waves having a deeply hypnotic effect.

'Good to see her relaxing a bit, eh!' Manos said handing a jug of iced water across the bar. He could feel the sombreness in Nikki's eyes before she looked up.

'Yes,' she said softly, briefly glancing towards the prone body with the ash-blonde hair; and she meant it. Pulling down on the pump, releasing the chilled beer, she filled the tall glass and handed it across the bar. She took the money in return and rang it into the till distracted by her thoughts.

'Aye,' Manos said, sucking through his teeth. He reached around Nikki's shoulder, pulled her sharply into a fatherly-embrace and placed a kiss on the top of her head, keenly observing Ariana resting on the sand. She looked the most at peace she had done since her arrival, which had been more akin to an invasion. The transformation in Ariana's energy gave some hope. Teresa had never settled in the whole of her time on the island, but Ariana was different. She was more like Sophia than Teresa ever was.

He had watched Nikki and Ariana as they played volleyball, the tenderness in the way they looked at each other, the sincere smile that passed between them that spoke more than words ever could, the subtle lingering touch as they handed the ball from one to the other. He had seen it before too when they were teenagers. When Teresa wasn't around, Ariana would appear occasionally, and they would head to the rocks and fish or take a boat out or laze around on the beach and snorkel. The same look, the same smile, the same touch. They were in love then, and, it seemed, they were still in love. He chuckled, his cheeks flushing with his assessment of the two women. He loved them both. He always had done. 'Reckon she'll find a good reason to stay,' he said, his prophetic statement of fact not needing a response.

Nikki looked at him. She wasn't so sure, but she hoped above all hope that he was right. She watched Ariana closely, confused by the effect the woman had on her already. The anger that had driven her up the hill on the first day had defused as quickly as it had arisen. There was warmth in her chest, fuelled by the compassion she felt and something more. But, the feeling was constricted, contained, imprisoned. The fact that Ariana would be selling, and leaving, stopped her immersing herself in the joy that threatened her heart, for fear it would break again. She couldn't afford another broken heart, and yet, the touch of Ariana's skin, the soapy scent that was so familiar, the dark-penetrating gaze, and the ash-blonde hair that would sometimes fall around her eyes, it was already too late. Nikki's heart ached, and there was nothing she could do to alleviate the sensation. In fact, with every hour passing, in the company of Ariana, the ache deepened.

'Can feel it in me waters,' Manos continued, justifying, heading onto the beach. 'And old Sophia was never wrong,' he added with a tilt of his head, the large carving knife waving ceremoniously in his hand.

It was correct, Sophia was never in doubt that Ariana would return. Whether she had gone so far as to assert that Ariana would make the island her home though was unclear, and most likely pure conjecture, but in Manos' mind, it was a fact, and therefore the truth. Nikki smiled, but it was a strained movement, lacking integrity. Manos meant well, but sometimes, with the best will in the world, one had to accept reality, and that was, the sale of the white house on the hill.

The sound of a guitar grabbed Nikki's attention from her troubled thoughts, and she smiled warmly. Soph was sat on a small rock, adjacent to the driftwood bench, rocking as she strummed, her eyes smiling at the object of her attention. Gianna, gazing back at her with a beaming grin, looked awestruck. Nikki glanced from Soph to Gianna and back again, and sighed.

The music drifted into Ariana's awareness, and she stirred, covered her eyes from the sun with her hand and blinked them open. She pulled herself up and watched her daughter, a warm feeling spreading across her chest. She knew Soph had a gift and it had pained her that her mother and husband had blocked Soph from going to Music College. At least that would change soon. She was determined to make sure that Soph got the education and support she needed to develop her talent. It was the least she could do.

'Here.' Nikki said, handing her a glass of wine.

'Thanks.' Ariana said, staring. Nikki's tanned legs; her arse; her waist; her chest, and eventually into her eyes as Nikki lowered herself to sit.

'Food is ready when you are,' Nikki said, laughing, pointing at Manos. He was dancing, singing, and wielding his carving knife at the large lamb joint, cutting chunks as directed by each guest in turn.

'He always was a charmer,' Ariana laughed. 'He has a good voice too,' she said, heartened by the jovial and relaxed atmosphere that encapsulated the west-cove. The contrast with the east-cove, where they had moored, and the ledge where she had dozed just two days ago, couldn't be greater. Nikki moved, and her arm brushed against Ariana's, shifting her from her thoughts. The tiny hairs on her arm rose instantly, and a shiver tracked up into the back of her neck. She shuddered.

'You okay?' Nikki asked.

The strumming stopped. The cacophony suddenly quieted. All ears tuned to the sweet, haunting voice, and an acoustic rendition of, *Time After Time*.

Lying in my bed, I hear the clock tick and think of you.
Caught up in circles, confusion is nothing new.

Nikki stared in Soph's direction, captivated by the pure quality in her voice, but Ariana was visible through her peripheral vision, and she couldn't stop the light feeling that invaded her chest or the tingling heat vibrating in her core. The warmth of the sun, the heady effect of the wine, the sheer fun of playing volleyball with Ariana by her side, it was almost perfect. She swallowed against the lump that formed in her throat and fought the rising emotion wetting her eyes. Soph's voice drifted across the silence. As she glanced around, even Manos rubbed at his cheeks, accusing the smoke from the fire pit, naturally. She chuckled to herself.

If you're lost, you can look and you will find me, time after time.

Ariana became aware that Nikki was staring at her. The intensity in Nikki's eyes had darkened her natural hazel colouring, giving it a deep, rich quality that drilled right through Ariana, causing her breath to hitch and her mouth to dry. The sensation that fired through her body, culminating low in her crotch, caused her to groan, and heat to flush her already burned cheeks. Nikki continued to hold Ariana with her eyes, unwavering, assessing, asking, longing. Ariana tried to extract herself from the silent inquisition, but she couldn't. The way Nikki was looking at her. She had never been looked at like this since leaving the island. Since Nikki last looked at her this way. Only Nikki made her feel like this. She tried to swallow, but couldn't.

Hands clapped as the song drew to an end, the sound pulling Nikki from the trance. Her smile seemed more reserved than the message her eyes had sent. The light relief enabled Ariana to breathe. Gianna was wiping at her eyes and laughing; Soph was teasing her, pulling her into her arms and hugging her. They looked happy.

As Ariana scanned the audience, others were shedding a tear too. Bursting with pride, sniffling with emotion, she grinned.

'She has an amazing voice,' Nikki said, her tone a fraction lower than her normal resonance.

Ariana nodded. Overwhelmed, conflicted, she still couldn't speak.

8.

Ariana stood on the shaded kitchen-balcony, sipping her coffee. The sun hadn't long risen in the east-cove and wasn't visible on this side of the house yet, but the temperature was already hot, and especially on the burnt skin on her nose and cheeks. The sea looked bluer, and especially the point where it kissed the sky on the horizon, darker. The contrast between the sand and rocks, on the far side of the west-cove, seemed sharper than usual. The warm salty air, infused with sage and samphire from the garden below, was becoming a familiar scent this side of the property, overlooking the taverna. She breathed in the fragrant aroma, her eyes wandering to the bench-tables on the beach and watching intently.

The sight of Nikki appearing from the bar caused Ariana's heart to flutter. She watched as Nikki started clearing the tables and tidying the beachfront from the evening's party, feeling a sudden urge to rush down to the taverna and help her, to be with her, to chat to her, and explore the warm fuzzy sense of comfort that seemed to accompany Nikki's presence. The rush of excitement felt so different from the hurried, panicked state that she had lived by for so long. It was lighter, freer and altogether more exhilarating.

Yesterday, for the first time in a very long time, she had laughed, she had had fun, and she had felt happy. She hadn't wanted the night to end, but when it had, she had returned to the house and slept deeply. She pressed her hand against her thumping heart, a lazy grin firmly implanted on her face. *Mmm!*

'You alright?' Soph asked, her voice groggy, squinting quizzically at her mother.

Ariana jolted out of her reverie. She turned and took a couple of paces towards Soph. Reaching up she tenderly swept the scruffy hair from Soph's face and cupped her already tanned cheek. 'I'm fine,' she said.

Soph eyed her mother suspiciously. She'd never seen her like this before, but it was kind of cool. She looked, almost, relaxed.

'Ready to do some painting?' Ariana asked.

Soph's eyes rolled. Maybe not that relaxed then! 'What's the rush?' she asked, defensively.

'No rush,' Ariana replied softly, and she meant it.

'I got stuff on with Gianna,' Soph said, though with no idea what that stuff might be.

'Okay,' Ariana said. She looked as if she were locked in some other time and space, her dreamy world, besotted.

A broad grin appeared on Soph's face. 'Cool,' she said, suddenly feeling a rush of relief at not being forced into decorating tasks that she had no desire to undertake, with or without her mother's help.

'Coffee's in the pot,' Ariana said, pressing a kiss to Soph's head as she passed, dropping her cup in the sink, and heading out of the house.

Soph watched her mother depart, filled a cup with coffee and headed for the balcony. Staring out over the water, she sipped. She could get used to this place, she mused with a contented smile.

Ariana stepped out of the house and studied the shutters on the living room window, to the right of the front door. She entered the garage and dug out the rough sandpaper she had seen, ambled back to the window and started rubbing at the loose paint. The top of the shutter out of reach, she walked back to the garage and returned with a short ladder. Propping the ladder against the wall, she climbed and continued rubbing the small piece of sandpaper on the painted wood.

Nikki slowed as she reached the top of the slope, glanced out over the west-cove and gathered her breath. See, it's as beautiful as ever, she said, to the box in her hand. She followed the path to the right, tracking the low walled garden, leading up to the front of the house. Passing the steps down to the lower floor, she stopped suddenly and placed the box carefully on the wall. She gazed up with a stunned frown. 'What. Are. You. Doing?' she asked, her deliberate punctuation and tone laced with bemused amusement bringing Ariana's hand to a stop.

The ladder wobbled with the sudden rush of insecurity that startled Ariana, and she grabbed at the wall. 'What the...' she blurted, unable to turn her face from the whitewashed stone and appreciate the beaming grin on Nikki's face.

Nikki stepped closer and held the ladder firmly. 'You okay?' she asked, biting on her lip to prevent the laughter escaping.

'I...' Ariana started, gripping more tightly at the rails of the ladder.

'Climb down slowly,' Nikki instructed, her eyes suddenly entranced by the bare legs above her head. She coughed to clear her throat, only averting her gaze at the last minute, enjoying the view as Ariana descended.

Ariana moved slowly. Absorbed with sanding the wood, she had lost sight of the fact that she was up a ladder, and she wasn't that fond of heights. One pace at a time, she made her way down. Nikki stepped aside as she reached the bottom, giving her the space to put her feet on solid ground.

Nikki assessed Ariana's flustered face, the small piece of rough paper in her hand, and then the partly sanded shutter. The impact of the sandpaper was barely noticeable. 'Hmm,' she said, starting to chuckle.

Ariana slapped her on the arm, 'What?' she asked, defensively.

'You redecorating then?' Nikki asked, sporting a scrunched up nose, squinting again at Ariana's handiwork.

'Yes,' Ariana retorted, waving the tatty piece of sandpaper at Nikki.

Nikki's eyebrows rose. She scanned the other four sets of shutters on the wall, squinted again as she processed the remaining windows in the house, and grinned mischievously. 'Well, that's going to take you the best part of a year,' she said, with a sympathetic laugh. 'Just doing the windows,' she added, 'and then there's the walls,' she continued.

Ariana studied the chipped pink nail vanish and picked at the broken nails on her right hand. She started to chuckle, her eyes slowly rising and meeting Nikki's. 'What do you suggest?' she asked.

Nikki looked at the shutters again, with a carpenter's eye. 'I can take them down and work on them in the workshop,' she offered.

Ariana's smile widened. 'Really!' she said excitedly, and then just as suddenly, a wave of rejection passed through her, leaving a dull feeling in its wake. Why would Nikki want to help her, when to do so would result in her selling and leaving the island sooner rather than later? The smile fell from her lips, and the feeling of emptiness dived into the space created by her thoughts. 'Are you sure?' she asked, in a more reserved tone.

'Sure,' Nikki replied with a shrug. If Ariana intended to do-up the house before selling, the least she could do would be to ensure she didn't kill herself in the process, and with the amount of work that needed doing, she could bank on Ariana being around for the rest of the summer. 'Is there a screwdriver in the garage?' she asked.

Ariana nodded. She watched as Nikki disappeared and reappeared carrying a multi-piece toolset, a hand-drill and extension cable, and a beaming smile.

'Right,' Nikki said, heading for the ladder. 'Where's the socket?' she asked.

Ariana indicated to the wall, just inside the front door

and Nikki plugged in the cable. 'I'll undo the top screws first. You'll need to help support the shutter,' she said, nodding for Ariana's affirmation. She leapt up the ladder.

Ariana had nodded back, though she hadn't quite heard all the instructions, pleasantly distracted by the long tanned legs directly in front of her eyes. She noted the lighter skin of the creases at the back of Nikki's knees, the firm muscles of her calf and hamstrings, leading to the join between the top of her legs and buttocks. As Nikki reached up, so her shorts inched up a fraction, and a new, sweet scent caught Ariana by surprise.

Nikki descended the ladder, removed the drill from its box and inserted a screwdriver head. She squeezed the trigger, and the head spun. 'Good,' she said, jumping back up the ladder, drill in hand. 'You need to support the shutter,' Nikki said again, louder this time, coaxing an entranced Ariana into the task.

'Sorry,' Ariana said, her voice broken. She moved away from the tantalising aroma and view, to the side of the ladder and held the bottom of the shutter. She didn't hear the noise of the drill, and when the shutter dropped from the top, it caused her to jump, bringing her attention into sharp focus.

'Have you got it?' Nikki asked with urgency, gripping at the top of the wooden structure before it fell and ripped out the lower hinge.

Ariana clung to the wood, pressing it against the wall for stability. 'I think so,' she said, less than convincingly.

Nikki scampered down the ladder and quickly helped to suspend the shutter against the wall. She stood a couple of inches taller than Ariana, so her reach was higher, but the position had Ariana clamped to the wall as well as the shutter. The proximity drew a smile to Nikki's lips. 'Mmm,' she mumbled, clearing her throat. She waved the drill in the air and pressed the trigger. Ariana was directly in front of the hinge Nikki needed to access.

Ariana gulped, the heat from Nikki's body flaming through her, scorching the skin where they touched. She had stopped breathing, Nikki's scent sending her spinning, delirious, and intoxicated. 'Oh!' she exclaimed, suddenly aware that she needed to shift her position across so that Nikki could access the screws. She moved sideways.

Nikki groaned. It was an involuntary response and directly related to the sensations building low in her core. Ariana's dark eyes had been so close, her full, rosy lips so kissable. It had taken every ounce of restraint to not make a fool of herself right there and then. She directed the head of the drill. 'Hold on to that,' she said, pointing to the exact point on the shutter. Ariana complied. Nikki supported the upper part of the shutter with one hand and unscrewed with the other, allowing the rusty screws to drop to the floor. As the last one fell, the shutter dropped, and she pressed it hard against the wall, lowered the drill and took a firm grip on the slatted wood. 'You okay?' she asked.

Ariana nodded. She was floundering. 'Fine,' she said, gripping with all her might and following Nikki's lead, lowering the shutter to the ground.

Nikki shifted the ladder to the other side of the window and began the process again. By the time the second shutter lay on the floor, Ariana felt dizzy. 'Do you want a drink?' she asked, hoping the more cooling air inside the house and a little space from Nikki might bring her back to her senses.

'Sure,' she said, wiping a bare arm across her forehead. The sun favoured this side of the house in the morning, creating a suntrap. Her mouth was feeling parched. She smiled, her head on a tilt, watching Ariana escape into the house.

Ariana took in the fresh air, heading towards the kitchen, trying hard to stem the flow of thoughts that challenged the plan she had devised for her and Soph's future. The smell of Nikki lingered. She poured two tall glasses of water, her hand shaking. The urge to kiss Nikki was so intense, to feel her soft lips, sweet taste, her strong arms holding her close. She wanted to scream. She blew out the air that had stopped in her lungs, shook her thoughts from her mind and clamped down on the feelings that had her behaving like a teenager, buried them back inside her chest and closed the lid on the box. Now was not the right time, or place for sentimentality, she reminded herself. Walking back down the corridor, drinks in hand, she felt strong again. She handed over the glass, her eyes locking onto Nikki's and congratulated herself.

'Thanks,' Nikki said, taking the glass and downing the water in one long slug. 'By the way, I brought this,' she said, reaching for the small, simple, wooden box and handing it over.

Ariana slowly lowered her gaze to the urn, the hollow, empty feeling returning to her chest, sliding, and forming a dense weight in her gut. The reality dawned like a tonne of bricks. She took the box tentatively.

'Sorry,' Nikki said softly, with a compassionate smile. 'With the... decorating, I forgot,' she said, her hand indicating to the shutters resting against the wall.

'It's okay,' Ariana said quietly, her attention on the apologetic, hazel eyes, suddenly struck by a profound sense of loneliness. 'Do you want something stronger to drink?' she asked, feeling the need to dampen the rising negative emotions and the company of someone she trusted.

Ariana had turned back into the house before Nikki could answer. She placed the box on the kitchen table as she passed and headed straight for the freezer. She pulled out the chilled bottle of ouzo and two glasses from the cupboard, poured one shot and downed it on the spot. The burning pain at the back of her throat took her breath away, but it was also a welcome distraction from the turmoil that plagued her: the lustful thoughts as she stared at Nikki on the ladder, the reality of Sophia's ashes in the box, and then the future. Her heart had already started to gain her attention, and it was driving a wedge between her thoughts and her feelings. She could barely breathe with the confusion.

'Maria not here?' Nikki asked, glancing around the room.

Ariana paused. 'She's taking a paid break,' she answered, a wave of guilt adding to the anxiety churning in her stomach.

Nikki nodded. 'She deserves one,' she said. The comment helped a little.

Ariana forced a smile. She picked up the chilled bottle and the two small glasses and headed onto the balcony. She poured the drinks and handed one to Nikki.

Nikki stood, looking out over the water, sensing the shift in Ariana's demeanour. Even she still struggled with Sophia's absence, and she had had the time to adjust. Ariana, on the other hand, hadn't yet begun to grieve for her loss. She leaned against the walled edge. 'Such an amazing view,' she said, scanning the territory she knew well, around to the jetty where the ferry sat, and beyond to the far edge of the west-cove. Then out to sea, Ithaka visible in the distance, the warm breeze transporting the essence of the sea. 'Beautiful,' she mumbled as if to herself.

Ariana moved across the small space and stood, following Nikki's gaze. 'It is,' she said, her tone calmer, her posture softer.

Turning towards Ariana, Nikki studied her. She coughed to clear her throat. 'You okay?' she asked, tenderly.

Ariana nodded slowly, turned to face Nikki, reached out and placed her hand on her arm. 'Thank you,' she said.

Nikki shrugged. 'For what?' she asked.

'Last night, the shutters, the ashes, everything,' Ariana rambled.

Nikki stared into Ariana's sadness, her senses consumed by the lightness of the touch on her arm and the piercing dark-brown eyes that ran a direct line to her heart. She had spent the best part of the night trying to rationalise all the reasons why getting involved with Ariana would be such a bad idea, but none of them had convinced her then let alone after the close-contact incident they had just shared against the shutter. Ariana felt it too, of that she was sure. 'Do you want a hand,' she asked, hoping the answer would be yes.

Ariana frowned, confused by the question.

Nikki's heart felt as though it was melting under pain of Ariana's expression. She studied the lost look with renewed determination. No matter what had happened between them, that was in the past. If Ariana needed to sell to create a life for herself and Soph, then Nikki owed it to them both, and Sophia, to help her. For once in her life, Ariana deserved to have someone backing her decision, whether they agreed with it or not. And Nikki didn't agree with the sale, but above all else, Ariana's future happiness was the most critical factor in the whole damned equation.

Ariana stared vacantly at the fire in Nikki's eyes, her mind distracted by the feelings driving her to do something she might later regret. She would most definitely regret. 'Sorry,' she said, reminding herself there was a question to be answered, one that she couldn't remember.

'With scattering the ashes,' Nikki said, tapping the side of her head as if to admonish herself for her lack of clarity. 'Can I help in any way?' she asked again. Sophia had often talked about having her ashes spread around the rose bushes, and they had joked about her keeping an eye on the place from the other world. Nikki drew a long breath and released it slowly.

Ariana turned towards the sea. She didn't want to think about scattering the ashes. She closed her eyes, gathering her thoughts.

'Sorry, I just thought you might want some company,' Nikki explained.

Ariana nodded, she would. 'Yes,' she said, her voice broken.

'There are quite a few rose beds around the garden,' Nikki added, trying to inject a little light-heartedness.

'Yes there are, and she knew how much I hated gardening,' Ariana said, with a wry smile. She was beginning to feel a little woozy from the stiff drink and starting to enjoy the carefree feeling that had blocked her thoughts and released the delicate heat that slowly spiralled down her spine.

Nikki tilted her head, her lip curling up on one side. 'She'll be watching and telling you how to do it,' she quipped.

'I wouldn't put it past her.'

'I'm free now if you want,' Nikki offered.

Ariana nodded.

*

'Hey,' Gianna said, swaggering towards the music on the cliff top, a large bag slung over her back.

Soph stopped playing, turned and couldn't help the smile that appeared, or the warmth that invaded her chest. 'Hey, you! She pulled her feet up from the cliff's edge and stood. 'What's that?' she asked.

'We're going snorkelling,' Gianna replied, with a chuckle and a wicked grin.

Soph paled.

'You'll be fine. You get to stay on the top of the water,' she said, dropping the bag at her feet and resting her hands on her narrow hips.

Soph licked her lips. Gianna's assertiveness, her dark eyes, the crop-top and short shorts that hung off her slim hips, were all having a stimulating effect on her lower regions. Her mouth was dry, and she had already stopped processing the idea of being in the water with fish that bite and other sea creatures that might attack her. Her eyes were busy, and her mind was on a very different track.

'Come on, let's go,' Gianna said, picking up the bag and heading towards the house. 'I'll wait here while you drop your guitar,' she said.

Soph ran down the slope and into the house, Gianna, a pace behind her waited outside the front door.

'What are you doing?' Nikos asked, approaching from the olive grove.

'Going snorkelling,' Gianna responded.

'Don't you have work to do?' he asked, knowing the answer.

'I'll do it later,' Gianna said, trying not to get drawn into his obvious annoyance and coming across as conceited. He had barely spoken to her in the last few days and when he had he was always telling her off for something. Her mama had done nothing but complain about being on paid leave, which she didn't get. She would have snapped Ariana's hand off for the chance to be paid to take a holiday. And, anyway, they didn't pay her that much in the first place. She could take a week off and no one would notice.

'Be sure that you do,' he said, turning and walking away from her.

She huffed, tried to ignore the sick feeling that niggled at her. She had always got on well with her papa, but ever since they found out about the sale, he had been grumpy, and she understood that; but since she'd started hanging out with Soph, he had become really irritable. Did it matter whether she did her stupid work or not if they were soon to be out of a job anyway?

'Ready?' Soph said, drawing Gianna from her frustrations.

Gianna picked up the bag and threw it over her shoulder. 'Come on,' she said, heading down the track to the east-cove at a pace.

'You okay?' Soph asked, assessing Gianna's gritted teeth and pinched features. Something was endearing about the petulant look, she mused, her lips curling at the thought.

'Fine,' Gianna grumbled.

Soph had spotted Nikos talking to Gianna, from the house, and it was clear he had been giving her a hard time about something. 'Your papa doesn't like me much,' she stated.

Gianna stopped walking, turned and held Soph's eyes. An electric current fizzed down her spine, and she couldn't find the words she wanted to say. She could feel the pressure building behind her eyes, threatening to spill onto her cheeks.

'It's okay,' Soph said, with a shrug. 'He doesn't need to like me,' she added, taking Gianna's hand in hers. 'As long as you do,' she added. She smiled mischievously, her eyebrows rising and exposing the whites of her eyes.

Gianna's breathing settled and her shoulders sat an inch lower than they had done a moment ago. She tried to smile, but her jaw was still too tense to comply.

'Does he know you're gay?' Soph asked, squeezing Gianna's hand, drawing her eyes.

Gianna nodded. 'He doesn't like it,' she said, her voice quiet, 'but he knows,' she said with certainty.

Soph shrugged. 'Definitely me then,' she said, with a chuckle, releasing Gianna's hand.

'He's giving me a hard time for not working,' Gianna said, cursing at the discomfort that jammed her mind.

'Do you need to go and work now?' Soph asked, her eyes lowered, hoping the answer would be no.

Gianna's eyes lowered to the dirt track, and she kicked aimlessly at the loose stones.

'G!' Soph nudged her in the arm.

'He knows I like you,' Gianna mumbled, her eyes never leaving her feet.

Soph looked up at Gianna, clocking her unease, and then a smile started to form and grow, building into a sneaky grin. 'Good!' she replied.

Gianna raised her head slowly revealing her sparkling eyes and a coy smile. 'You're cool,' she said.

Soph laughed. She'd never thought of herself as cool before. 'I like you too,' she said, trying to hold back a blush, and failing.

Gianna's grin continued to widen. She grabbed Soph's hand and led her down the track.

'Remind me, how does snorkelling work?' Soph asked, nudging her shoulder into Gianna, playfully.

9.

Ariana collected up the urn from the table and carried it to the side garden. Nikki followed her. The rose garden stopped just short of the cliff edge and sat directly below the master bedroom; Sophia's room. She stood on the large lawn, assessed the rose beds that surrounded it on three sides of the square, and sighed. Sophia had insisted that her ashes be scattered around each rose.

'They are beautiful,' Nikki remarked, her eyes feasting on the display of colour, her nose inhaling the heady sweet scent that hung in the air. If the rose were a drug, they would both be high by the time they finished!

Ariana placed the urn on the ground, next to the first rose bush on the left-hand side of the square. She gazed at the yellow petals, perfectly formed, leaned in and pressed her nose to the flower. From Nikki's angle, it looked as if Ariana was kissing the rose. Ariana pulled back and caressed the petals. 'We need a trowel or something to dig with,' she said.

'There's a shed,' Nikki said. 'I'll go,' she offered.

Ariana rested on her knees, gazing at the beautiful flower, entranced by the strong scent, her emotions wavering until Nikki returned.

'You okay?' Nikki asked, holding out a hand fork and trowel.

'Not really, but I have to do this,' Ariana said.

Nikki dropped to her knees and started gently turning the fine soil at the base of the rose bush.

Ariana opened the lid on the box and gasped. Nikki's concerned gaze was on her. 'I've never seen...'

'It's okay,' Nikki said, softly. She reached out and placed a hand on Ariana's arm and squeezed.

Ariana's heart slowed as she studied the silver-white dust in the box. She had expected something akin to the colour of dirt, but this was nothing like that. And there was a lot of it, too! She reached into the box, allowing the coarse granular substance to filter through her fingers, entranced by the silver sheen that glistened in the sunlight.

Nikki watched.

Ariana frowned. 'Seems strange to think this is her.'

'It is surreal.'

Ariana nodded. Taking a deep breath and blowing out hard, she turned her attention to the prepared rose bush. She took a small handful of the dust and scattered it around the base, sat back and stared at the silver-white particles.

Nikki was already preparing the next bush in the row. Ariana sighed, grabbed another fistful of ashes and scattered them, more liberally this time. Noting the difference between the first and the second, she added another small smattering of ashes to the base of the first bush. Satisfied that they looked similar, she moved on, following Nikki's lead, until they reached the end of the row.

'Drink?' Nikki asked, standing and stretching out her back. Her forehead glistened with the beads of sweat that had formed, a slow trickle making its way down the side of her temples. Her cheeks had taken on a healthy glow too. 'Looking good,' she said, assessing their work. Silver circles bounded each stem along the row, giving the appearance of a constellation of stars. She set off for the kitchen, observed by Ariana, and wandered back again with two glasses of water.

'Did you know her well?' Ariana asked as Nikki approached.

Nikki stalled, images sprung to mind of the evenings Sophia had spent at the taverna laughing and chatting with her and Manos until the early hours, and the years they had helped with harvesting the olives. She smiled through a wave of sadness. 'Yes,' she responded, softly. 'She was like family to me,' she added, handing over the water. She sipped at her glass, thankful for the cold drink to ease the pressure at the back of her throat.

Ariana stared at her as if she had a thousand questions to ask and didn't know where to start. 'Do you miss your parents?' she asked, curiosity getting the better of her. Ariana had asked the question about Nikki's parents one time when they were younger, when she had escaped to meet Nikki on the rocks below the house and they had talked and made plans together. Nikki had simply shrugged saying, 'They died when I was four.' Other than knowing they were both killed in a boating accident, the conversation had stopped there and had never come up again.

Nikki picked up the hand-fork and continued to turn over the soil. 'I don't remember them,' she said, matter-of-factly. Pops has been kind of like a father to me, so I don't feel I've missed out on anything. I guess you can't miss what you've never had,' she said, stopping and looking up at Ariana.

Ariana nodded. She didn't know why she missed her mother, it didn't make sense, but she did miss her. Or maybe she just felt so alone, and even the thought of her mother provided some bizarre sense of comfort. She flinched.

'You okay?' Nikki asked with concern.

'I'm glad Sophia had you,' Ariana said, her tone carrying the solemnness she felt in her heart, her eyes holding Nikki's gaze with tenderness.

'I'm glad I had her too,' Nikki replied with a genuinely appreciative smile.

They continued to work in silence, rhythmically digging and spreading the ashes, the last red-rose bush getting a little more dust than the rest and the empty box sitting on the grass.

'Thank you.' Ariana said. She stood, leaned against Nikki's shoulder, gazed around the three sides of the square, and sighed. From the sky above it would look a lot like a silver-white arch. A door to the other side, she mused silently.

Nikki wrapped her arm around Ariana's shoulders and pulled her close. 'She'd love it,' she said, smiling and nodding her approval.

'I hope so.'

'Deserving of a glass of wine,' Nikki added, squeezing Ariana tightly.

Ariana let herself be squeezed. She was enjoying the genuinely affectionate contact. Being with Nikki now, like this, it was as though they had never parted. 'Good idea,' she said, with enthusiasm.

Nikki laughed. She pressed a tender kiss to Ariana's temple before the thought even registered, and then forgot to baulk at her spontaneous, intimate reaction, though she probably should have.

Ariana snuggled closer.

*

Nikki sipped at the chilled wine, savoured its zesty aroma on the back of her tongue then swallowed, the cool liquid going some way to quench her thirst. She leaned against the kitchen-balcony wall, under strict instruction to be waited upon, and gazed out around the west-cove and across to Kefalas. Laughter and music echoed around the rocks, interspersed with the low hush of the gentle waves and the chirping of the crickets. Lunch was always a casual affair on Sakros; life was a casual affair on Sakros.

Watching Pops and Chrissy busying away, serving, she smiled contentedly. Her eyes closed, enjoying the warmth of the sun on her face, and memories drifted into her mind's eye.

'Do you think you'll ever leave,' Ariana asked, lazing back on the warm sand, staring into the deepest-blue sky she had ever seen.

'Why would I want to leave?' she asked, staring into the same blue sky, her hands resting behind her head, the sun hot on her skin. She closed her eyes. 'It's the most beautiful place in the world.'

'What if you fall in love?' Ariana asked, her tone quiet, serious even.

Nikki turned onto her side, rested on her elbow and scanned Ariana; her long blonde hair, slightly fairer skin than her own, and the dimples that made her look like she was smiling. She leaned in and placed a soft kiss on the red-painted lips. 'I already did,' she said.

Nikki blinked her eyes open, released the air from her lungs, and turned her attention to the cluttering sounds in the kitchen behind her. Ariana was still preparing food for them, in Sophia's kitchen. She observed, Ariana, navigating a room she didn't know and a skill she hadn't quite mastered. She couldn't conceive the life she had led, sheltered to the point of virtual imprisonment. But, at least Ariana had Soph, and that wasn't such a bad thing. Soph was an interesting kid; smart, easy-going, a little squeamish, she smiled, and definitely into Gianna. The smile shifted. When the Carter-Cruz' left the island this time, it would be for good. Gianna would be devastated. She swallowed down the thought, but the discomfort in her chest remained.

'Hey.' Ariana said softly, holding out a bowl of large, green olives, a tender smile lighting up her eyes.

'Hey,' Nikki responded, her gaze landing softly on Ariana's smile, admiring the red lips she still longed to kiss. The discomfort in her chest transformed and the light fluttering sensation that replaced it caused Nikki's breath to pause.

Ariana gasped, she couldn't stop the quiver in her lip or the bowl in her hand from trembling. It was an unconscious response to something intangible in Nikki's gaze; a significant force drawing them together, connecting them.

Nikki didn't waver from Ariana's lips, her gaze deepening as Ariana wetted them, bit down on the top lip and then the bottom. Time had slowed, and the movement held fascination. Her head tilted a fraction, and her eyes squinted as she continued to assess the impact of the last twenty years. Yes, Ariana looked older, of course. But there was something even more alluring about the mature woman she had become. Nikki bit down on her lip, unconsciously mirroring Ariana's movements.

Ariana cleared her throat, breaking the spell, and placed the bowl on the table. Swiftly, she returned to the kitchen, aware that Nikki's eyes were still on her. 'More wine?' she shouted, picking up the cheese board and her empty glass and returning to the table on the balcony.

Nikki grinned. She'd barely touched her glass, but the idea of dumbing down her feelings in a boozy lunch held some appeal. 'Sure.'

Ariana shot back into the kitchen and returned with the wine and a basket of bread.

Nikki's grin widened. Ariana looked flustered, but not in the same way she had when she first arrived, not a stressed kind of fluster, more like a nervous, excited response. Nikki could feel the difference. She sat on the wicker chair and plucked a delicious olive from the bowl. 'Are these from the estate?' she asked, knowing the answer.

Ariana nodded as she sat, words escaping her.

'You selling the land as well, I assume?' Nikki asked. There was no anger in her tone.

Ariana nodded and took a long sip of her wine.

'How much do you think you'll get for it?'

Ariana shrugged. 'I don't know,' she said evasively, the conversation diverting her thoughts and shifting the energy between them. 'I need to arrange for the agent to visit.' She didn't want to have this conversation, not now, not at any time. The sale's contract was agreed before she arrived at the white house. The agent's visit was a mere formality. The deal had already happened, and nothing could change that fact. Her hand rose to her face, her fingers kneading at the pressure in her forehead and temples as if to force reality to the back of her mind. She couldn't tell Nikki; she didn't know how to, without causing even more distress and discomfort.

Nikki nodded, unaware of the source of Ariana's anxiety, and sipped at her wine, churning over the possibilities in her mind. She didn't know if she would be able to raise the money needed to buy the place, but she couldn't see it sold to a complete stranger without giving the idea considered thought. 'Here, taste this,' Nikki said, holding out an olive.

Ariana took the fruit into her mouth, the subtle touch of Nikki's fingers against her lips, sending a shock wave down the back of her neck and spine. She could barely breathe, let alone swallow. She bit down gently, her mouth watering at the distinctive, salty taste, and Nikki's touch. 'They are good,' she said in a broken voice.

Nikki popped another one into Ariana's mouth. It didn't help.

Nikki watched with pleasure, the pimples rising on Ariana's neck, her touch, unnerving Ariana in the most exquisite way, tenderly, adoringly. She hadn't realised how much she had missed the intensity of this feeling, until now. The sense of Ariana's soft lips on the tips of her fingers igniting and pulsing through her, Ariana's entranced gaze, frozen in a time they had shared together; an unfulfilled past, and an opportunity to reconnect. There seemed to be a slither of light appearing, the possibility of a future together. There was a mutual desire that had never waned. She would get the funding to buy the house, no matter what.

'Mmm,' Ariana mumbled, her eyelids flickering as she ate.

'They're the best,' Nikki said with a warm smile. 'We've only ever stocked Sophia's olives, and our lemons and limes, and our eggs and vegetables come from here too,' she added with a frown. Almost all of their fresh ingredients came from the estate.

Ariana held Nikki's gaze, resolved not to be dragged deeper into a conversation for which she had no answers. 'Do you have a girlfriend, partner?' she asked suddenly, flinching as her mind challenged her emotions on the inappropriateness of the question, a brief vision of Chrissy appearing. She flushed, thought about apologising, but Nikki's response stalled her.

Nikki's skin darkened and she cleared her throat. She hadn't seen that question coming. 'No,' she responded, avoiding eye contact, cutting a small piece of feta cheese and popping it into her mouth. She swallowed it down with a sip of wine. 'No, there isn't anyone,' Nikki said, her tone sober, reflective.

Ariana's heart raced. She had assumed there would be someone after all these years. 'I'm surprised,' she said, watching Nikki's reaction.

Nikki looked up, held Ariana's gaze firmly. 'There was someone special,' she said, staring at the only woman she had ever loved, hoping that Ariana would sense the truth. 'It was a long time ago,' she added.

'Oh!' Ariana's heart landed with a thud in her gut, leaving a painful burning sensation where her heart should have been. She hadn't expected to react to the idea of Nikki having been with someone else, but there it was, plain and clear, for everyone to see. She pressed her hand to her chest, hoping to hide the gaping wound from Nikki's probing eyes.

'You okay?' Nikki asked, regaining her composure.

Ariana stopped rubbing her chest. She reached for the cheese on her plate, but her fingers just stayed there and fiddled with the food. 'I'm sorry, I have no right to pry,' she said.

Nikki shrugged. 'Hey!'

Ariana looked up.

Nikki was smiling kindly. 'Fancy a walk around the grove?' she asked. 'We can find the tree that these came from,' she added, light-heartedly, pointing at the olives in the bowl, her grin strengthening.

'I'd like that,' Ariana said, still pondering the significant person that had once been in Nikki's life.

*

Nikki stopped at the ledge on the side of the rock, facing out over the east-cove and sat. She hadn't walked around the grove in a long time. It seemed more expansive than she remembered, and even more dusty. She sneezed. 'They're having fun,' she remarked, pointing down to the beach and the two girls snorkelling in the water.

Ariana eased herself to the ground next to Nikki. Nikki's scent struck her. 'Mmm,' she moaned, challenged by her body's response to the sweet, spicy aroma.

'Soph's gay, right?' Nikki asked, observing the two young women in the water.

'Yes,' Ariana replied on a sigh, her tone tinged with remorse.

Nikki blew out a deep breath. 'I bet that went down well,' she said, with no intention of hiding her sarcasm.

'Like a lead balloon,' Ariana replied, knowing that Nikki was referring to Teresa's response to Soph's sexuality.

'She's very talented. Did she study music?'

'No. My husband and my mother decided she should have academic schooling, to set her up for a proper job. I fought against them, and lost.'

'She's bright too,' Nikki said.

'She is. But, her passion is music and I've failed her.'

Nikki turned sharply, cupped Ariana's cheeks firmly, and held her gaze. 'You have not failed her,' she said, with a blend of determination and frustration. 'Don't say that Ariana, please,' she added.

Ariana's dark-eyes darkened and lowered, her cheeks still lodged in Nikki's firm grip. She couldn't watch the pain in those hazel irises. 'Soph wanted to go to music school,' she whispered.

Nikki released Ariana, rubbed her thumb across Ariana's cheek tenderly, sweeping away an errant tear. 'She still can, if that's what she wants,' she said, softly

'That's why I need to sell,' Ariana responded.

Nikki nodded, but her jaw had tensed.

'We have no money, Nikki. Everything is tied up in the estate. I don't even have any money for Soph's 18th birthday,' she said.

'When is it?' Nikki asked.

'Just over three weeks, 28th July.'

Nikki reached out and clasped Ariana's hand. 'We'll think of something,' she said, softly. 'I can help, Ariana, if you'll let me,' she offered.

Ariana sniffled, wiped at her face, her head shaking back and forth. 'No, I need to stand on my own two feet,' she replied.

Nikki released the shaking hand. Now wasn't the time to argue the point. She leaned back against the grassy bank and pulled Ariana into the crook of her arm. 'Let's enjoy the sun,' she said, closing her eyes. She needed time to think.

Ariana breathed in the sweet, spicy scent and relaxed into the warmth of Nikki's semi-exposed skin. She felt safe. It didn't take the problems away, but it was enough for her mind to calm.

*

Soph spat out the breathing tube, pulled the goggles from her eyes and raced out of the shallow water onto the safety of the warm beach. 'That was brilliant,' she said, her face shining with the broad smile that spanned from ear-to-ear.

Gianna giggled, dropped her snorkel, and slumped her wet body onto the soft sand. She had known Soph would love snorkelling, but seeing the joy on her face and hearing the excitement in her voice made her feel all kinds of strange things, feelings with which she didn't quite know what to do. 'It was aaaamaaazing,' she said.

'So many fish,' Soph said, slumping down next to Gianna and staring out to sea. 'I didn't realise it was so rocky out there,' she added.

Gianna watched Soph's eyes, darting, sparkling; replaying the images that had captured her imagination. The warmth in her heart bathed her eyes, her soft gaze shifting to Soph's shoulder, trailing down to the pert breasts, the blue piercing in her bellybutton, and the glistening beads of seawater resting on the taut, tanned stomach. Her mouth dry, her heart racing, she glanced away to control her urges.

'I've never seen a jellyfish before,' Soph said, turning to look at Gianna. 'They're so...' she squirmed, her eyes drawn back to the sea, images flooding her mind.

Gianna laughed, then stopped. She couldn't help herself. She reached out and traced a line down the side of Soph's back, her finger admiring the slight curve at her waist, amused by the skin rising along the trail of her touch.

Soph shivered, her mind stopped and her mouth dried. The tingling sensation down her back, creating a sense of urgency so powerful, she froze. She gulped for air. Gianna's finger tracking along the line of her shorts and up the centre of her spine wasn't helping. It was driving her wild. She tried to speak, but all that came out was a guttural groan. She could hear Gianna moaning softly too, and that wasn't helping. She couldn't get involved with her, even though she wanted to. She couldn't hurt Gianna.

Gianna's heart racing, her fingers captivated by the touch of Soph's soft skin, she reached her free hand up and turned Soph to face her. Soph's eyes were darker than the darkest sea, almost black, and the way she was staring at her touched her deeply. She held her gaze steadily and allowed the feelings to build, the fluttering in her chest, the fire in her belly, and the pulsing even lower. She tried to swallow.

Soph inched closer.

Gianna gasped.

Soph stopped, her eyes seeking permission, her arousal driving her on. She was barely breathing, her heart pounding fiercely in her chest.

Gianna had stopped breathing altogether.

Soph hovered. Gianna moved towards her. There was no going back. Soph moved slowly, halted only by the feel of Gianna's tender lips against hers. She groaned softly.

Gianna's heart exploded with the light touch. The silky softness of Soph's lips, the smoothness of the skin on her face. She had never experienced anything as exotic as this. She leaned into the kiss, her mouth responding intuitively to Soph's lead. When Soph's tongue touched hers, she moaned again.

Soph deepened the kiss, her tongue probing delicately, her hands gripping at the loose sand, exercising restraint. She eased out of the kiss, smiling.

Gianna opened her eyes and stared, lost in the blue headlights gazing at her, momentarily stunned. A smile started to grow, and she took a deep breath. 'Mmm.'

Soph continued to stare at Gianna's warm, happy smile and the glow that surrounded her; her cautious thoughts swept out to sea, her mind entranced by the blissful moment. 'Mmm,' she replied.

Gianna giggled, sucked her bottom lip into her mouth, and stared. 'Wow!' she exclaimed.

Soph gazed at Gianna's profile, her fingers reaching across the sand and covering Gianna's hand. Suddenly she jumped on top of her, pushed her flat to the sand, sprung to her feet and sprinted towards the water. 'Race you to the rocks,' she yelled.

Gianna struggled to her feet, laughing. 'You!' she yelled back, diving into the sea and gaining two yards on Soph in an instant.

Soph couldn't swim for laughing, but flapped her arms and moved her body forward the best she could. By the time she arrived, Gianna was sat on the rock watching her. 'I really like you,' Soph said, squinting up at her.

*

Nikki smiled as she watched, a warm wave flowing into her chest, with the antics on the beach, memories of the time she and Ariana had spent together; teasing; playing around, having fun, flooding her awareness.

Ariana's eyes were flickering, and the light of the sun made her lashes look almost white, against her sun-bronzed skin. Her nostrils made the smallest of movements with the movement of her breath, her full red lips resting closed. She looked as peaceful as an angel; her hair sprawled out freely on the sand. Nikki couldn't take her eyes off the girl she had just kissed. Ariana's lips twitched, forming a broad smile, and then a chuckle, her white teeth, brighter in the sunlight. Nikki wanted to kiss her again, and again. She wanted to feel that soft, warm pressure against her lips forever.

Ariana squinted one eye open. 'What?' she said, her body moving with the laughter that had gripped her.

'You're beautiful,' Nikki said, grinning broadly.

Ariana harrumphed.

Nikki closed the space, pressed her mouth to Ariana's, excited by the fiery contact she groaned into the kiss, daring to explore further.

Ariana fell into the kiss, lost in the tenderness of the touch, the taste of Nikki on her lips, the feel of her tongue teasing her, probing her. The sensations were building, hot like a white flame and sparking like a firecracker, and like nothing she had ever experienced. She groaned.

Nikki eased out of the kiss and resumed staring. Ariana's eyes remained shut. *I'm in love with you.* Nikki's words never reached Ariana's ears.

Ariana stirred with the squealing sounds from the sea and opened her eyes. She eased away from Nikki's shoulder looking slightly disorientated.

'Hey,' Nikki said, smiling at Ariana's ruffled look, the sleep marks lightly marking her cheek, her drowsy eyes endearing.

'Sorry, I drifted,' Ariana apologised.

Nikki shrugged. 'It was nice,' she said.

Ariana's smile was tight, and she suddenly pulled herself up to stand. 'They're still playing?' she asked, with unwarranted urgency.

Nikki nodded. 'They're into each other,' she said, standing, facing Ariana, her eyes asking the question. *What about you, Ariana?*

Ariana fidgeted her hands, unsure of what to do with them. 'I need to get back, I've got things I need to do,' she said, reactively, defensively.

Nikki tilted her head and stared at Ariana, willing her to open up. Her heart ached at the pain in those dark eyes, the distance that seemed permanent, but for a few brief glimpses into the person she knew existed beneath it all. Nothing was that urgent, she mused, and especially not this late in the day. 'Sure,' she said, smiling warmly, heading up the path to the white house.

Ariana followed a pace behind, her eyes settling on the very short, denim shorts, swaying tantalisingly in front of her. Try as she might, to look away, they kept drifting back to the slightly faded blue material, and the golden-brown muscular legs below. Still somewhat drowsy from the short sleep, her guard partly down, and driven by something beyond rational thought, her imagination kept presenting her with images of Nikki, naked. She shook her head to chase the pictures away and gain some composure, but Nikki's perfume, drifting down the slope, just enhanced the desire to touch her. By the time she reached the house, her pulse was racing, and her hands were clammy. Her eyes skittered everywhere, avoiding Nikki's curious gaze.

Ariana looked edgy. 'You okay?' Nikki asked.

Ariana nodded, but the tears forming in her eyes betrayed her.

Nikki stepped closer and pulled her into her arms confidently. 'Hey,' she whispered, her hand holding Ariana's head into her chest. 'It's okay, you can talk to me,' Nikki said.

Ariana stiffened at the feel of Nikki's bare skin against her cheek, the scent of her stronger, the warmth hotter. The comfort she had felt with the first embrace, just days ago, had been replaced by something far more uncomfortable. The truth. She was in love with Nikki. She still wanted her. As she pulled out of Nikki's arms and locked onto the hazel eyes, her resolve faltered. She was shaking.

Nikki had felt Ariana initially flinch at the close contact, but something else had given her an entirely different message. Intuitively, instinctively, whatever it was driving her sense of knowing, she knew. She definitely knew. She didn't want to stop gazing into those dark eyes. 'Hey, I'm going fishing later, you want to come?' she asked, hoping to shift the energy between them.

Ariana shook her head.

'Go on; it will be fun. It's so peaceful at night,' she said.

Ariana looked up, entranced by the genuine kindness and consideration Nikki conveyed. She was perfect.

'And, you did promise you'd chill out for a bit while you're here,' she persisted, with a doe-eyed look in her eye.

The doe-eyed look caused Ariana to chuckle. That was so not Nikki! 'Okay,' she conceded, secretly enjoying the thought of the tranquillity that came with the night, and just being with Nikki.

'Great! I'll meet you at the rocks about eight,' Nikki said, her feet suddenly filled with energy as she hopped excitedly from one foot to the other.

'Okay.' Ariana chuckled.

10.

'Good lunch?' Manos asked, sporting a broad grin and staring at the clock on the wall. 'Is that the time?' he teased.

Nikki poked her head up from inside the boat, her face sticky with grease and sweat. 'I've been back an hour at least,' she defended, waving her arms at him, holding back on the chuckle that was tickling her ribs.

'Aye,' he replied. 'Here,' he handed her a bottle of beer.

She took the drink and downed half of it in one slug. 'Damn, that's good,' she said.

'How's she coming along?' Manos asked.

Nikki frowned, heat flooded her body, and she took another slug of the beer.

'The boat,' Manos clarified, pointing to a large hole in its side that still sat, untouched. 'Lot to do,' he stated, biting on the toothpick in his mouth.

'We've got some shutters to repair too,' she said with a coy smile, her eyes indicating to the panels resting against the back wall of the workshop.

'Aye,' Manos quipped. He sucked through his teeth and twiddled the toothpick.

'I said we'd help. She's got a lot of work to do if she's going to bring the house up to scratch,' Nikki said.

'Thought you were going to stop her selling,' Manos said, matter-of-factly. He sipped at the clear liquid in his glass.

Nikki locked onto his calm, soft eyes. 'I know,' she said. He just smiled sweetly, approvingly.

'Need any help?' he asked, turning to the panels and studying them. 'They all this bad?' he asked, with a chuckle.

'Can you help me shift them? If I can work up at the house I will, but some will need repairing here,' she explained.

Manos nodded, twiddled the toothpick again and sipped from his glass. 'Anything else?' he asked, knowing there would be more to it than a few shutters in need of repair.

'External walls; internal painting,' Nikki replied with a tilt of her head. She sipped from the bottle and wiped the sticky sweat from her forehead.

'Anything else?' Manos continued.

'Yeah, need to pick up more wood for this. Might have to get it from Lefkada,' she said, appraising the inside of the boat, below her feet. 'There's no rush,' she said, with a shrug.

'How's she doing then?' he asked, referring to Ariana, with genuine concern.

Nikki's eyes wandered with her thoughts. 'Depends, I guess. She's chilling out, a bit. Two-steps forward, one step back,' she offered, her eyes scanning the sky.

'Hmm! Shame to see her so withdrawn and... so uptight! She was always so light-hearted, high-spirited, mind,' he said with a warm chuckle, 'Like her mother,' he added, with more than a hint of fondness.

'Teresa, high spirited!' Nikki challenged, shaking her head. As far as she could remember, the woman was stuck up, aloof, and hell was she uptight.

'Teresa wasn't always that stressed,' he said, with affection. 'When she was younger, she was good fun,' he said, his eyes sparkling and his cheeks flushing with his recollections.

Nikki studied him curiously and smiled. 'You had a soft spot for Teresa?' she asked, her grin broadening.

'Aye. A long time ago, mind,' he said, with a tilt of his head.

Nikki chuckled. 'Well I never knew,' she remarked, tickled by the idea of Pops having a crush on someone. He'd never had a lady friend in all the time she'd known him. Then again, neither had she! Manos had been her father's best friend, as had their father's before them, and had a small share in the

Kefalas business. When her parents died, he had taken guardianship of her and managed the businesses held in trust for her. They had had each other, and they had the taverna, the boat restoration, and the harbour management, and it worked.

He raised his hand as if to brush her off, in a jovial manner. 'Long time ago,' he said, sucking on the toothpick.

'We're going fishing tonight,' Nikki said.

'Aye,' he replied, but he seemed to have wandered, and his focus was with another place and time. His white-haired face twitched, and his eyes shone.

She smiled.

*

Nikki sauntered across the sand, laden with her fishing gear and an extra rod. The sun sat low in the evening sky, shards of orange and red lazing on the horizon, and in places, the water looked as black as death. Heading to the rocks below the white house, a halo of white hovered above the rose garden. She smiled at the thought of Sophia's on-going presence at the house and then started to chuckle. She was still smiling when she reached the rocks.

Ariana walked hastily down the path, heading for the water's edge, her heart racing and her stomach tight. She didn't know whether she felt nervous or excited, but she knew why. She had sat on the balcony for hours, working through the pros and cons of being with Nikki. There weren't too many cons, but one of them was a big one. But that didn't seem to make sense to her heart, which ignored the logical, rational approach entirely. The lightness and ease she felt around Nikki made her feel safe, secure. She hadn't felt any pressure or rushed in any way since she'd arrived. She couldn't remember the last time she had felt so at peace, if ever. In just three days it was as if some magical transformation process had taken place, and yet, she still hadn't solved the real problem.

'Hey.' Ariana started chuckling. Nikki was chuckling. She didn't know why they were chuckling and it didn't matter. The sound of Nikki's happy, giggly laughter was enough.

'Hey. Have you seen that?' Nikki asked, pointing up to the light hue over the rose garden above them.

Ariana looked up.

'She's watching you know,' Nikki remarked, with a wry smile.

Ariana gazed at the sight. 'I do believe she is,' she said, with fondness. Suddenly struck by a wave of sadness, 'I wish I'd seen her before she died,' she said, softly.

Nikki reached out, placed a hand on Ariana's shoulder. 'She understood, you know,' she said, reassuringly.

Ariana nodded. 'Are we set then?' she asked, switching her attention to the task of fishing.

'Take this,' Nikki said, handing her a rod. 'You remember how to fish?' she asked.

Ariana smiled mischievously. 'I bet you...' She paused, pondered an appropriate wager.

Nikki was laughing loudly. 'I've had a few years practise you know.'

'Twenty Euros?' Ariana dared.

Nikki held out her hand. 'Deal,' she said.

Ariana shook it. Enjoying the feel of Nikki's fingers wrapped around her own, she continued to hold Nikki's hand until Nikki released her. She coughed lightly to clear her throat, grabbed the pole from Nikki and stepped across the rocks. Finding a suitable spot, she eased the rod back and then whipped it forward, the reel spinning and the line unfolding.

'Three-seconds,' Nikki remarked, commenting on the time it had taken for the float to land. She chuckled, fixed her line, found her spot, and cast out. 'Four seconds,' she said, for Ariana to hear.

'Twenty Euros,' Ariana said, holding back a laugh. Nikki grinned.

Ariana rested her rod against the rocks and sat, drawn by the setting sun more than the bobbing float. In truth, the chances of them catching much would be slim. It wasn't like their expeditions out at sea when they were younger, but it was still fun. 'What's it like living here?' she asked, out of the blue.

Nikki startled. She didn't quite know how to answer the question. Island life, with trips to the likes of Lefkada, which was just a bigger island, was pretty much all she knew, and it suited her. 'I like it,' she replied. 'What was it like in London?' she asked.

'Not like this,' Ariana said, glancing at the thin red line that represented the last of the setting sun. The soft whooshing of the waves was a stark contrast with the cacophony of noises on the City streets, the rumbling and grating of steel heard in the underground, and the ever-present oppressive fog of pollution. 'This is so much more relaxing,' she said, softly, the lightly salted air, fresh and enlivening, sitting on her tongue.

'I guess,' Nikki said. She had never thought of it as relaxing or otherwise. It was home. The pace of life was what it was. There was nothing to rush for, unless there was an accident of course, or someone was seriously ill, but even those events happened rarely. 'I don't have anything to compare it with,' she added, having never lived anywhere else for any length of time.

'Would you ever leave here?' Ariana asked.

Nikki laughed, an involuntary response.

'What?'

'You asked me the same question a long time ago,' Nikki said.

Ariana shook her head. She didn't remember.

'And?'

'No, I wouldn't,' she said, her voice reflecting the tension that gripped at her stomach. The fact that she would never leave Sakros had clear consequences for any life she might have with Ariana.

Ariana stood, wound in the reel and re-cast her line. She remained silent. Nikki half-watched her, her other eye on the bobbing float.

'Where will you go?' Nikki asked, eventually.

'Huh?' Ariana had been lost in thought and missed the question.

'When you sell, where will you go?' As much as Nikki didn't want either the sale or Ariana to leave the island, she wasn't going to deceive herself into to thinking things wouldn't turn out that way.

'I, umm, I don't know,' Ariana said, in almost a whisper. She hadn't thought that far and she didn't enjoy the feelings that had arisen as she processed Nikki's question. 'Europe somewhere, I guess.'

'Were you happy?' Nikki asked. 'While you were away, I mean,' she clarified.

Ariana's legs lost their strength suddenly and she stumbled, dropped the line, and used her hands to break a near-fall, easing herself down onto a rock.

'Whoa, you okay? Nikki asked. She went to put down her rod.

'I'm okay,' Ariana said, holding up her hand as if to say carry on fishing.

Nikki ignored the signal, placed her rod carefully on the rocks, sat next to Ariana and placed an arm around her shoulder. She was shivering.

'I'm happy I have Soph,' she said. She had never been happy in her marriage, and her mother had controlled her life for far too long. 'And I'm enjoying being here, now,' she admitted.

118

Nikki squeezed her close.

Ariana eased out of the grip and turned to face Nikki. She reached up and traced a line from Nikki's high cheekbones, to the outside of her jaw and her chin, and eased her thumb slowly across Nikki's full lips. 'The happiest I have ever been in my life was when I was with you,' she said, her voice barely audible.

Nikki's lips twitched. She tried to swallow, but her mouth was dry. The twitching turned into a coy smile, and the tingling on her lips lingered.

Ariana reached up, swept Nikki's hair back behind her ear and smiled. 'You're so kind,' she said.

A whizzing sound and the rattling of a fishing rod dragging across the rocks pulled both women out of the moment. Nikki dived to grab the escaping pole, catching it just before it submerged. She shot it under her arm and worked the reel to gain control of the line.

Ariana jumped to her feet, a sudden rush of adrenaline heightening her competitive spirit. 'You got it; you got it,' she shouted.

Nikki laughed, mindful of the previous fish that got away. 'Not yet, but that twenty is looking hot for my pocket,' she teased. Easing the line in, she brought the fish close to the rocks and over the net. Holding the fish in position, she lifted the net and relaxed the rod. 'Got it now,' she said, facing Ariana with a smile that was about more than catching a fish.

Ariana leant into the net and unhooked the fish. 'Grey Mullet,' she said.

'Supper tomorrow,' Nikki said.

'I'll cook,' Ariana offered.

Nikki laughed. 'Can you remember how to gut it?' she asked.

Ariana pursed her lips, trying to look offended. 'Of course,' she said. 'Hasn't been that long.'

'And twenty Euros, remember,' Nikki said.

'I'll have to owe you,' Ariana retorted, smiling broadly.

'Payment in kind,' Nikki teased.

Ariana raised her eyebrows. 'Really, Ms Kefalas! What do you take me for?' She was finding it hard not to laugh.

'About twenty Euros,' Nikki replied.

'This bet's not over yet,' Ariana retorted, picking up her rod, reeling it in and re-casting it with determined focus.

Nikki laughed, baited the hook, cast out and sat. 'Double or quits?' she asked.

'Deal.'

*

'I'll carry the fish up,' Nikki said, dropping her gear at the beach by the bottom of the path to the white house. Three mullet was an excellent catch, and weighing heavily on her shoulder.

'That was fun,' Ariana said as the clambered up the path with the energy of a teenager.

Nikki was only half-smiling, shaking her head, still mystified at the fact that Ariana had hauled two fish to her one. Having trebled the odds for the last bet, she now owed her a hundred and twenty Euros. 'Hmm,' she responded, enjoying the tease. It had been more fun than she had had since probably the last time she and Ariana had fished together. She had lost the bet then too.

'You want a nightcap?' Ariana asked as she opened the front door.

'Umm, okay,' Nikki replied, following Ariana into the house and dumping the fish onto the sink drainer. Studying Ariana, her stomach flipped. She blinked several times to focus.

'Ouzo, right?'

Nikki grinned. 'Thanks.'

Ariana pulled out two glasses and poured them both a shot. Handing one over, she took her glass to the sink, took a sip and then reached for the knife. 'Sit,' she said, her back to Nikki.

Nikki took a slurp of the drink, the burning in her mouth instantly awakening her to her arousal. She swallowed. Absorbed by the deftness with which Ariana cleaned the fish, time stopped. Ariana plated the fish, covered them, and placed them in the fridge. As the door closed, Nikki's presence returned. 'You haven't forgotten, then,' she remarked, standing as Ariana returned to the sink, washed her hands and picked up her drink.

Ariana stared into the soft hazel eyes. She had needed to stay very focused and work quickly to clean the fish and control the rippling sensation in her stomach that had led her hands to shake. Now, the focus of her attention was causing her whole body to tremor. She had never wanted anyone as much as she wanted Nikki, and yet, she had never been more scared of anything in her life. Even living the life she had, with a dominant husband and mother hadn't been as frightening as this woman standing in front of her now. Wearing yes, but not threatening, not in this way. She didn't know how long she had been biting down on her lip, but the subtle taste of iron alerted her, and she took a short sip of her drink, wincing as the alcohol eased into the small open wound.

Nikki closed the space between them. The fire in her throat didn't compare to the longing that gripped her. She could still feel Ariana's cheek resting against her chest, her thumb teasing her lips, her dark eyes caressing her body. She knew. Ariana was trembling. She reached out and took the hands, cold from the water, raised them up and intertwined their fingers, eased closer and leaned towards her. Ariana's lips sat apart, and her breath was coming fast and shallow. Nikki could taste the warm aniseed air passing between them, its lure intoxicating.

Nikki continued, eliciting a soft groan at the feel of Ariana's lips against her own.

Ariana's breath hitched at the contact. So soft, so…

'Mum!' The single word had the same effect as a finger in an electric socket, throwing the two women apart, immobilising them and rendering them speechless.

Soph stood in a crop top and knickers assessing the two women with a coy smile. 'Hey, Nikki,' she said, aiming to sound casual but coming across as something closer to thrilled.

'Hi,' Nikki croaked, her face flushing, her hand flicking through her hair, her pulse thundering.

'It's late,' Ariana said sharply, then realised two pairs of eyes were looking at her as if to say, 'And?'

Nikki started to chuckle.

Soph grinned as if to say, 'Got ya.'

Ariana crossed her arms, uncrossed them, smiled, chuckled and then started to laugh.

Soph glanced from Nikki to her mum and back again and shrugged. She grabbed two tall glasses, filled them with cold water and headed back out the kitchen door.

'Did you see what I saw?' Ariana asked, somewhat perturbed.

Nikki closed the gap again, this time with a greater sense of urgency. 'They'll be fine,' she said, silencing Ariana with her mouth.

Ariana fell into the kiss, spellbound, her tongue exploring, resuming a dance that felt so familiar, and so right. Her hands cupped Nikki's head, pulled her closer, kissed her with tenderness, and for a brief moment opened to her. Then, without warning, she jolted out of the kiss and took a pace back. What was she thinking? 'Sorry, I,' she stammered, violently and pushed Nikki away.

Nikki froze. 'I… I… I'm sorry,' she stammered. 'It's my fault,' she stated, shaking her head, admonishing herself, her hands raised to her ears, fire coursing through her veins, frustration flaring. Had she misread the signals? She pinched at the bridge of her nose, trying to process the last few minutes, the hours, the day, failing to come up with anything that made sense. What was she thinking? Slowly and calmly, lowering her hands to her side, she held Ariana's worried gaze. 'I'm sorry, Ariana. I didn't mean to push you.' The sharp pain piercing her chest spiralled deeper, penetrating her heart, draining the blood from her body, and the spirit from her soul. She turned slowly and walked away.

Ariana tried to respond, but the words were stuck, and unwilling to budge. Before she could bring them to the surface, Nikki had walked out of the kitchen and out the front door.

11.

Nikki stood at the top of the track leading down to the beach. She stared through glassy eyes at the moon shimmering on the water, the dark sky littered with tiny stars, trying to swallow back the anger and frustration that seemed to rise like waves, stirring and muddying her mind. At that moment, the few seconds of the kiss, she had never experienced such clarity, such purity. And then, in the next, the walls had collapsed, and here she stood, more wounded than she dared to admit.

Every pace felt laboured, her foot treading the dirt track cautiously and with a weight more substantial than the mass of her body, her stride shorter and purposeless. She paused at the bottom of the path, collected the fishing gear and trudged her way across the sand.

Manos studied the despondent form approaching. He didn't need to ask what had happened, Nikki would tell him in her own time. His eyes drawn to the light glow above the rose garden, he nodded, as if he understood something that could only pass between those with utmost faith. He sipped at the clear liquid in his glass, leaned back and rested his eyes, enjoying the relative silence and the low hum of the night insects.

'Pops!' Nikki muttered, in acknowledgement, as she passed by the lounger and dropped her gear at the entrance to the bar.

'Aye,' he replied.

Nikki turned back to the beach and walked out to the water's edge. She stripped to her bikini, strode into the sea, and dived as the water reached her knees.

Manos squinted to get his bearings, sipped, swallowed, and closed his eyes again, his ears tuning into the new sound accompanying the light ripple of the waves.

Nikki's arms thrashed, her legs thrashed, and her head stayed under the water until her lungs reached bursting point. She thrust her head out of the sea, gasped for air and spluttered at the intensely salty taste caught in her throat. She wanted to scream, she wanted to cry, but most of all she wanted to be held, comforted and loved. Diving back under the water, the burning in her eyes exacerbated by the salty liquid, she pulled herself down, as low as she could go.

Manos gazed out at Nikki's cry for help, his heart aching with his inability to alleviate her pain. He had seen Nikki like this before, just the once and it had broken his heart then too. He sipped at his drink, sighed and sucked through his teeth, his faith tested.

Nikki broke through the surface of the water, drew in a deep breath and started to swim. She would swim out until her arms and legs burned. Only then would she turn around and make her way back to the shore. She had done it before, she could do it again, and in that time, the hour or more it would take, she would let go of the past. She would help Ariana to renovate the house, and sell because she had promised - and maybe she could raise the funds to buy - but nothing more. She pounded the surface of the water, gliding at a fast pace out to sea, energised by the decision she had taken.

Manos waited.

*

Ariana slumped against the kitchen sink, her free hand covering her mouth, her heart racing and her head spinning. What just happened? How could a day that was going so wonderfully end so catastrophically? Already a fog had descended on her mind, and she didn't know what, if anything, to believe. *What was real?* Her stomach squeezed into a tight ball and her chest followed, and she struggled for breath. She

125

gasped, coughed, and swallowed the bitterness that burned more than her throat. Tears burst uncontrollably from her eyes and streamed down her cheeks, and she couldn't stop her shoulders convulsing with the sobs.

She filled a glass with chilled water, tried to ease the fire in her throat, and her eyes welled up again. Another eruption of tears and the shaking took over her body and sapped her of any remaining strength. She slumped to the floor, held her head in her hands, and wept.

Scene after scene appeared in her mind's eye: Teresa berating her for being an ineffectual mother; her husband criticising her for not providing for his needs; her life, a failure on every level. All of it, as clear as if the events were all happening now, simultaneously ripping through her, stripping her of everything she might have been. Her body continued to shake violently, her mind spun, and she screamed out. But there was no one to hear the voiceless woman in the corner of the room. Everyone she had ever loved had let her down, and now she was alone.

She wasn't sure for how long she had sat on the cold tiled floor, her back to the sink cupboard, but the tears had dried, leaving a white residue on her skin and her head pounded; the house was silent.

She pulled herself up to stand slowly, gripping at the sink for support, her knees reeling under the pressure of the stress involved in standing upright. Her eyes refused to focus, declined to settle, and a wave of nausea drew a groan from her lips. Fighting, she waited for the feeling to pass, the dizziness to reduce and her strength to return.

She turned on the tap and splashed the cool water on her face. Taking deep breaths, she stood taller, her chest expanding more rhythmically with each inhalation. Her legs taking the strain, she walked out onto the kitchen balcony and stood, raising her head into the balmy air. *What am I doing?* She hadn't meant to push Nikki away so forcefully, to reject her so vehemently. She didn't want to reject her at all. On the contrary, she wanted her, needed her. She loved her.

She glimpsed the edge of the rose garden, the halo of light still visible by the light of the moon, the night sky dark but for the stars glittering, and sighed. Knowing Sophia wasn't there, yet feeling her presence, helped to ease the tension in her mind. Her ears tuned into the hushing sound, the rhythmical, gentle ebb and flow of the sea drawing her eyes to the small white foamy squiggles that formed at the water's edge, she stared, entranced.

*

Soph rammed the earphones deeply into her ears, to the point of pain, turned up the volume on her phone, and huffed. Music was preferable to the wailing she had had to suffer, which thankfully had now stopped, but she hadn't been able to sleep, the space next to her having lost its comforting warmth. She reached across the bed, her hand caressing the sheet, Gianna's scent reminding her.

She had tossed and turned for hours, worry vying with irritation as her thoughts drifted to the years of pain she had endured with her mother. Years of sadness. Years of dysfunction. Years of hurt. She had come to realise Ariana wasn't a bad mother, just a depressed one. She had heard the arguments between Ariana and Teresa. Her grandmother had always won, and at first, and she had taken sides with Teresa until it had dawned on her that her grandmother was nothing other than a manipulative bully. Her father had barely been around, but when he had he hardly ever spoken to Ariana, without it ending in a shouting match and, most often her mother's tears. He had never given Soph the time of day, and she hadn't been close to him, and especially since he hated the fact that she played music. She had grown to hate him too.

She sat up, finished the dregs of water in her glass, rubbed wearily at her heavy eyes, and clocked the time on her phone. 3 am. Her eyes burned and the pressure in her head was shouting at her to sleep, but she couldn't rest. She lay back on the bed, eased her hands behind her head and stared at the ceiling, steering her thoughts to Gianna.

*

Nikki stopped, suspended, thankful for the buoyancy of the salty water assisting her to stay afloat, her arms making sweeping motions, her legs resting, barely paddling. The darkness of the water merged with the dark sky all around. She tilted her head back, her body rising to float, and studied the stars, barely a sound registering as her ears dipped under the surface of the water. Her body felt exhausted, but the extreme exertion had swept away the frustration, and she felt calm and more at peace.

The intensity of the last few days, seeing Ariana and resurrecting all the old memories, and emotions, had diffused a little and she could see more clearly. Ariana was in pain, that much was obvious. Conflicted even. Nikki hadn't misread the signals; of that, she felt convinced. A closed-lip smile slowly formed. She knew Ariana, intimately, the shift in the colour of her irises when she was excited, sad, angry, and aroused. The way her cheeks shone when she smiled, and the dimple that formed in her right cheek when she laughed. The way her tongue toyed with her top lip and her teeth with her lower, and the seductive smile that would sparkle and bring depth to her eyes. She knew it all. And she had seen it, in the last few days. She had definitely seen the old Ariana, the one with whom she had fallen in love. The stress, the drama, the angst, that wasn't

Ariana. That was who she had started to become, under the constant influence of her mother. *She just needs time.*

Nikki righted herself in the water, moved onto her front and started the long swim back to shore. Smooth strokes and a renewed determination to be there for Ariana would make the swim back to shore a pleasant one.

*

A new movement in the water caught Ariana's attention from the surf breaking on the shoreline. Her eyes widened and her pulse raced at the sight of Nikki striding out of the sea and flicking the hair from her face. She couldn't deny the impact seeing Nikki had on her body. It was automatic, persistent, and happened every time she thought about her. She watched, Nikki collecting her clothes from the beach, Nikki strolling across the sand and then stopping next to the lounger. She hadn't noticed Manos there before now. He must have been waiting for Nikki. He must have been worried. What had she done to Nikki? A wave of guilt struck her. Nikki didn't deserve to be treated that way. She needed to go to her, explain, apologise. Her heart raced with the sense of urgency driving her to make good the damage she had inflicted.

Ariana ran through the kitchen and out the front door. Down the path, she slowed her pace, careful not to make a wrong step and stumble. Reaching the sand, she tried to increase her stride again, but the soft sand sapped the last remaining energy from her legs, and she faltered. Dragging her feet, one step at a time, she pushed on. As she approached the taverna, the lounger was empty. The doors too were locked. She made her way around the side of the bar, to the rear of the building, and stood in front of Nikki's apartment. Her heart, pounding in her chest, she froze. Glancing around, she took in the layout she hadn't seen before. The workshop sited to the left of the apartment and in direct view from the side of the bar. It looked as if Nikki was working on an old fishing boat, and the two shutters she had removed that day lay propped against the wall. There was something familiar about the boat, but she couldn't quite place it.

'Good morning, Ariana,' Manos said, in a hushed tone.

Ariana's feet almost left the ground as his voice registered, and she gasped, her hand covering her mouth to stem the scream she would have otherwise released.

'Sorry, I didn't mean to make you jump,' Manos said. His smile was warm, his eyes heavy with concern.

Ariana slowly relaxed her hand, her heart still pounding. She tried to speak, but Manos interrupted her.

'Nikki could do with some sleep,' he said, with compassion. He wasn't pushing her away; he was making sense. 'She'll be fine,' he added, with a reassuring grin.

Ariana nodded, stepped closer and collapsed against Manos' strong chest. He folded his arms gently around her and held her close. She was exhausted, and maybe that's why she allowed herself to be held by him. She didn't have the energy to fathom it, and she didn't care why she had fallen into his arms. Maybe it was his quiet maturity or his genuine kindness? He always seemed so stable, so constant, and reliable. As far back as she could remember he had been there at times when her mother hadn't. Something about his demeanour felt reassuringly familiar, and had given her permission to be comforted, and supported. Her eyes closed for a moment before she pulled back. 'I need to go,' she said softly.

'Aye,' he whispered, watching her as she made her way back to the beach. He released a long breath, his head rocking subtly with his thoughts, sucking through his teeth, hoping Sophia had been right in her assessment of her granddaughter; hoping Ariana would make the right choice.

12.

Ariana's eyelids flickered, her ears adjusting to the grinding sound outside her bedroom window. The harder she tried to open the lids the heavier they seemed to be, so she stopped trying and rested into the pillow. In the absence of any struggle, her muscles softened, and the tension in her head melted away, the sense of relaxation bringing with it a tiny smile. She hadn't realised what it felt like physically, to not be tense. The grinding noise stopped and then started again. Curiosity got the better of her, and she eased herself up from the bed, noting the increased temperature in the room. Squinting, daylight streaming through the gaps in the shuttered window, she stood and stretched.

As she opened the shutters, the noise increased, and she stepped onto the balcony, her ears guiding her eyes right, to the window next to hers. 'Manos!' she exclaimed.

Manos stopped the sanding machine and smiled at her. 'Sorry,' he said. 'I thought you'd be up already,' he added, his eyes avoiding her scantily dressed body.

Ariana pulled her arms around her chest, even though she would be revealing more flesh if she were wearing her bathing suit. 'I didn't realise you were...' Ariana's voice faded, her eyes searching the side of the house. She couldn't see Nikki.

'I offered to help Nikki,' he said, juggling the toothpick in his mouth.

'Can I get you a drink?' Ariana asked, wondering if Nikki might be working on the front of the house, and curious to find out.

'Yes, please,' Manos responded, but Ariana had escaped from the balcony before he finished the short sentence.

'Afternoon,' Soph said, with a wry smile, as Ariana entered the kitchen.

Ariana flushed, a wave of embarrassment sweeping through her at her behaviour the previous night. 'Hi,' she said, unsure how or whether to apologise. 'I'm sorry if I disturbed you last night,' she said, remorsefully.

Soph shrugged, downed the coffee in her cup and stood. 'Coffee's in the pot,' she said. 'I'm going to the beach with G,' she added.

Ariana smiled warmly, pulled Soph into her arms and squeezed her tightly. 'I love you,' she said.

Soph tensed. She hadn't expected that and didn't quite know how she felt about her mother's overt display of affection towards her. 'Right, I gotta go,' Soph said.

'Right, sorry,' Ariana fussed, releasing Soph. The last thing she intended was to offend her daughter. 'Have fun,' she said, to Soph's back as she exited the kitchen.

'You too,' Soph shouted back.

Ariana smiled; Soph looked happy. She poured a coffee and a glass of water, stepped out the front door, glanced around, and then took the external steps to the side of the house, to the shuttered bedroom on the ground floor. No sign of Nikki.

'Thanks,' Manos said, taking the glass and emptying it in one shot. 'Coming along eh,' he said, his hand caressing the exposed wood.

Ariana glanced at the sanded shutter, sipping fervently at the drink in her hand. The wood did look better, even though it hadn't yet been painted, but her attention was elsewhere. Manos was grinning suspiciously.

'She's gone to Lefkada,' he said, his eyes still on the wood in his hand.

'Oh!' Ariana replied; the word laced with disappointment.

'You want to start painting these?' he asked with a slight tilt of his head. 'These aren't as bad as the ones at the front, he said. 'I can remove the shutters there while you paint,' he added, his grin widening. He wasn't going to take no for an answer.

Ariana nodded. The panels she and Nikki had removed had needed far more attention than the ones Manos had sanded down. She would need to get a coat of paint on them before the sun was fully around the hill though. 'I'll do my best,' she said.

'Aye,' Manos said. 'Me too,' he added with a chuckle.

Ariana smiled.

'I'll get the paint,' he said.

'Do you want a coffee?' she asked.

'Good idea,' he replied with a nod, heading up the steps, Ariana following him.

By the time Ariana returned with two fresh cups of coffee, Manos had the lid off the paint and was inspecting the brush in his hand.

'This'll do it,' he said, placing the brush on the low wall and taking the offered cup. He gazed out across the west-cove, sipping at the drink. 'Beautiful, eh,' he said.

Ariana stopped and studied the view, the lower level providing a different aspect to the kitchen-balcony above her bedroom. Shrubs and bushes partly obscured the beach, narrowing the span, the insects seemed more vocal too, and yet it also felt very cosy and private. 'It is,' she said, with sincerity. She sipped at her drink, immersed in the ambience.

'Your mother used to love exploring over there,' he said, pointing to the rocky outcrop on the opposite side of the cove.

Ariana flinched. Not only was there more than a hint of affection in his tone, she had never imagined her mother enjoying any aspect of being on the island. She couldn't think what to say.

'When she was younger,' Manos clarified as if to answer the question in her mind. 'We used to explore a lot back then,' he said, sucking softly through his teeth.

Ariana was still struggling to process his comments. Her mother had always been so keen to leave the island and never return, and even though Teresa's obsessive desire had never made any sense to her, she had never sought to ask why. 'Why did she take me away then, if she loved it so much?' she asked.

Manos paused, his eyes remaining fixed on the rocks on the other side of the cove. 'It's complicated,' he said.

Ariana frowned. That was no answer.

'The estate wasn't always what it is now,' he started. 'And, Teresa became ambitious,' he said with a sense of admiration. 'You know she used to love to sing, but singing in the bar,' his eyes drifted to the taverna, 'just wasn't enough for her. She wanted to sing, to travel, to enjoy fame and fortune, and at that time the estate was barely providing enough for them to survive. But, then.' He paused.

He talked as if he held deep affection for Teresa and sympathy for her too. But, the bigger surprise was the fact that Teresa used to sing. Ariana had never been aware of that, ever! A flash of anger passed quickly through her, with the images of her mother stopping her from singing as a child, and the vehement opposition to Soph going to Music College. Her jaw sat agape as she continued to hang off Manos' words.

'A young man turned up here one day, Aaron Carter.' His tone shifted to something closer to dismay. Bemusement? 'He charmed your mother with his ideas of a multi-million dollar lifestyle, made promises that excited her more than life here, and she decided that marrying him was the best option for her.'

Ariana's jaw had dropped, and her mouth sat open wide and in danger of catching a passing insect.

'It happened very quickly; the marriage I mean.' There was something in his tone she couldn't place. 'But then he left her here while he travelled to set up his business empire. I don't think Teresa was expecting him to do that when she married him, and she became angry and bitter.' He was shaking his head, his eyes pitying, his lips pressed tightly together for a moment, and then he took a deep breath and continued. 'The truth was, at the time Aaron arrived here, he had nothing but a dream. Then you were born, and that made life difficult for Aaron to fund, so Teresa stayed here for Sophia to provide the support she needed. He came to visit as often as he could, as you know, but the promises he made were very slow to materialise. At one point we thought Teresa might never leave, but then he hit the jackpot and she went to him. She had stopped singing long before she left the island, mind,' he added with a resigned shrug.

There was regret in his tone, and as he turned to face her, the sheen on the surface of his eyes spilt a tear onto his cheek. 'You were fond of my mother?' she asked, in a pitch higher than usual.

He swiped awkwardly at his damp cheek. 'It was a long time ago,' he said. 'And, yes, I loved her very much.' He reached out and with tenderness, tucked Ariana's hair around her ear and lifted her chin between his thumb and finger. He studied her with genuine warmth. 'She loves you dearly,' he said, 'she's just never been very good at choosing love over money.'

Ariana studied the depth in his dark-eyes, the tenderness of his touch even though his fingers were coarse, and he released her chin.

'Better get painting before the sun gets too hot,' he said, looking skyward.

She nodded. Only after he had disappeared back up the steps did she reach for the paintbrush and realise her hands were shaking.

*

'You okay?' Gianna asked with concern, her keen eyes failing to pin down the cause of Soph's evasive behaviour.

Soph sat, digging her toes into the soft sand, her knees clamped to her chest, picking at the calloused skin on her fingertips. She looked up briefly, tried to smile but ended up grimacing and releasing a huffing sound.

'What's up?' Gianna asked, leaning across, toying with Soph's hair and trailing her index finger down her jaw-line.

Soph moved her head into the tender touch, her mouth finding Gianna's fingers and pressing her lips to them. Gianna's sweet scent filled her as she breathed, stirring a deep sense of longing. 'Do you get on with your parents?' Soph asked, her voice quiet, pensive.

Gianna pulled her hand away and leaned back on her elbows, stared out to sea. She hadn't ever thought about whether she got on with her parents or not, they were just her parents and often a pain in the arse. But she loved them all the same. 'I guess so,' she said, trying to be honest. 'Don't you? Your mum seems cool,' she added, hoping to lift Soph's solemn mood.

Soph let out a weighty sigh. 'I guess,' she said, reminded of the times her mum had defended her, even though she had always been over-ruled by either her father or her grandmother. Her mum had also been the one to allow her to get the tattoo, and the piercings. But that wasn't the cause of Soph's low mood. The effect of Ariana's sadness over the years had created a deep scar. She was left feeling she wanted to run from her and be held by her, at the same time. The inner turmoil had her feeling more alone, isolated, and lonely. 'Does your mama get sad?' she asked.

Gianna shook her head. 'Angry sometimes,' she said. 'Papa gets angry too,' she added.

'Yeah, my dad used to shout, a lot,' Soph agreed. 'It's arse,' she added, with a nervous chuckle.

Gianna huffed. 'They aren't perfect,' she stated.

'I guess not,' Soph said, holding Gianna's bright eyes, the dark liner shaping them drawing her in, triggering the tingling in her neck and the warmth in her chest.

'My mum got sad a lot,' Soph admitted, suddenly feeling the urge to share her worries.

'That must have been hard,' Gianna said, softly.

'Depression! She used to cry all the time, for years,' Soph continued, her gaze fixed on the horizon out to sea.

Gianna quieted and watched. The colour seemed to drain from Soph's cheeks, and her blue eyes lightened and narrowed.

'She was crying last night,' Soph said, hugging her legs and dropping her gaze to her feet in the sand.

Gianna eased next to Soph, put an arm around her shoulders and pulled her close. The body in her arms began to shake, and she squeezed tighter, finding it hard to hold back the tears in her own eyes.

Neither of them spoke for what felt like an eternity.

Soph lifted her head. The tears had stopped with the comfort of Gianna's warmth, and a wave of relief lightened her spirits. She rubbed at her damp cheeks, chuckled at her embarrassment and turned to face Gianna. Her heart stopped at the intensity of the almost black irises staring directly at her.

The sharp pain ripping through Gianna's heart transformed instantly as the girl she was falling for looked up at her through teary eyes, and she couldn't prevent what followed. She lurched forward, her mouth finding its target with precision and force. Her lips pressed down hard, her tongue, responding to Soph's, dancing synchronously, exploring hungrily. She pulled Soph into the kiss. Soph's hands were around her head and pulling her to the ground, Soph released a guttural groan as her back hit the sand and Gianna landed on top of her, their mouths continuing to explore. Seeking out Soph's hands, she intertwined their fingers and pressed Soph's hands to the side of her head, her tongue continuing to investigate the soft, warm texture at its tip. Gianna slowed her exploration as the emotional intensity driving her increased, causing her to tremble; tenderly, mindfully, nipping, and teasing, she took them deeper into the kiss.

Soph was drowning, and it was the most erotic sensation she had ever experienced. She could die now, and she would have lived. The sensual feel of Gianna pressed against the length of her body, kissing her, breathing new life into her, feeding her; she had found a home, a place of her own, and she didn't want the feeling ever to leave. The quality of the kiss, so intimate, so tender, made her feel safe, needed, wanted. Her body melted beneath Gianna's confident strength, moved rhythmically with the gentle rocking motion that had taken hold of them both, their contact shifting in waves from the lightest of touch to the most intense pressure, unhurried and yet driving her wild with desire.

*

Nikos sighed, turned his back to the scene on the beach and strolled into the olive grove, shaking his head.

*

Ariana stood back from the Mediterranean-blue shutters, brush in hand, wiped at the sweat on her brow and stretched. Admiring her work, the wet paint glistening in the sun, she smiled. It looked perfect and also showed up the not-so-white colour on the whitewashed walls. She rested the brush across the lid of the paint pot and wiped again at her salty damp face. It was hot! Picking up the pot and brush, she climbed the steps at the side of the house. Manos was nowhere in sight, but with three sets of shutters removed the front of the house looked decidedly bare.

Ariana dropped the paint pot at the garage, cleaned the brush in the kitchen sink and poured herself a glass of water. She wandered out onto the balcony overlooking the west-cove, and turned her head, her eyes closing into the light, warm breeze coming off the sea. Opening her eyes, she sipped at the water, placed the glass on the wall and rubbed at the tenderness in her forearm. Something about the exercise and the pleasing result felt good though. She congratulated herself, gazed out over the sea and across to the taverna, captivated by the easiness of life here. Manos appeared from the bar with plates in his hand, served them to the couple at the table and returned into the shade of the taverna. He had waited on her and Nikki once, when her mother had been sick, and she had escaped down to the west-cove, she recalled.

'And what would Miss Ariana like to eat?' he asked with a broad grin, his dark hair slicked back, the dimples showing beneath his bristly cheeks, a white cloth over his arm, and bowing as he spoke.

Ariana giggled, her feet dangling from the chair, swinging restlessly, the fizzing in her stomach reminding her that she'd better not get caught. She looked up to the white house, hoping her mother was still asleep. Grandma Sophia had said not to worry, that it would be their little secret, but that didn't make the tingling feeling go away.

'Can I have calamari?' Nikki asked excitedly, staring at Pops with a big toothy grin. Usually, she ate in the kitchen with him, or at the apartment; she hadn't been waited on like this before, but then Ariana had never visited before, and she rarely saw any other children on the island.

'Miss Nikki would like calamari,' Manos repeated, pulling out the pad from his pocket and scribbling a note.

'I'll have calamari too,' Ariana said, but she wasn't quite sure what it was.

'That will be two calamari for the young ladies at table number 5,' Manos said, with a warm smile. He wandered into the bar and returned with two glasses of orange juice and two blue straws.

'Thank you,' Ariana said, politely, dipping the straw in the drink and sipping eagerly. Nikki was watching her with dark eyes and a broad smile. She looked pretty with her dark wavy hair and light coloured eyes.

Nikki jumped up from the table. 'Want to collect shells?' she asked.

Ariana looked concerned.

'It's okay. We can play until the food comes,' Nikki said, with a shrug.

'Really?' Ariana questioned. That would never happen in her mother's presence and the wave of guilt that churned her stomach told her she probably shouldn't be getting up from the table until after she had eaten.

'Come on,' Nikki insisted, grabbing her bucket from the sand and running towards the water, squealing with delight.

The urge was too strong, and Ariana leapt from the table and chased Nikki to the water's edge. Nikki was already picking at something in the soft, wet sand.

'What are you doing?' Ariana asked.

'Finding new shells,' Nikki said. 'I haven't got one like this,' she said, holding up a smooth, oval-shaped shell that shone like a rainbow. She rubbed it against her t-shirt, inspected it, and put it in her shorts pocket, her eyes eagerly seeking out more gems from the sand.

Manos watched the two girls playing, and waited.

Ariana hadn't known how long they had searched for, but with a half-full bucket of shells and stones and grumbling tummies they made their way back up the beach and tipped the

contents onto the table to inspect them. Moments later Manos
appeared with two plates of calamari and a bowl of fries.
It had been the best day ever.

Ariana sighed, a warm feeling bathing her chest. Driven by an overwhelming desire to repeat the experience, she wandered out of the house, ambled down the slope, and meandered across the beach.

'Ariana!' Manos greeted, sporting a welcoming smile. 'The blue looks good,' he said, his eyes indicating to the bedroom shutters she had painted.

She turned to look, smiled at the shiny, fresh colour, standing out from the untreated shutters at the other windows. 'Yes, they do,' she agreed. She was still smiling as she turned to face him. 'Can I get a table, please?' she asked.

Manos' grin widened. 'Of course.'

Whether by intent or fluke she couldn't decide, but he led her to table number 5, held out the chair she had sat on as a child, and handed her a menu. 'Calamari and fries, please,' she said, without looking at the options. 'And a glass of white wine, please,' she added, grinning broadly.

The sparkle in his eyes and the slight twirl in the hair on his dimpled cheeks told her he had remembered. She sat, in the shade of the awning, and it dawned on her, she had stopped worrying. It was a liberating experience, and, for a brief moment, she felt like the ten-year-old child who had played on the beach, collecting shells and dining like royalty. 'Thank you,' she said with a soft smile, as Manos placed a glass of wine in front of her.

Facing the empty seat across the table, the absence of Nikki brought with it a wave of sorrow. She sipped at the wine, tuning her into her heart. The ache she found there caused her stomach to flip, the sudden burst of anxiety that would typically have her fleeing, feeling so familiar, so comforting in a dysfunctional way, and so wrong. She couldn't go there again. She couldn't allow her life to be dominated and controlled by that kind of fear. She sipped at the wine, and focused on the aching sensation in her chest, for the first time in her life accepting the message her heart conveyed. She was in love with Nikki. The truth was undeniable, painful and incredible at the same time, and she knew she could no longer avoid it, no matter how scary it might feel. She had nothing to fear, except fear itself. She gazed out to sea, hoping to spot the returning motorboat, her heart fluttering at the image in her mind's eye of Nikki ambling across the beach.

The sea was calm. There was no boat in sight.

Manos approached with a large plate of calamari and a basket of fries and placed them on the table. He stood, gazing out over the beach, the toothpick dancing on his lips. 'Beautiful day,' he said, not expecting a response.

The rich aroma, with a hint of lemon and garlic, evoked a pleasant feeling, drawing a soft smile. Ariana hadn't realised how hungry she was. She popped a battered ring into her mouth and it melted on her tongue, the delicate creamy taste of the soft seafood eliciting a groan of approval. 'Mmm, that's so good,' she said.

'Good as you remember, Miss Ariana?' he asked, with a coy smile and a half-bow.

She chuckled. 'Better,' she said, dunking a fry into the garlic mayonnaise.

Manos nodded. 'Aye,' he said, and turned back to the bar.

13.

Nikki gazed down from the aircraft window, the white surf lining the small rocky islands contrasting with the deep blue sea, thousands of miles below her feet. Dotted across the expansive ocean, some very tiny, they looked spectacular and strangely hypnotic. She settled back into the hard, uncomfortable seat, trying to ignore the irritating, deafening and persistent noise, thankful the flight to Athens was a short one. She released a long breath, her thoughts drifting to that moment with Ariana, the brief kiss they had shared, and the truth revealed in Ariana's dark eyes as she had held Nikki's gaze earnestly. She smiled, her mind quieted by the certainty that she had come to believe in spite of the rebuff, that Ariana was in love with her.

She hadn't reckoned on going to the mainland to source the funding she needed, but the bank manager in Lefkada was limited in what he could offer, and in the end he couldn't help. He had at least made the call to the business department of Alpha Bank and set up the introduction, and he had also made sure her file had arrived there. But, that didn't stop the anxious feeling dancing in her stomach, or the tension compressing her head. She hated flying, and she hated the city, and there was a good chance she would have to spend a few days in Athens to get the approval she needed and the contract paperwork signed. A week away from Ariana; the thought didn't sit comfortably, and she fidgeted anxiously in the seat.

She closed her eyes, hoping the white noise would induce sleep. It didn't, her thoughts occupied by the procession of illogical doubts passing through her mind. What if her absence caused Ariana to distance herself further? What if Ariana didn't want to be with her? What if Ariana didn't allow her to buy the house? She had convinced herself that Ariana

143

hadn't meant to push her away, but she could be wrong. She had left Sakros before Ariana had woken, how could she be sure that Ariana felt something for her? But Ariana did, didn't she? Question after question challenging her newfound belief in Ariana, she bolted upright in the seat, her eyes wide open, beads of sweat on her brow in spite of the air-conditioning. She released a deep sigh and turned her attention to the deep blue sky outside the aircraft window.

'Can I get you a drink?' the hostess asked, her attention on the trolley in front of her as she passed down the aisle.

'Coffee, please.' Nikki took the drink, sipped from the cup and continued to gaze. Catching sight of the mainland, memories of the last and only other time she had travelled to Athens came to mind.

'You want to buy me a drink?' the fair-haired young woman asked, her eyes glassy, her stare unfocused.

Nikki didn't, but for some inexplicable reason she nodded, and the woman ordered within seconds.

'You come here often?' the woman asked, her light-blue eyes still trying to assess Nikki through the alcoholic haze that obscured her vision.

'No,' Nikki croaked, suddenly unable to find her voice.

'Shame.' The girl shrugged disappointedly, and disappeared into the stream of women, lingering and chatting, between the main door and the bar, leaving Nikki to pick up the tab for the drink.

Nikki released the breath that had stopped in the presence of the young woman's alluring light-blue eyes, a sense of relief passing through her, ordered another beer and scanned the room with curiosity, her heart racing with the adrenalin pumping through her veins, the voice in her head questioning whether she should be in here.

She'd never been in a woman only bar before. In fact, she'd never known any other gay women. It was intriguing, exhilarating, and more than a little intimidating, but, she was twenty-one now, nearly twenty-two, and having just taken on legal ownership of the Kefalas businesses, perfectly capable of making her own choices. Why shouldn't she have some fun? She wondered briefly what it would be like to be in this place with Ariana, and then tried to dismiss the idea for the random thought that it was, but Ariana's image wouldn't leave, pulling her attention from the women in the room.

It had been almost six-years since Ariana had left the island, and with no word since. Ariana had got married and had a child, Sophia had told her as they had gathered the ripe-olives from the branches. It had been a hot, sticky day, and the fruit had fallen quickly, the essence of burnt salt filling the air and tingling her tongue. It had been a good harvest that year, but the news of Ariana's marriage had cut deeply, leaving a gaping wound, the salt stinging and increasing the pain. Sophia had noticed her shaking and wrapped her in the warmest, most comforting embrace, and held her until the tears stopped flowing. Unsteadily, transfixed by the news, she had continued to pick the olives, but something had changed. Hope. The realisation that Ariana had already made a life for herself and would never return to the island had descended like a dark cloud, placing a shadow over her heart, squeezing it, crushing it, until she could no longer breathe. Hope was gone. Sophia had tried to convince her differently, and she wanted to believe her, but Nikki had already died inside, and she needed to find a way to be reborn. She needed to make a life for herself, one that would never include Ariana.

The sombre thought, so final, so surreal to her emotional mind, had shaken her from the memory, but the event had left its mark even six years on. She scanned around the bar, trying to find the optimism that had driven her through the door earlier *that evening. She swallowed back the tears that wanted to display themselves, to demonstrate to the world the hurt that lay buried in a shallow grave, hidden by the sturdy veneer she presented to the world, and downed the beer in her hand. The chill against the back of her throat helped; the music from the bar slowly penetrating her awareness.*

She had downed the third beer, and then a fourth, in quick succession, until the distant memory faded entirely and her head was beginning to float, her inhibitions abating; she was swaying with the music that filled the small space. A dark-haired older-looking woman, maybe in her thirties, she couldn't tell, placed another beer in her hand and started to move with her, their eyes meeting, fleetingly, frivolous smiles passing between them, connecting their worlds on a carnal level. Nothing else mattered. Their bodies touched to the rhythm of the music and flames flared through Nikki, captivating her, seducing her. The move was swift, the kiss hard, deep, penetrating, hungry. The sugary taste of the woman's breath mingled with the heady scent that filled the space, the kiss never ending. She hadn't needed to come up for air; she hadn't needed to breathe; she had needed what this woman offered.

Nikki allowed herself to be dragged from the bar, out into the street, down a side alley and pressed firmly against the wall. The anticipation, desire, and need, adding to the thrill of being taken by the older woman, whose mouth consumed her with confidence and assurance, whose deft hands were exploring her legs beneath the skirt that stopped high up her toned thighs. Silently, the message was clear.

Nikki had groaned as the woman parted her with her fingers, their mouths never losing contact, and when the woman entered her, she gasped and froze. The feel of the woman inside her stunned all her senses, her mouth stopped kissing, her mind had forgotten how to process, and her legs unable to hold her weight. Her body had been taken over by a force so strong, she felt paralysed by the sensations emanating from her core, parts of her pulsing, but what scared her more was the craving. The addict starved of the drug, she wanted as much as this woman was able to give, and more.

Her wild screams, piercing the night sky, lost in the cacophony in the city streets, didn't fill the void though, and she staggered away from the woman with no name, away from the bar, and into the night, more lost and alone, the shadow over her heart even darker than the darkest night sky. She had sobbed herself to sleep, not for the first time since Ariana had left. And when she opened her eyes in the cold light of day, the poison that had infiltrated every cell in her body, causing her head to implode and her stomach to churn, paled by comparison with the feeling of resentment and shame that caused the tears to tumble, again.

Nikki jolted out of the graphic memory, her heart racing. She sipped at her drink, her hands clammy, and stared around the cabin. It may have been a long time ago, but some visions were as vivid as if they happened only yesterday. That void had remained with her, until just a few days ago. Ariana had filled that emptiness, and Ariana had the power to create it again. It had always been Ariana, and it always would be. The truth was terrifying.

*

'Stay for tea,' Soph pleaded, as they reached the top of the slope, her eyes pining for a few more hours together, her hand squeezing Gianna's.

Gianna's bronzed cheeks shone. She didn't want to go home either, not now, not ever. She nodded excitedly and was instantly swept away as Soph yanked her enthusiastically through the front door and into the more cooling air. 'Can you cook?' she asked. There was so much she didn't know about Soph, and yet she felt as if she had known her forever.

Soph raised her eyebrows and shrugged. She'd never tried cooking. 'Dunno,' she said. 'Not sure what's in the fridge,' she added, bounding into the kitchen and opening the fridge door. Three pairs of fish eyes stared back at her, and she frowned.

Gianna glanced over her shoulder and chuckled at the sparse contents and the googly eyes staring blankly at them.

'Ah!' Soph shuddered. Her favourite species of all time, not, glared unblinkingly and directly at her and she pondered, clueless as to what to do with them. She could feel Gianna's breasts pressed against her back, the fingers tracing her spine, and she shuddered again, for an altogether different reason. 'Do you know what to do with these?' she asked, her voice challenged by the impact of Gianna's proximity.

Gianna nodded. She loved cooking, and the thought of presenting something delicious for Soph filled her with delight. Excitedly, she reached across Soph, pulled the plate of fish from the fridge and rested it on the work surface. 'Drink?' she asked as if presenting Soph with a task to help her to feel useful.

Soph flustered, opened the fridge again and pulled out two bottles of beer. She flicked the lids with the opener and rested one on the work surface next to the fish, watching Gianna as she searched around the kitchen. She seemed to know exactly where to look and pulled out various ingredients of which Soph only recognised the small onions and garlic.

'Play me some music,' Gianna said, dumping the vegetables and herbs on the side and sipping at her beer.

Soph dived out of the kitchen. Gianna started chopping. By the time Soph returned, the pan was sizzling and a gentle aroma of garlic and samphire filled the room. 'Smells amazing,' Soph said, perched on the kitchen table and strumming lazily.

'What shall I play?' she asked, her attention on the strings, her fingers toying with the tuning pegs.

When Soph was deeply engrossed in putting the words to a tune, creating music, Gianna found it intensely erotic, not that she had told Soph that, yet. 'Make something up,' she replied, biting down on her lip, secretly turned on by the idea.

Soph started to tinker with the notes.

The sound caressing Gianna's ears immediately stirred something exhilarating far lower and she released a soft groan as she worked. Drawing her concentration to the food, she tossed the fish into the hot pan and dived sideways to avoid the spray of burning oil that jumped out at her.

Soph stopped playing and studied Gianna intently, a coy smile appearing at the dancing chef. She rubbed at the light humming sensation beginning to press her temples and yawned, feeling tired.

Gianna swirled the ingredients around the pan with confidence, coating the fish with aromatic oil. Within what seemed like seconds, she had lifted the pan from the heat and rested it on the side. She picked up her beer and sipped. 'You ready to eat?' she asked.

Soph beamed, her teeth brighter against her sun-tanned skin. She placed the guitar on the table, jumped up, and grabbed the cutlery from the drawer.

Gianna squeezed fresh lemon onto the fish, served them onto the plates and followed Soph out of the kitchen.

Soph slumped into the wicker chair and studied the fish in front of her, which seemed to have more of a glazed look in its eye than it had done in the fridge, and started to chuckle. The zesty, fresh aroma and her grumbling stomach getting the better of her less-pleasant thoughts about the mullet, she picked up her fork.

Gianna had already started eating. 'Go on, try it,' she said, watching Soph poke at the dish. 'It's not going to bite you,' she said, with a laugh.

Soph took a large mouthful of the succulent dish, and the flavours danced on her tongue. She groaned. 'It's good,' she said, her fork eagerly seeking out the next bite.

Gianna flushed. She took a sip of her beer before sampling another mouthful, her eyes lovingly on Soph.

Soph's plate of bones appeared before Gianna's, and she lazed back in the seat. 'That was awesome,' she said, with a satisfied grin, her starry-eyed gaze fixed on Gianna, her heart fluttering. 'I really like you,' she said, suddenly.

Gianna smiled reservedly. 'I really like you too,' she said, but she was lying, holding back from the truth that had kept her awake at night and had her rushing to the house before the crack of dawn, and not wanting to leave Soph at the end of the day. She placed her fork on the plate and leaned back in the seat, studying Soph in silence.

Soph closed her eyes, comforted by the feeling of a full stomach and the company at the table, the almost deafening but soothing hum of the cicadas and the low hush of the sea. 'I love this place,' Soph said. 'It's so peaceful.'

Gianna gazed at Soph, admiring the colour in her tanned cheeks and her sun-bleached hair. It suited her. She leaned back in her seat and closed her eyes.

'What was Sophia like?' Soph asked, her eyes remaining shut, her head resting back in the seat.

Gianna paused. 'She was a legend,' she replied.

Soph squinted one eye open. 'Really?'

'Yeah, she was pretty amazing. Built this place up from nothing after her husband died. Everyone loved her. The estate is a big part of the island,' she said, smiling with something between fondness and respect.

Soph listened.

'She used to sing, too,' Gianna added, after a moment's thought. 'Used to sing in the bar regularly, and she'd get everyone singing along with her. Your voice is a lot like hers,' she said, with a broad grin. 'In fact, you're a lot like her.'

'How?' Soph asked, sitting up and opening her eyes. She hadn't given Sophia any thought, though she had seen some of the photographs dotted around the house. It seemed suddenly intriguing to her, that Gianna had known her great-grandmother. It was as if she had missed out on something - someone - special, and Gianna was a small link to that person. There was comfort in that, and the feeling of connection too.

Gianna faltered at the dark-blue eyes that were holding her gaze intently. 'She was really happy and liked to have fun. She was friendly and kind, and she would always help someone if they were struggling.' She shrugged. 'She wasn't scared of being bitten by a fish,' Gianna said, laughing. 'She liked nature, a lot, especially her roses,' she added, with a warm smile.

Soph chuckled, pressed her hand to her chest, feigning offence at the reference to her fallibility. Her great-grandmother sounded nice.

Gianna grinned affectionately, reached across the table and took Soph by the hand, pulling her to stand.

The intensity in Soph's eyes etched the smile on her face with seriousness. She moved to speak, but no words came.

Gianna gazed into the deep blue pools knowingly and led Soph slowly towards the bedroom. She swept the hair from Soph's face and studied her intently. 'Can I stay with you tonight,' she whispered.

'Yes,' Soph said, captivated by Gianna's tenderness. She'd never felt more vulnerable in her life than she did right now, and yet, she'd never felt more certain about anything either.

Gianna smiled softly, traced a finger down Soph's cheek and jaw, and brushed across her lips. 'Good,' she whispered.

Ariana sat in her bikini on the large rocky outcrop at the furthest edge of the west-cove from the white house, beyond the jetty and the leisure boats, her feet dangling in the deeper water, gazing out to the west in the direction of Lefkada. It seemed strangely disconcerting to think that her mother had enjoyed this spot with Manos at some point in the past. She couldn't imagine it and dismissed the more recent images of Teresa that threatened to spoil the moment.

Her clothes lay where she dropped them at the water's edge and the snorkel and mask that Manos had left out for her, as she slept away the afternoon after the calamari lunch, hung over the pointed edge of a barnacle-covered rock. She had snorkelled for the best part of two hours, the soundless, weightless, environment providing the respite she needed, the salty water both refreshing and surprisingly cathartic to her aching muscles. She smiled to herself.

The other side of the rocky outcrop a steep rock face emerged from of the water, its length defining the coastline that formed a significant section of the northwest side of the island. Sometimes, locals would be seen jumping and diving from the ledges along the jagged rocks. She had watched them once, as a teenager, but never ventured to join them for fear of injuring herself, or worse still, getting caught by her mother.

She stared at the lowest ledge, not too far from where she sat, studied the water below it, and a wicked grin cut across her face. With fearless determination, she stood and inched her way up the side of the rock. Reaching the ledge, she pressed her back to the jagged cliff and winced at the sharp stone against her skin. She tried to stand taller and breathe deeply to relax, but watching the waves kissing the base of the rocks below had her heart pumping fiercely. The exhilaration was almost too much to bear, and she considered heading back to the safety of the rocks from which she had just stepped. She dismissed the idea; the difficulty of descending the tricky slope backwards filled her with more terror than the thought of jumping. The only way was to take a leap of faith and launch forward. Standing, staring out in front of her, avoiding the shimmering surface that made the sea look too far away, she took in a deep breath, pinched her nose, closed her eyes, and jumped.

'Yes!' she screamed out, as her head broke through the surface. She swam to the rocks and started the climb again, with increased confidence. She shouted out excitedly as she jumped, a beaming grin on her face as she hit the water. Emerging, she lay on her back, floating, feeling like a fifteen-year-old exploring for the first time, and she was. She returned to the rocky outcrop, pulled herself out of the water and sat. Grinning, her heart lighter, and her resolve stronger, she breathed deeply, her chest expanding effortlessly. Freedom felt so good.

She strained her eyes into the night sky, searching the horizon seeking out any tiny lights that might suggest a returning boat. Nothing. The calm sea swayed to its tune, undisturbed, its quiet hush mesmerising, the white foam brushing softly against the rocks, bathing her legs, soothing. She rubbed at her tired eyes, yawned, and glanced casually towards the white house, and the light-glow hovering over the rose garden. She chuckled, shaking her head back and forth. *Really?* The idea of Sophia looking over them from the rose garden was undoubtedly alluring, but common sense wouldn't allow her the luxury of such a comforting thought.

'Don't tell your mother; it will be our little secret.'

She smiled wryly, shaking her head at her grandmother's words, and stood. One last glance out to the sea and she eased her way off the rocks, through the shallow water and onto the beach. Picking up her clothes she sauntered lazily, barefoot, across the sand. Manos was relaxing on the lounger, glass in hand, the taverna silent but for the gentle purr of music emanating from the bar behind him.

'Beautiful eh!' he said, sipping at his drink.

She stopped, gazed at him and smiled warmly. 'Yes, it is,' she said. 'Very beautiful.'

'Drink?' he asked, picking up the second glass from the sand, pouring and handing over the nightcap before Ariana could refuse.

She smiled with a tilt of her head, took the drink and sipped. 'When's Nikki back?' she asked.

'Maybe a few days,' he said, studying her response carefully. 'She's had to go to Athens, for business,' he added. The news didn't land any softer for the justification.

'Oh!' she replied, her tone giving away her disappointment again. She had assumed Nikki would be back from Lefkada within the day, not heading to Athens. She finished the drink in her hand and placed it on the sand next to the bottle, her heart weighing heavier.

'I'll start repairing the wall tomorrow,' he said, referring to the house.

'Okay,' Ariana said, but she hadn't heard him, distracted by the empty feeling in her chest.

'Nikki will finish the shutters when she gets back,' he said.

The mention of Nikki's name drew Ariana out of the trance, and she smiled. 'Right,' she said. Perhaps, if she got stuck into the decorating time would pass quickly, and then Nikki would be back. *Nikki, Nikki, Nikki.* 'Night Pops,' she said, softly.

'Night Miss Ariana,' he replied, with a warm smile.

Ariana strolled across the beach and up the path, the light-heartedness she had felt snorkelling, swimming and jumping into the water, overshadowed by the thought of Nikki's prolonged absence, and something that hadn't dawned on her until now. What if something terrible happened to Nikki? The thought caused her heart to stop. She knew she would never survive if something dreadful happened to Nikki. She wanted Nikki close, unharmed and close. Now.

14.

Gianna snuggled against Soph's back, her eyes blinking as she adjusted to the early morning sun, Soph's scent eliciting a groan of satisfaction and enticing her closer. Soph was snuffling and it was cute. Gianna opened her eyes, leaned up onto her elbow and gently swept Soph's scraggly hair from her face, admiring the soft lashes, fair eyebrows and the sparkling stone in her nose. Soph twitched and groaned at the gentle disturbance. Gianna smiled, leaned in and pressed a kiss to the suntanned cheek. She smiled adoringly at the white panda eyes that had spent a good part of the previous day protected by the snorkel mask.

Soph groaned at the soft lips against her skin, wriggled herself onto her back and opened her eyes slowly. Squinting at Gianna's dark-smile, 'Hey, she said, her voice groggy from sleep.

'Hey' Gianna responded, tenderly brushing the loose strands of hair clinging to Soph's face.

Soph lifted her head off the bed and rested back on her elbows, stopped, and then slumped back on the bed. 'My head's thumping,' she said, with a sad face, pressing her palms to her temples.

'Too much sun,' Gianna said, moving to massage Soph's temples.

Soph groaned at the gentle pressure, Gianna's scent stirring her senses.

'Want some pills?' Gianna asked. She made a move to jump up from the bed, but Soph stopped her and pulled her down on top of her.

'In a minute,' Soph said, locking onto Gianna's dark eyes, holding her inches from her face. Soph ruffled Gianna's hair with her hand and pulled her closer until their mouths touched. Tenderly, she pressed her lips against Gianna's then released her and drew her into her arms. 'Thank you for staying,' she whispered.

Gianna's lips tingled at the sensitive touch that had sparked a burning fire in her core. She snuggled into Soph's shoulder, resting her head on Soph's chest, savouring her scent and the warmth from her skin. There was no other place she would rather be. Easing out of the hold, she pressed a quick kiss to Soph's lips and leapt out of bed. 'Where's the Paracetamol?' she asked, beaming a smile, her face flushed.

'In the kitchen, cupboard to the right of the sink, I think,' Soph replied, leaning onto her side, smiling at Gianna as she hurried out the door. She relaxed onto her back, releasing a guttural groan at her erotic thoughts.

*

Ariana poured the coffee into her cup and sighed. She rubbed at her tired eyes. She had tossed and turned all night, her thoughts oscillating from the joyful day she had spent relaxing and reminiscing, to the fact that Nikki had just disappeared on her and wouldn't be back for days, and then to the reality of the house sale. Her head had spun all night and without resolution. She needed to explain the situation to Nikki, but maybe Nikki wouldn't want to listen. Ariana had pushed her away and now worried that perhaps she had pushed Nikki too far. She could feel the tension rising, frustration slipping to the surface and needing to find an outlet. *Damn! Damn! Damn!* She slammed the pot down heavily then jolted.

'Gianna!' Ariana exclaimed.

Gianna stopped suddenly, and equally as quickly heat darkened her face. 'Oh! Hi Ariana,' she stammered, her eyes searching for anything to focus on besides Soph's mother.

'Sorry,' Ariana apologised, her hand on her chest, thrust from her irritating thoughts. 'Sorry, I wasn't expecting... Is everything okay?' she asked, suddenly aware that Gianna's eyes were scanning the room.

'Yes, Soph needs something for a headache. I think it was the sun,' Gianna said.

'Ah!' Ariana replied, a brief wave of concern causing her to ponder the fact that she hadn't given Soph much attention since they had arrived. 'Meds are in the cupboard,' she added, heading out of the kitchen and down the corridor.

Ariana descended the stairs in a state of mild confusion. She liked Gianna and the fact that Soph seemed happy, but the idea of Soph not needing her and needing someone else, caused a disconcerting feeling to lodge in her stomach. She stood in the open doorway, gazing at her daughter lying in the bed.

'Hi mum,' Soph said, squinting through half-open eyes.

'Gianna says you're suffering from the sun. Are you okay?' Ariana asked, crossing the room and reaching out for Soph. She perched on the side of the bed, swept the hair from Soph's face and studied her intently.

'I'm fine,' Soph insisted dismissively, somewhat taken aback by her mum's interest. 'Honest,' she added, hoping to reassure her. The last thing she wanted was her mother stopping her fun with Gianna, just because she'd had too much sun. She needed to be careful for the day, and she would be fine.

'Are you sure you're okay,' Ariana asked, still stroking Soph's face, still in need of reassurance, eyes searching her daughter.

'I'm fine. I'll stay in a bit today, maybe we can do some painting,' she offered, optimistically.

Gianna walked into the room, pills and water in hand. 'Here,' she said, holding them out to Soph.

Ariana stood, gazed from Soph to Gianna and back again and cleared her throat. 'I'll get some breakfast ready,' she said.

'Thanks,' Soph said, holding Gianna's gaze with tenderness as she took the pills from her, and then nodding to her mum.

Ariana left the bedroom and climbed the stairs. Soph seemed different, more grown-up, and she didn't know how she felt about that. Soph had had girlfriends before, but the way she looked at Gianna, she'd never seen her look at anyone that way before now. She knew what the look meant; she'd seen it in Nikki's eyes and had no doubt Nikki had seen it in hers too.

She stood in the kitchen, her heart racing and anxiety churning her stomach. She knew that sensation well too; it was telling her she was out of control, and afraid. She tried to breathe, attempted to rationalise the competing thoughts that seemed to constantly challenge her emotions. On the one hand, Soph was happy and enjoying life here, Christ it was even starting to feel like home to Ariana. On the other hand, there was the not so small issue of the fact that they would be leaving the island, and that would mean Soph leaving Gianna behind. The thought that her daughter would experience a broken heart seared through her as if it were her pain, and maybe it was. *Breakfast*, she told herself and started busying around the kitchen, laying the table. *I wish Nikki were here.* The thought popped into her mind, followed by an empty feeling. She chased it away; she had a meal to prepare.

*

Heading out the front door with increased determination, Ariana nearly upended Manos as he passed by, weighed down by a bucket filled with a wet sandy looking substance. 'Whoa,' he said, swinging away from the potential collision, and chuckling. 'Got a boat to catch?' he teased, chasing the toothpick from one side of his mouth to the other.

'Sorry,' Ariana said, stopping, flicking her fingers through her hair and then finding a smile. 'I'm just getting the paint,' she said, pointing towards the garage. 'The girls are going to help,' she added.

'Aye, I'm starting on the south-wall,' he said, indicating in the direction he was walking, towards the rose-garden. The sidewall of the house scaling the three levels of the property and facing directly south across the sea was always the worst affected by the weather.

'Right,' Ariana said, pacing, with the sense of edginess that was driving her to distract herself in the work that needed doing. 'I'll get the paint then,' she said.

'Aye,' he replied, continuing on his route. 'Coffee would be nice,' he added, with a chuckle.

'I'll bring one out,' she said, stepping into the garage. Hunting around, she picked up the pot of apple-white and a pot of pure white paint and lugged them back to the house. She left the apple-white at the top of the stairs leading down to the bedrooms on the ground floor and put the white paint in the living room. Heading to the garage again, she returned with brushes, rollers and paint trays. Maybe the girls could paint Soph's bedroom or the living room. She would continue with the shutters. Into the kitchen, she poured two coffees and carried them out to the rose garden. The strong scent of rose slowed her, and she breathed in the heady aroma. *Did they always smell this sweet?*

'Thanks,' Manos said with a deep smile, taking the drink, sipping as he rubbed his hands over the surface of the damaged wall. It was as if he were caressing rather than assessing it. 'You know this was her favourite spot,' he said.

Ariana knew to whom he was referring. 'Yes,' she said, in a whisper.

'Sophia had the roses imported. Reminded her of Charles,' he said.

Ariana hadn't known that.

'Your grandfather was British,' he said.

Ariana had known that, but he had died long before Ariana had been born so she had no connection to him and she hadn't heard Sophia or Teresa ever talk about her grandfather.

'Loved him with all her heart,' Manos said, sucking through his teeth, his head tilting. 'The estate was his passion, and he never got to see it in its full glory, you know. It took old Sophia years to develop, but she did it, and for the most part she did it all on her own,' he reminisced with fondness and esteem.

Ariana sighed, feeling a slight sense of deja-vu with the conversation.

'The island depends on the estate,' he said. 'It's not just the olives.' He smiled. 'Beyond the grove, there's the fruit, vegetables, herbs, and the olive plant itself. Still uses the traditional pressing method,' he added with a proud smile.

Ariana swallowed hard; her head was spinning with information, as she reconciled the impact of the sale on the livelihoods of the Islanders. Why did it suddenly matter to her? She had briefly seen the plans for the development. The hotel complex with its new marina and it's suite of detached holiday homes, its array of swimming pools, tennis courts, and aqua sports facilities; all modern, all built to the highest specification, all increasing tourism to the island. Before she had returned to Sakros, the proposition had seemed perfect, for her and for the Islanders. It hadn't mattered then. Her mother had insisted it would be the best thing all round too, and Ariana had had no problem believing her. She had signed the contract. *I've already signed the agreement*, she wanted to say, but she didn't.

'It's going to look beautiful,' Manos said, starting to apply the render to the wall, apparently oblivious to Ariana's shift in attention.

Ariana felt her throat clench, the pressure at the back of her eyes, the tension in her neck, and she wanted to scream.

Not the joyful shout as she had jumped from the ledge the previous evening, a sharp yell that comes from a wounded animal flailing helplessly. She turned away. The short walk back to the house under the weight of the burden she could no longer ignore, seemingly taking forever, making every pace more challenging than the previous. Even the sound of music and laughter coming from the kitchen-balcony didn't penetrate the dark feeling that had taken root in the pit of her stomach.

Soph gazed at her mother, unsure whether she wanted to ask the question as to her welfare, on the basis that she didn't want to hear the answer. Gianna frowned. 'Is everything alright?' Soph asked.

Ariana smiled weakly. 'Sure. How's breakfast?' she asked, changing the subject.

Soph shrugged, scanning the yoghurt and fruit on the table. 'Good. Head's better too,' she added, with a healthy smile.

'Good,' Ariana said, distracted by her concerns. Selling was one thing, destroying the island, which she now realised the proposed development would do, was something entirely different. Why had Teresa been so insistent on her selling, when to do so would be so devastating to everyone? It would quite literally destroy Sophia's life's work. 'I left the paint at the top of the stairs if you want to do your room?' she said, her flat voice mirroring her vacant gaze.

Soph slumped in the seat and crossed her arms, trying to ignore her mum's sombre mood.

'That'll be fun,' Gianna chirped over-excitedly, determined to keep Soph out of the sun for the best part of the day.

Soph glared at her but couldn't hold the expression, which turned swiftly into a sensual grin.

'I'm glad you're feeling better,' Ariana said with a sincere smile, her attention momentarily with her daughter. 'I'll be painting the shutters,' she said, turning out of the kitchen and stepping out the front door.

Soph stared at Gianna and shrugged. 'She doesn't look happy,' she said.

Gianna shrugged and smiled. She had no measure of Ariana's moods, by which to judge her. 'Have you painted before?' she said, with a mischievous smile.

'No,' Soph replied. 'How hard can it be,' she stated, her arms still crossed.

'You can do the roller bit, and I'll do the edges,' Gianna said.

Soph didn't have a clue what she was talking about, so nodded and smiled.

*

Ariana worked her way cautiously down the ladder, paint pot wavering in one hand, the other supporting her as she descended. She wiped at the sweat on her brow as she studied her work from the ground.

'It's looking good,' Nikos said, the tension in his voice spoiling the compliment.

Ariana turned towards him. He looked as tense as he sounded, and it was all her fault. She smiled, trying to soften the atmosphere between them, but even her jaw was too tight. 'Yes, it is,' she said, her voice jittery.

He continued to stare at the paintwork, loitering as if he had something he wanted to say, but didn't know where to start.

'Would you like a drink?' Ariana asked. 'I'm just going to get one,' she added before he could find a reason to refuse. He had stayed away from the house since she had arrived, and with good reason.

He nodded, held her gaze, sorrow weighing heavily on

his eyelids and the dull look in his eyes suggesting he had other things on his mind.

'Is everything okay?' Ariana asked as he followed her through to the kitchen. She poured two glasses of water and handed him one.

He took the glass and sipped, his large hands shaking, his eyes darting around the room, reflecting his fractured thoughts. 'I'm taking another job,' he said, his voice broken. 'We'll be moving to Lefkada,' he added.

Ariana struggled to swallow the water in her mouth and started to cough. It hadn't been that long since she had given them the news of the sale and asked Maria to take paid leave. This was the last thing she had expected, but then, why wouldn't Nikos look to find other work? But, this quickly! She rubbed at her temples, trying to process the consequences of him leaving but they were too enormous to conceive. She had no hold over him; he had no reason to offer her any loyalty. On the contrary, she had technically destroyed his life. She couldn't even persuade him to stay on the basis that the new owner would continue with the estate because that would be a downright lie.

'Maria's brother has a place there,' he continued.

Ariana nodded, unable to speak. What could she say?

'I'm sorry,' Nikos said.

He looked genuinely devastated by the news he was imparting, the decision that had been forced upon him, by her actions. The voice in Ariana's head persisted. This was all her doing, all her fault. *Gianna!* Ariana gasped. Soph wasn't going to take this news well either. 'Does Gianna know?' she asked.

Nikos shook his head, his eyes on the glass in his hand.

'You know she and Soph are close?' Ariana asked.

He nodded. When his eyes lifted and locked onto Ariana's, his pain was even more apparent. 'She's going to get her heart broken,' he said, his eyes welling up. 'I never wanted that for her,' he said, with deep sadness.

'They like each other a lot,' Ariana said. He didn't speak again, just stared at her knowingly. Warmth filled her cheeks. 'When will you leave?' Ariana asked, quietly.

'At the end of the month,' Nikos replied.

Ariana nodded silently, a deep sense of grief filling her aching heart.

'Thanks for the water,' Nikos said, placing the glass on the drainer. His eyes acknowledged her briefly as he passed her and exited the front door.

Ariana stood silently for a few moments, trying to reconcile her thoughts. She couldn't, so she walked out to the balcony and stared out over the west-cove, hoping the reassuring sight and the light breeze would settle her mind. Even the waves didn't crash as loudly as the voice in her head, pounding, ricocheting, admonishing. She felt trapped, a failure, irritated and upset, all at the same time. The familiar feeling flowed through her veins, feeding her insecurities, reinforcing her mother's words; her husband's words, and her own deeply ingrained beliefs. *Why would Nikki want anything to do with her?* Tears threatened, but the sound of Manos clearing his throat blocked the flow.

'Wall's patched up,' Manos said, squinting at the pained expression on Ariana's face.

She tried to smile but her jaw, too firmly clamped, prevented her. She tried to speak, but the words wouldn't come. Her eyes locked with his, so warm, so soothing, and tears trickled down her cheeks.

Manos approached Ariana and pulled her into his arms. He sighed deeply, Ariana's head swaying with the movement of his chest. 'It'll all work out,' he said, with confidence that Ariana couldn't comprehend.

She pulled back, wanted to shout at him for thinking things would turn out fine. *How could they?* Her mouth moved, but his eyes stopped her from speaking. He was smiling warmly, reaching up and tucking her hair behind her ear, with tenderness.

'It'll all work out,' he said again, softly, his eyes conveying the certainty in his tone, the hair on his cheeks curling with the smile on his lips.

Ariana released a long breath. He didn't know the half of it, she mused.

'That front shutter's looking good,' he said, shifting her attention.

Ariana nodded and wiped at her wet cheeks.

'Only a dozen more to go,' he added, with a twinkle in his eye and a chuckle.

She sighed, and a smile formed.

15.

Nikki toyed with the teaspoon in her hand. The fruit and yoghurt sat untouched in the white china bowl in front of her, the coffee in her cup unfinished. She gazed around the breakfast room, the voices of other diners merging, the soup of noise surrounding her failing to drown out her anxiety. Her heart skipped a beat. *What if the bank refused to give her the loan?* She dipped the spoon into the yoghurt, swilled it mindlessly around the dish and the rested the handle carefully against the lipped edge. The waiter approached and filled her cup, and she smiled graciously. She released a long breath and lifted the cup to her lips. She didn't want to think of failure, but her mind had focused on nothing else in the last few days. *What if Ariana sold, and left the island again?* The thought was too painful to consider, yet, it trickled unopposed through her body leaving a gluey residue that wouldn't shift.

When she had left Sakros, the light in Ariana's bedroom had been visible through the slats in the shuttered windows. Torn with the idea of going to her then and telling her she would buy the house, begging Ariana to stay, she had stalled. Only then had it occurred to her that until she had an agreement with the bank, she had no plan, just a dream. The truth had caused a tight ball of fire to lodge itself in her stomach. She had turned sharply and started back up the beach to her apartment, intending to detract from the idea, and accept that Ariana would leave the island. Then, her eyes drawn to the hazy light above the rose garden, she slowed her pace and stopped. The pounding in her chest, induced by the fear of losing Ariana again, had driven her back to the boat. She hadn't looked back as she sped across the water, but with each day since, each day away from Ariana and an opportunity to reflect honestly, the doubts had crept in again. The thought of the proposal rejected by the bank was one thing, but it was nowhere near as painful as the broken heart she would be left with if Ariana deserted her again. She admonished her concerns and sipped at the coffee, and drifted.

Ariana, Ariana, Ariana! She smiled adoringly at the image. Ariana with her ash-blonde hair that carried a little curl under the right side of her chin, the dimple in her right cheek that came alive when she smiled, her dark-brown eyes sometimes like the darkest chocolate with the shine of a highly polished mirror, her full shapely lips and slightly curvaceous body. The way she marched that body across the sand when she was angry, throwing what little weight she possessed with even less conviction, and then melted with the exhaustion of the pretence.

She had noticed the shift in Ariana, even in the short time since her arrival on the island, and it had given her hope. Glimpses of the passion they had once shared for each other had filtered through the cracks in that charade, and in those brief moments, they were stronger than ever. The sense of completeness she had felt when they kissed had revealed something more profound, something intangible. They belonged together. Nikki had never doubted that fact. Sophia had never doubted either. Even Manos knew it. The question was, would Ariana wake up, or flee again? It was a question Nikki didn't want to think about. Ariana had to come to her senses; she had to!

Nikki finished her coffee, stood swiftly from the table and exited the hotel. With every pace on the dusty city street, her heart raced, and as she approached the tall, soulless building the anxiety in her chest filtered down to her legs. She rubbed at her temples, trying to breathe deeply, calming her nerves, the intensely oppressive heat, pollution and constant assault of beeping horns and industrial clanging noises, doing nothing to help the low-grade headache that had accompanied her since disembarking the flight.

She released a long breath, rubbed at her sore eyes, stepped up to the bank, and into the air-conditioned building. Thankful for the colder air on her skin, her eyes searched the large foyer, seeking out the desk she needed. Forcing her legs to carry her, she approached a man in uniform who seemed to be guarding the door. He pointed in the direction of a glass-partitioned area in the far corner, away from the tellers and the queues. The fish-bowl room was empty, so she waited outside the door, her heart pounding in her chest, a queasy feeling turning her stomach. She tried to stand taller but looked very much like the fish out of the water that she was. Floundering, unsure, thrown by the alien environment in which she found herself. The city wasn't her world, it never would be, and she couldn't wait to get home. She rubbed her cool-clammy hands together and waited.

'Ms Kefalas,' the deeper voice said.

'Yes,' Nikki replied, smiling at the young, clean-shaven face, and dark-blue eyes. He was smiling kindly at her, his free hand held out, his other hand carrying a paper file. She took the offered hand; his skin was softer than her own; dry and warm, she noted.

'Please, do come through,' he said politely, opening the door to the room. His voice echoed around the small space, disorienting her as she followed him. She stopped at the front of the desk as he made his way behind it. He urged her to sit, and she did. He gazed briefly at the computer screen in front of him, tapped on the keyboard, placed the file on the desk, rested his hands on top of it and looked up at her. 'My name is Mr Loukas; I'm the assistant manager here at the bank,' he started. He blinked several times before continuing, and she couldn't help but notice his unusually long eyelashes. 'I understand you are looking for a business loan,' he said.

Nikki sat upright. Even though the man opposite her didn't look much older than fifteen, which was a little disconcerting, he was currently the person that separated her from a future with Ariana, and on that basis alone, she needed him. 'Yes,' she replied, her smile tight with the anticipation.

'I have looked at your application, Ms Kefalas.'

Nikki waited on his words. If he could hear her heart pounding, he didn't let it show. She tried to swallow, but her mouth was dry and her muscles paralysed.

'I'm pleased to say, from the information you have provided, we can offer you a loan of three-hundred-and-fifty-thousand-Euros,' he said, with a happy smile.

Nikki's heart stopped, her ears silenced, and a rush of adrenaline drowned her in excitement. Mr Loukas' mouth was still moving, but the words weren't registering. Whatever the details were, she would sign the contract and take the money.

'Do you understand?' he asked. He smiled, closed the file in front of him and started tapping on the keyboard.

Nikki nodded. 'Yes,' she said.

'The paperwork will be ready for you to sign in a couple of days unless you want me to get it sent out to you?' he asked.

'No, I'll come back and sign it,' Nikki said, unable to contain her enthusiasm. She would tolerate another two days in Athens for the sake of completion.

Mr Loukas stood, and she mirrored him, only then realising her legs had the consistency of jelly, but in a more positive way than when she had walked into the building. He held out his hand, a professional smile on his face, and she shook it again. 'Thank you,' she said, feeling strangely delirious.

'You are welcome. I will see you here on Thursday at three-thirty,' he said, opening the door.

Nikki floated out of the room and out of the building. Even the intensely oppressive heat, the pollution, and the noise didn't touch her. As if floating on air she made her way into the bustling city, her grin broadening with the bubble of excitement, holding back from shouting out with joy. She was feeling hungry, for the first time in almost a week, and wanted to enjoy the achievement, but that celebration would be far more fun with Ariana present. She would wait.

*

Ariana sat on the large double bed in her grandmother's room, her feet out in front of her, her head resting against the simple wooden-headboard, enjoying the scent of rose that filled the room.

The shutters she had managed to finish were looking pristine, and the newly painted wall gleamed, reflecting even more light onto the rose-garden. The thought that Sophia would be aware of the changes to the property tickled her. Her body ached from the hard physical work, but there was also an unfamiliar feeling that felt good: satisfaction, from doing something productive. She smiled and raised the glass of wine in her hand.

'Cheers,' she said, to no one in particular.

She studied her fingers curiously as they traced the embossed lettering on the front of the photo album on the blue pillow, curiosity tempting her further. She sipped at the wine in her other hand. She'd consumed too much already, but she'd needed to, to build the courage to come up to the room and look through the albums. With nervous anticipation, she turned the cover, revealing four photographs underneath the inner plastic sleeve. Her eyes locked on to the curly, white-haired lady, with wrinkled, bronzed skin, and a big white smile. She looked radiant, content. Her sky-blue eyes shone through the page, connecting the observer with her vibrant, replete life. Ariana sighed. *Sophia!* The date had been handwritten underneath the photograph, five years earlier. Sophia looked healthy and a lot younger than her seventy-eight years. Ariana traced her index finger across the image, willing Sophia to come back to life. She sipped at her wine again, swallowing back the lump in her throat and turned the page. She continued to study the pictures and moved onto the second album, Teresa as a child. Ariana gazed, recognising her mother's sharp features, bemused by the happiness that oozed from her laughing eyes and rosy cheeks.

She picked up another album, a white-covered large volume that looked a lot like it might contain wedding photographs. She opened the cover and studied the images on the first page. It wasn't a wedding, but it was a party, and, even though it was dated before she was born, there was no mistaking the venue was Kefalas. Her breath stalled at the younger version of Sophia. It could have been Soph, such was the similarity between them. Her heart skipped a beat then warmed. She turned the page again.

Teresa, older than in the previous album, stared out at her. There was something noticeably absent in her eyes though, even though she was grinning enthusiastically for the photographer. She didn't recognise the man's hand Teresa was holding at first, the long, jet-black hair and dark beard tricking her mind. *Manos!* She studied the details of the image carefully. It was definitely Manos; his warm, engaging smile was unmistakable and... but, they were cutting a cake. They were together. *What?* Her mind spinning, she was struggling to reconcile the situation captured by the photograph, which was contradictory with what she knew of her mother's life. She turned the page, revealing more photos of the two of them together, smiling, dancing, and... kissing. She slammed the album shut, her eyes scanning the room like a child about to be caught out. She sipped at the unstable glass in her hand. Manos had made no secret of the fact that he had once loved Teresa, but he never so much as implied that they had been, what looked like, engaged to be married.

She jumped up from the bed and started pacing the room, unsure what, if anything, Manos' history with her mother meant. It shouldn't make any difference to her, but for some strange reason, it did. The date of the party, just two years before her birth and eighteen months before her mother married her father! Had Manos been engaged to her mother when Aaron Carter turned up and swept Teresa off her feet? Is that why Teresa kept her away from the taverna and the west-cove all those years? Anger flared, and she wanted to hit out. She threw herself onto the bed, buried her face into the throw and pounded her fists, screaming silently.

*

'You girls look like you could do with a drink,' Manos said, eyeing the paint-streaked faces and beaming smiles, with a warm smile of his own.

He had watched the two young women strolling across the beach, their pace perfectly synchronised, their proximity close, their bodies connecting as they swayed on the unstable sand; their hands clasped, their heads dancing together, laughing, animated. There was no doubt in his mind; Soph and Gianna were in love.

Both women nodded simultaneously at the offer of a drink.

'Beer?' he asked, heading to the bar.

'Thanks,' they said.

Soph wandered over to the driftwood bench, sat and gazed out over the quiet sea. The sun, low in the sky, had cast red-orange streaks across the horizon already, leaving the space to the east with a near charcoal appearance. 'What's that?' she asked, pointing to the hazy-light over the rose garden.

'Your great-grandmother,' Manos answered with a chuckle, handing out the bottles clasped between the fingers of his left hand.

'Eh?' Soph glared at him as if he'd lost his marbles. Gianna laughed.

'Her ashes,' he added, as if the justification would make his previous response make absolute sense.

Soph scrunched up her face, even more confused.

'Ah!' Gianna exclaimed, nodding her appreciation. She sipped from her beer, gazing at the ghost-like haze.

Soph tutted, shrugged, and sipped. *Bonkers!*

'Here,' Manos said, pulling an acoustic guitar from behind his back and presenting it to Soph.

Soph's eyes widened. 'Wow, it's a Gibson, 1930's original. Where did you get it?' she asked with excitement.

Gianna swooned at Soph's joy.

'Your great-grandmother acquired it,' he said, with an air of mystical reverence. 'It's yours,' he added. 'She would want you to have it.'

'I can't,' Soph said, almost throwing the guitar back into his arms.

He refused to take it and backed off, smiling reassuringly. 'I insist, Sophia would insist,' he said, the white-bristles around his dimples curling with his broad grin. She had given him the guitar after her final gig at the bar, a year before she died. He had played it a bit, but he was nowhere near as proficient as Soph.

Soph caressed the guitar with tenderness, admiring with expert eyes every inch of the solid Sitka spruce top and mahogany back and sides. She sat it across her lap, tweaked the tuning pegs, plucked at the strings, and beamed a grin that spanned her face and made her blue-eyes a shade darker. Within moments, sweet musical notes filled the evening sky and drifted hauntingly around the cove.

Gianna flushed, her dark eyes darkening, the gentle vibrations tingling in her stomach tracking upwards, causing the hairs on her neck to rise. She gazed, entranced, loving the music, and in love with the musician.

Manos started to sing, his tone low and his voice slightly out of tune. Soph encouraged him with a nodding head, quieted her voice and winked at Gianna. Gianna giggled.

As Soph wrapped up the song, Manos started clapping and bowed. 'Aye,' he said, turning and walking back into the bar. 'It belongs in your hands,' he added. He stopped, reminded of Sophia's days singing in the taverna and looked back over his shoulder. 'You should play here regularly,' he said, his tone hopeful, his eyes pleading.

Soph chuckled at the suggestion, rested the guitar against the bench and reached for her beer. 'Let's explore,' she said, holding out a hand to Gianna.

'Do you like heights?' Gianna asked, grabbing Soph's hand, squeezing firmly, and dragging her in the direction of the rocky outcrop the other side of the jetty.

Soph allowed herself to be dragged, the nerves chasing from her chest to her stomach. She wasn't that fond of heights. The only reason she could sit on the edge of the cliff next to the house, was because there was a ledge directly below her feet that made the cliff feel as though it wasn't the final edge. If she fell off of it, the worst she might do is sprain an ankle as she hit the lower ledge. If there were a straight drop to the water, she would undoubtedly freak out. But something about Gianna gave her confidence, made her feel she could do anything. She broke into a jog, and then a sprint, pulling Gianna along, giggling and laughing when their feet splashed the shallow water. 'Are there any fish in here?' she asked, scanning her submerged feet.

'Yes, and they bite really badly,' Gianna said, teasing her, pulling her close and placing a tender kiss to her lips.

The touch lingered after their lips parted, and when Gianna gazed at her, her eyes were darker. Soph had forgotten about the water and the fish. She leaned in and tenderly pressed her lips to Gianna's again. Easing out of the kiss, 'You serious?' she asked, 'about the fish.'

Gianna's lips remained parted, the fizzing sensation tracking south taking her words with it. Soph was pressing a finger to her lips, preventing her from speaking. Gianna pulled the finger into her mouth, teased it with her teeth, clasped Soph's hand and kissed her palm. 'No,' she said, with a coy smile, lowering their hands and pulling Soph into the deeper water, edging them towards the rocky outcrop.

Soph didn't feel the chill as she dived forwards and started to swim, her heart flaming with desire. She pulled herself up onto the rocks and followed Gianna to the other side.

Gianna stepped cautiously, one eye ensuring Soph was close to her. She stood on the farthest edge of the outcrop, the cliff face visible, spotlighted by the setting sun.

Soph closed the gap and stood next to Gianna, her eyes feasting on the new landscape. 'Wow!' Red shards bounced off the shiny-black rock, and shadows danced on the rippling sea. Surrounded on three sides by water, the moon throwing light from the east, and the bizarre silver-light over the rose garden, there was something oddly spiritual about the place, haunting, awe-inspiring. She placed her arm around Gianna's waist, leaned into her shoulder, staring at nothing in particular, captivated by the ambience and the soft hush of the waves against the rocks.

'It's spectacular,' Gianna said eventually, breaking the trance.

Soph released her grip. 'It's incredible.'

Gianna turned suddenly, enthusiastically stepping towards the sharp rock face, and started to climb.

A sudden burst of anxiety thrust Soph to her senses. 'Where are you going?' she asked, in a state of near panic.

Gianna turned to face her with a beaming grin. 'Come on?' she said, looking for the next foothold.

Soph froze. She couldn't have moved even if she had wanted to. She watched, the whites of her eyes widening with every step Gianna took, her heart racing.

Gianna passed the lower ledge and continued to climb. Exhilaration was driving her forward and within a few moments, she stood on one of the upper shelves, turned to face Soph with a broad grin, and waved.

Soph blinked, but her lips refused to smile.

The scream that pierced the night, silenced as quickly as it started.

Soph gasped.

Gianna hit the water.

Soph waited for her to surface. Nothing. She stared. Still nothing. Panic took her breath away, her eyes darting across the dark water for a sign. She tried to think, thought about jumping in, dismissed the idea, thought about it again, and jumped. The deep sea was colder than she imagined. She pulled herself to the surface, frantically scanning for Gianna. Nothing. Her heart pounding and her eyes burned with the salt, she dived under the water then came back up again. It was too dark to see anything. She wanted to scream but couldn't. She spun round in the water, looking for a break in the surface, anything. The seconds that passed felt like minutes. She tried to reassure herself, knowing Gianna was a strong swimmer, but that wasn't what concerned her. She hadn't seen what had happened, just heard the squeal, and then the silence, and then the splash. Her head was spinning, her pulse racing she found her voice, 'Gianna,' she screamed.

The tap on her shoulder stopped her heart instantly and clamped her lungs, triggering a shriek that could have woken the dead, followed by a spluttering sound as her head dropped under the water and then emerged, the screech still projecting through her constricted breath.

Gianna startled, wiped the water from her eyes, her feet paddling hard to keep her afloat, and glared with concern.

'You scared the shit out of me,' Soph protested, her heart still pounding and her legs sapped of energy, drowning in a cocktail of anger, sadness and relief.

Gianna trod water effortlessly. 'I didn't mean to scare you,' she said, with regret. She reached for Soph, but Soph flung her off, her arms flailing as she swam for the rocks.

Gianna followed with slow, lazy strokes.

Soph pulled herself out of the water, fuelled by rage, and something far stronger. She wanted to scream at Gianna, and yet she wanted to hold her so close and never let her go. She'd never felt that way about anyone in her life. She bounded across the rocks to the other side of the cove, slipped into the water and swam to the beach.

'Soph, I'm sorry, I didn't think, I'm so sorry,' Gianna babbled, chasing her up the beach.

Soph stopped dead and turned.

Gianna almost collided with her, Soph's wild eyes glaring, causing her breath to catch in her throat.

'You could have died,' Soph said, realising how dramatic she sounded but unable to stop, her heart still thumping, her eyes burning fiercely.

Gianna reached up tentatively, stroked the hair from Soph's face, her eyes full of apology. 'I'm so sorry, Soph, I didn't mean to scare you. I always stay under the water for a bit after jumping; it's just nice down there,' she said, her thumb brushing across Soph's wet cheeks.

'I don't want to lose you,' Soph said weakly.

'You won't,' Gianna said, with a gentle smile.

Soph threw herself into Gianna's arms and squeezed her tightly. 'I love you so much,' she whispered.

Gianna eased out of the hold and stared longingly into Soph's dark-blue eyes. 'I love you too,' she said, her grin broadening with the expanding fuzzy feeling in her chest.

Soph moved first, closed the gap quickly, joining their lips in an impassioned kiss, the hum of the waves lapping against the beach drowning out their low moans.

16.

'Mum!' Soph shouted, bounding into the house. 'There's a man here to see you.' She continued down the stairs, leaving him standing in the doorway.

The man lingered uncomfortably, his eyes scanning the newly decorated façade curiously, in his short-sleeve, pristine-white, shirt, his scrawny neck encumbered by the thin tie squeezed tightly around the starched collar, a black leather briefcase held firmly to his chest.

'Coming,' Ariana shouted, descending the stairs from the master bedroom, wiping at the rose-white paint on her hands. Her eyes lifting from her fingers, she stopped, stared at the man and sighed. There was no mistaking who he was, or more importantly what he represented. Ariana flicked her fingers through her hair, pulling it from her eyes and glared.

'Mrs Carter-Cruz?' the man asked with a nervous smile, releasing one hand from the case pinned to his chest. 'I'm Jasper Soloman,' he said, holding out his hand. 'I'm here to check over the estate,' he added, not that he needed to explain for Ariana's benefit.

Ariana reluctantly took the offered hand. 'Can I get you a drink?' she asked, courteously, turning and walking away from him before he could speak. She reached into the fridge and pulled out a bottle of white wine, poured two glasses and handed one to him.

He took the glass tentatively and placed it on the kitchen table. 'Maybe I could look around first,' he said, his lips thinning, his smile tighter, his demeanour more edgy than when he had introduced himself.

Ariana took a long glug of the wine, hoping the slightly acidic sensation would distract her from the tightness in her throat and the effects of the alcohol would act quickly on her brain so that she could forget this whole experience ever happened. 'Of course,' she said. 'Where would you like to start?' she asked.

'I see you're decorating,' he said, quizzically.

Ariana stayed silent.

'I hope you don't mind me saying,' he started, trying to control the slight stammer in his voice, 'but I think it is only right that we manage our expectations, and just to say, the work you are doing, whilst it clearly enhances the aesthetics of property, won't add anything to the valuation that was agreed by my client. 1.5 million Euros is a very fair price for the plot you have here,' he added, patting the briefcase. He squeezed his lips together as if the words had been a real effort.

Ariana breathed deeply; the words had been harder for her to hear than for him to say. She took another long slug of the wine. 'Perhaps you'd like to start outside,' she said, swallowing down her annoyance. 'You are free to wander. It stretches further than you can see. If you walk out the front door and stay to the left of the path down to the cove, follow the grove to the production-plant and then track back on the inland side, you'll see the rest of the grounds,' she said, with disdain.

The man was nodding, mapping the route in his mind's eye. He turned sharply and scampered out the door; briefcase gripped to his chest.

Ariana reached into the fridge and pulled out the bottle of wine. Picking up her glass, she carried both to the ledge on the side of the slope, overlooking the east-cove. She needed to think, and, she might be able to spot the odious little creature from time-to-time as he trawled his way along the grove to the production-plant at the far end of the estate. She smiled ruefully. At least he would be gone for a good few hours.

As she stared out over the east-cove, she couldn't escape her niggling thoughts about Manos and the photographs. She sipped at the wine, observing the movie in her mind; the dark-brown eyes, the dimples in his cheeks, the rounded nose and finely shaped lips, and in the picture, his hair longer than now, curled under his chin, precisely as hers did. She sipped at the wine, refilled the glass and sipped again. His fondness for her, the way he had supported her as a child, it was starting to make some sense. But, why hadn't he stopped Teresa taking her away? Why hadn't he told her, if he were her father? She pressed her fingers to her temple and then pinched the bridge of her nose. The resemblance was too remarkable to ignore. She poured another drink and slugged it down. A profound sense of loss nestled in her chest, reinforcing her newly discovered belief. Aaron Carter had never shown her an ounce of interest in her; did he know the truth or was it another family secret? Gazing out over the expansive sea, she shivered, loneliness gripping her.

*

Nikki's grin widened, the motorboat swaying with the low waves, as she approached the island. As much as she loved her home, her heart didn't always race like this coming back from the regular Friday ferry trip to Ithaka, or even the regular Lefkada trips. The airy light feeling dancing in her chest, fuelling the smile on her face, was down to one thing; Ariana. She had done what she needed to; now she just needed to convince Ariana to sell the house to her and persuade Ariana to stay.

Approaching the shore, she killed the engine and flipped the motor out of the water. Stepping out of the boat, she pulled it up to rest on the sand, slung her bag over her shoulder and paced enthusiastically up the beach.

'Aye,' Manos greeted her, a beaming grin dislodging the toothpick between his teeth. He opened his arms and pulled her in for a hug. 'Good trip,' he asked, intuitively knowing the answer.

Nikki nodded, her eyes sparkling, her smile full with satisfaction. 'All good,' she said.

'Good,' he said, handing her a beer and sipping the clear liquid in his short glass.

'How've things been?' she asked, her eyes indicating to the white house.

Manos' cheeks twitched, his head tilted, squinting in the direction of the hill. 'Up and down,' he said, with faint amusement and then fleeting unease.

Nikki nodded and slugged hungrily at the chilled drink. 'Renovations coming along I see,' she said, assessing the newly painted, Mediterranean-blue shutters with an approving smile.

'Aye. Ariana painted those,' he said.

'Look good from here,' she said, with a warm feeling in her chest.

'Look pretty good from up there too,' he added, sipping from his glass. 'It's good to have you back,' he added, his eyes lingering on the white house.

'It's good to be home, Pops,' she said, softly. Words couldn't describe how good.

'The ones I removed are in the workshop,' he said, back to the topic of the shutters.

'And the walls?' she asked.

'Repaired and whitewashed the south facing wall,' he replied, with a proud grin.

'Hmmm, you've been busy,' she said, her head nodding in approval.

'You hungry?' he asked.

'Starving,' she replied. 'I'll just dump this and change,' she said, heading to the bar.

'There's kleftiko on the stove, I'll bring some out,' he said, heading into the kitchen.

'Thanks.' Nikki dropped the empty beer bottle on the bar, stepped through the back and into her apartment, and leant against the closed door, the butterflies in her stomach intensifying with thoughts of seeing Ariana. She breathed in the familiar air. It was so good to be home.

*

'Hey,' Soph said, her feet dangling over the edge of the cliff, her thumb softly strumming the guitar, aware that Gianna was approaching from behind. She turned towards the gentle footsteps; the loving smile stripped from her face at the solemn look on Gianna's face. 'What's up?' she asked, standing urgently, staring into Gianna's grief-stricken eyes. 'What's happened?' she asked, her voice more insistent, desperation causing her heart to pound. She put the guitar down and rushed towards Gianna, pulling her into her arms. 'What's happened G?' she asked softly. Gianna's limp body hung in her arms; sobs falling from her lips, tears streaming down her face.

'We're leaving,' Gianna stammered, barely able to breathe through the convulsions that were taking over her body. She had screamed and screamed at her parents, and now she had nothing left. Just an empty, hollow feeling, cast over her like a dark shadow.

'What!' Soph pulled back sharply, staring into Gianna's wet eyes in disbelief. 'What do you mean, you're leaving?' she asked, fighting the burning sensation building in her eyes.

'You're selling so we're leaving. Papa's going to work in Lefkada at the end of the month,' Gianna stuttered, through the sobs.

Soph tensed, inflamed with rage. 'Fuck,' she yelled, startling Gianna into silence.

Gianna stared quizzically. She hadn't heard Soph swear before. She hadn't seen Soph angry before, at least not like this. She studied Soph's thunderous gaze, her dark-blue eyes closer to black, the tears seeping onto her cheeks, the frustration driving her to pace back and forth.

'I'll go with you,' Soph said, with absolute determination. 'We can get a place together,' she added, without consideration as to how that might happen.

Gianna spoke softly. 'I don't have any money,' she said, 'or a job.'

'We'll get one; we'll make it work,' Soph countered, her enthusiasm unwavering. 'I'll get work and we'll find the money somehow,' she added, a half-plan formulating in her mind as she paced.

Gianna was shaking her head. 'I don't want to leave here,' she admitted.

Soph stopped pacing and studied Gianna. She suddenly looked so much younger than her nineteen years, so vulnerable, so exposed. Soph stared out to sea, then to the east-cove where they had dived and swum together. Shifting around to the west-cove where they had played volleyball and eaten at the taverna, and then to the far side of the cove, the cliff where Gianna had freaked her out. To the rocks below her feet now, where she met Nikki on that first night, fishing. She swallowed past the tightness in her throat. She didn't want to leave either. *Why did they need to sell?* 'I don't want to leave either,' she admitted. She turned and strode purposefully towards the house.

*

Ariana jumped at the screaming noise, unable to make out the words, but sure Soph was behind the sound that seemed to emanate from the top of the cliff, beyond the rose garden. She pulled herself to stand, her woozy head causing her balance to falter, picked up the half-empty bottle and empty glass and staggered quickly up the slope. Reaching the top, Soph bounding towards her, she stopped. 'Are you okay?' she asked, Soph's dark eyes assaulting her, causing her to flinch.

'We can't sell,' Soph blurted, barely stopping before she reached Ariana, encroaching on her personal space as she spat the words out. Gianna stood a pace behind Soph, her eyes red with tears.

'I...' Ariana paused with no idea what she might say to her daughter. 'I...' she tried again, but nothing, just her head spinning.

'I'm not leaving here,' Soph insisted, her body tense with frustrated determination.

The sound of tentative footsteps on the sandy path and the clearing of a throat caught their attention, and both women turned to face the little man in the collar and tie, still hugging his briefcase close to his chest. 'Hmm, could I take a look around the gardens?' he asked, his voice full of trepidation.

'Yes.'

'No.'

Ariana and Soph said, simultaneously.

The man looked from one woman to the other, his brows furrowed, his lips pinned together, and a trickle of sweat sliding nervously down his temple.

The crunching of grit drew their attention, and all eyes shifted in the direction of the path leading up to the house from the west-cove.

'Hi,' Nikki said approaching the group, her broad grin disappearing at the sight of the pained expressions on the faces glaring back at her.

'Go,' Ariana barked, indicating for the man to continue his appraisal, releasing a long breath as he disappeared from view, her eyes avoiding Nikki's questioning gaze.

Soph ran towards Nikki and threw herself into her strong arms. Nikki stumbled back at the ferocity behind the move. 'Whoa, what's up?' she asked, alarmed.

'I don't want to leave here,' Soph said, crying into Nikki's shoulder. Gianna stood behind Ariana tears spilling from her eyes.

'Whoa,' Nikki repeated, her eyes fixed on Ariana's. 'What's going on?' she asked, acutely aware that there was a half-suited man, with a briefcase who appeared to be assessing the grounds, two women in tears and Ariana obviously in denial carrying a bottle of wine and an empty glass. It would have been comical had it not been for the consequences. 'Ariana?' she questioned, with more assertiveness.

Ariana's eyes refused to settle on Nikki's. Her bottom lip was quivering, and she bit down firmly to create pain of a different sort. She had no answers; the walls were crumbling before her eyes, and she didn't know how to think let alone answer Nikki's questions.

'Ariana!' Nikki said, more forcefully, glaring, trying to wake her from the hopeless trance she appeared locked into.

Ariana forced herself to look straight at Nikki, her stomach dropping at the worried expression on Nikki's face. 'Can I speak with you?' she said, her voice barely audible.

Nikki released Soph and wiped the tears from her face. Holding her gaze with sincerity and affection, cupping her cheeks, 'It'll be alright,' she said. 'Let me talk to your mum.' Nikki was nodding her head as she spoke and Soph mirrored the movement, sniffling.

Gianna stepped up, took Soph's hand and led her towards the path to the west-cove.

Nikki stared at an evasive-looking Ariana, looking confused.

The man cleared his throat again, drawing two pairs of eyes. 'I'll be off then,' he said. 'Everything seems to be in order here,' he added, not that anyone cared. He scampered down the slope to the east-cove to board the boat that had brought him to the island from Lefkada.

Nikki continued to glare, shoulders raised, palms begging, seeking an explanation, demanding answers.

Ariana stumbled into the house her shoulders slumped, feeling nothing, numbness having stolen her mind and her body. She dumped the half-empty bottle of warm wine on the drainer, pulled a chilled bottle from the fridge and two clean glasses, and wandered out onto the balcony.

Nikki followed her, fighting the rage that threatened her sanity. She needed to tell Ariana about her offer to buy the house, but something in Ariana's posture felt distant, dark, and ominous, as if anything she offered now would be too late. Ariana looked at her vacantly, hopelessly, resigned to a fate that she didn't want, and it reminded Nikki of twenty-years ago when Ariana had held the same desperate and helpless look. Nikki wanted to shake her out of it. She wanted to scream at Ariana, but she couldn't get past her heart pounding in her throat, blocking the words.

Ariana's weak smile met Nikki's stern gaze. Slowly, she opened the bottle and poured the wine. Standing the bottle on the table, she picked up her glass and walked to the walled edge, her eyes locked onto the bustling taverna. 'He just showed up without warning,' she said, knowing the information was of little value.

Nikki stood, waiting, her blood slowly coming to the boil.

'He's from the property development company who bought the estate,' Ariana continued.

Nikki flinched, and her heart stopped. *Bought. Property development.* The words ricocheted around her mind, her heart unwilling to allow them to settle. She couldn't even think of any words to challenge Ariana.

'I sold before I arrived,' Ariana added. Her tone matter-of-fact, her body still numb, her eyes still on the taverna.

Nikki repeatedly blinked, her hands clasping at her head, ruffling her hair, her palms squeezing her temples.

'Today was just a cursory visit. I signed the paperwork months ago,' Ariana continued, her tone flatter.

Nikki was shaking her head, confusion and questions warring. 'Why?' she asked, reality starting to filter through her mind, her heart splintering and the tiny shards like teardrops, falling. She felt as if her heart was breaking all over again, only this time it was even more excruciating and painful. The embarrassment of even thinking she could try and buy the place was nothing compared to the sense of betrayal Ariana had inflicted on her. 'Why?' she repeated, her jaw clenched, her tone shifting to something more menacing. Anger had a hold on her.

Ariana turned slowly. Her heart stopped at Nikki's ghost-like appearance. The intensity of Nikki's glare floored her, ripped through her, caused her to feel again. 'I...' she stammered, the rush of sadness gripping her words and stopping them from airing. Her eyes fixed on Nikki; she wanted to run to her, hold her, be held by her. Tears seeped down her cheeks, her eyes never wavering from Nikki's shaking head. Shame flamed up her spine and coloured her cheeks, making it hard for her to find her voice.

'Why didn't you tell me?' Nikki demanded.

Ariana floundered. The question was a reasonable one, under normal circumstances. But these weren't normal circumstances at all.

She had agreed to sell the house at her mother's request on the basis that the development company would pay a lot more than the estate was worth. Ariana would be set for life and without a husband to provide for her - even though the one she had lost everything they had ever owned - it was in Ariana's best interests. Her mother's words hurt, like lightning striking and burning the tree from the inside out and gutting it.

It had always been about the money. Ariana hadn't even questioned her mother's intent, believing Teresa when she said how much the island would benefit from the tourism. Teresa hadn't said how much the island would lose for the privilege. Ariana hadn't known then what she had come to discover since, the photographs, the engagement, and then the timing of Teresa's marriage, and her own birth.

'I didn't know,' Ariana said, the words answering to the distracting thoughts of Manos that had consumed her day.

Nikki frowned. 'Didn't know,' she spat. 'You signed the contract,' she shouted, stunning Ariana out of the trance.

'I think Manos is my father,' she said, softly.

Nikki winced, her frown deepened, and her lips stopped moving, leaving her mouth agape.

'I didn't know,' Ariana said again, shaking her head back and forth. 'That's why Teresa encouraged me to sell to the development company.'

Nikki pressed her palms to her temples. This wasn't making any sense, and the rage had stopped her mind from working correctly. She didn't understand, and the information hitting her ears didn't fit with anything her brain could compute. 'I don't get it.' Nikki said.

'The plan is to build a large hotel complex, marina, swimming pools, tennis courts, and a restaurant. They've agreed 1.5 million Euros for the estate, including the production plant.' Ariana said, with detachment.

Nikki swallowed hard. The sting of the details punctured her lungs, leaving her breathless, and she slumped into the chair, defeated. She would never have been able to compete with that sort of money.

'Mother insisted selling was best for me, and for the island,' Ariana started.

Nikki looked up; her eyes as dark as steel, her face taut. 'Ariana, Teresa has only ever done what is best for her,' she said, each word punctuated to control the anger that persisted.

Ariana nodded sheepishly. 'I know that now,' she said, her voice broken. She slumped into the chair opposite Nikki, her elbows on the table her head in her hands.

Nikki stood, turned into the kitchen, and headed out the door.

The painful silence and increasing distance between them carved a hole so deep, dark and cold, Ariana couldn't breathe. She collapsed her head onto the table and sobbed.

17.

Nikki stormed out of the house and up the path, her ears ringing with her incoherent thoughts, fire driving her legs with purpose. She needed to be as far away from the white house as possible - as far away from Ariana as possible. Ignoring the route down to the beach, she continued inland, taking the path around the back of the taverna and out to the top of the cliff on the west-cove.

She slumped to the ground, her fingers scraping desperately, aimlessly, at the loose dirt. She threw a handful of stones into space in front of her, her eyes tracking the scattergun effect as the pebbles broke the surface of the water below. She wiped at the burning salt irritating her eyes, which did nothing to release the tension in her head.

The past playing out in her mind, searching for the signs, her heart ached with the added weight. The markers were there of course when she really looked. Manos had always treated Ariana as if she were his own, the way he smiled at her, attended to her needs, nurtured her in the absence of Teresa. She shook her head back and forth, plucked another handful of grit and threw it out into space, watched it forming a pattern, albeit briefly, on the water before attending back to her thoughts. She didn't understand why Manos hadn't said anything to her, or to Ariana? Why had he allowed Teresa to take Ariana away in the first place? He had been like a father to her when she had been a child and then a business partner with the wisdom of a thousand lives, over the later years. Why hadn't he trusted her enough to say something? She pressed the heel of her hands into her eyes, rested her elbows on her raised knees, and considered how she felt. It seemed strange to think of Ariana as Manos' daughter. That also made Soph his granddaughter. She released a long breath, and for the first time in as long as she could remember, she missed her parents.

She sat, staring at the sun's descent into the deep-blue horizon, taking the light to another place. She wondered, briefly, what that place might be like. She closed her eyes, tired from the strain, and lay back on the ground, the scent of pine and dry earth, and the constant chatter of the cicadas and the hush of the waves for company. They were good company too; they would never break her heart, that's what people did, not nature.

When she opened her eyes to the darkness of the night, a full moon, surrounded by thousands of flickering lights showered the cliff. She stood slowly, brushed the dust from her t-shirt and shorts and meandered down the steep track to the beach. She crossed the sand, grabbed the ouzo from the freezer, a glass, and her fishing gear and headed out to the rocks beneath the white house.

*

Ariana tossed and turned, eventually climbing out of bed and heading up to the kitchen. She filled a glass of water and slurped it hungrily, her head beginning to thump. She grabbed the pills from the cupboard and took two with another glass of water.

The oppressive feeling hadn't lifted and whichever way she turned, the future loomed menacingly. She had known before the development agency man had shown up that she didn't want to leave the island, didn't want to leave Nikki or the house. She had known, but her hands were tied. She pondered the stuck, trapped feeling that was so familiar and disconcerting. That sense of knowing what she wanted but thinking it was impossible to achieve. She'd had the same feeling twenty years ago. *Aarrgghh!* The silent scream reverberated around her head, but a sudden surge of inner strength and the swelling of her heart, overpowered and silenced the voice. She stood momentarily adjusting.

Compelled by the hazy light, visible through the window over the kitchen-sink, she stepped out of the house and around to the rose garden. The sweet scent hung in the warm night air, and she breathed deeply, lowering herself to the coarse grass. Some might think her behaviour strange; she found it mildly fascinating as she started talking to Sophia as if she were present.

Entranced by the soothing aroma, comforted by the soft-white haze she closed her eyes. Nikki's stern glare and abject disbelief diffused in her mind's eye, the image replaced by Nikki's light-hazel eyes, darker at the outer circles of her irises, holding Ariana intently, intimately. Nikki's soft lips brushing tenderly across her own, creating wave after wave of tingling shocks through her body, exciting her, obsessing her. Drifting, she could feel Nikki's fingers, delicately tracing down her jawline, sparking the tiny hairs on neck; tracking her collarbone down to the top of her breasts, gently, tantalisingly, discovering every part of her supple skin, her nipples rising at the sensation. She gasped, groaned, yearned for more. Opening her eyes, her heart racing, the urge to run down to Nikki's apartment, wake her and make love to her shocked her into a child-like grin. She clasped her knees to her chest, hugging tightly, rocking back and forth, her confidence growing. Tomorrow, she would tell Nikki she was in love with her.

*

Nikki rubbed the sandpaper aggressively over the newly repaired wood on the boat, her mood oscillating between fiery anger and profound sadness. She wiped at the tears trickling onto her cheeks, berated herself, for what, she wasn't quite sure, and continued rubbing fiercely. She cursed as the coarse paper ripped the skin off her finger, studied the sore spot vacantly until the red liquid oozed from the cut. Served her right for not taking better care, wearing gloves, slowing down. She ignored the small scrape and continued to sand down the wood, with a little less force.

She had drunk too much last night, but not enough to kill the pain. After returning from fishing, she had studied the copy of the finance contract then ripped it into tiny pieces, an empty gesture but symbolic nonetheless. Then she had tossed and turned all night, eventually falling asleep as dawn appeared. By the time she awoke, Manos had taken the ferry to Ithaka.

She stopped rubbing, studied her fingers, raw from the friction, and noted that her hands were shaking. Anger exhausted and the feeling of vulnerability encroached, guiding the shaking to her core. She doubled over, crumpling to her knees and sobbed.

Ariana gasped at the sound emanating from the workshop. She hurried through the bar and came to a halt in the open doorway, her mouth agape, her breath poised. 'Nikki!' she exclaimed, rushing towards the heap on the floor.

Nikki shrugged off the contact, turned away, silently screaming, the intensity of the pain increasing with Ariana's presence.

Ariana faltered at the rejection. She stood, for what felt like a lifetime, unsure of the right thing to do. If she walked away now, there would be no going back; they would have nothing left to repair. She had come down to the taverna to talk, to explain, to work out how to stop the sale. Dropping to the floor, she pulled Nikki into her arms with a quality of strength and confidence she hadn't known existed within her.

Nikki's initial resistance softened in the warmth and security of the embrace, Ariana's arms firmly clasped around her body telling her she wasn't going to let go, her head pressed against Ariana's chest.

'I'm not leaving you,' Ariana whispered.

Nikki continued to whimper unable to process the words she so desperately wanted to hear.

'I'm not leaving,' Ariana repeated.

The sobbing stopped, the rocking continued.

'I love you,' Ariana said, placing light kisses to the top of Nikki's damp hair, squeezing her tightly. Nikki felt so good in her arms.

Nikki could feel her breathing relax as the sobs abated, and the warm sensation against her cheek felt comforting and reassuring. Ariana's sweet scent transformed and transfixed her at that moment, and her world shifted on its axis. The dense darkness that had pushed her to the floor was slowly lifting, a light, airy feeling bringing with it a new, fresh, wave of tears. She eased out of the hold, Ariana's arms still clinging around her waist, searching for a visual affirmation of the words she had just heard. She smiled wearily through the tears, at Ariana's wet face.

Ariana smiled affectionately and started to chuckle. 'I love you,' she said. 'I don't want to leave, no matter what happens with the house,' she said.

Nikki's smile grew slowly, and she rubbed at her wet cheeks. 'I love you,' she said, in a whispered voice.

Ariana leaned in closing the gap between them. She needed to feel Nikki's lips on hers. 'I love...'

Nikki's mouth stole the words from Ariana's lips, crashing down and connecting them with such intensity that nothing else mattered. Nothing else existed. She pulled Ariana deeper into the kiss, seduced by the salty taste on her lips and the feel of Ariana's tongue playing with her own, her hands pulling Ariana's body closer.

Ariana eased out of the kiss and gazed into Nikki's eyes, her fingers tracing the line of her cheek and jaw, her voice soft. 'What am I going to do?' she asked.

Nikki hadn't heard the question. Ariana was in love with her. The words circled, built, settled. That was all that mattered. 'I love you so much,' she said, with a smile that lightened her hazel eyes. She leaned into the fingers caressing her face, closed her eyes, and cupped Ariana's hand to her mouth.

Goosebumps flew up Ariana's arm and down her neck, and she shuddered. 'Mmm,' she murmured, the tingling down her spine continuing to light up her core.

Nikki stood, pulled Ariana to her feet, swept her into a firm hold and studied her adoringly. The intensity in her dark brown eyes seemed to open a path directly to Ariana's soul. The dimple in her flushed cheek revealed the depth of the smile on her red lips. The delicate lines caressing her almond-shaped eyes highlighted the sun-tanned skin of her cheeks. And then her ash-blonde hair, bleached by the sunlight. She looked stunning. Intoxicating; so beautiful. Engrossed in Ariana's sweet scent, Nikki drew closer, her lips touching Ariana's, delicately sensing her, calling to her. She caressed Ariana's mouth with her tongue, tasting, testing.

Ariana groaned softly, her mouth eager to respond, paralysed by the seductive touch to which Nikki was subjecting her. She hadn't realised how much she had missed this feeling, longed for this connection, this sense of oneness. Completeness. Nikki's soft lips were pressing against hers, and her strong hands were holding her with such assurance and yet such tenderness; it felt perfect. Nikki was perfect.

'Huhum.' Soph cleared her throat, observing the intimate embrace with embarrassed amusement.

Ariana eased away from Nikki's lips, but not from her arms. 'Hey,' she said, her eyes soft, her smile warm.

'Hey Soph,' Nikki said, her tone displaying the vulnerability that still lingered. She leaned closer to Ariana and placed a tender kiss on her head.

Soph's grin widened. 'Sorry, I was just coming to see if we could take a boat out and fish,' she said, directing the statement at Nikki.

'Sure,' Nikki said, nodding towards the beached motorboat to the right of the jetty. 'Make sure you wear life-jackets,' she said, with mild authority.

'Sure,' Soph said, bouncing back through the bar and informing Gianna. The two young women chased across the beach, squealing with delight.

Nikki sighed wearily and pulled Ariana into a hug. 'She looks happier,' she said.

'I told her we're not leaving,' Ariana replied with a warm smile.

'What about Gianna? Nikki asked. 'Manos mentioned Nikos has another job,' she added.

Ariana took in a deep breath and released it slowly, her head resting heavily against Nikki's chest. 'I don't know what to do about the sale,' she said.

Nikki nodded. 'Later,' she said.

Ariana nodded.

'Want to help me prep for lunch?' Nikki asked. She didn't want the house sale to cast a shadow over Ariana's decision to stay.

'I'd like that,' Ariana said, easing out of the hug a fraction and pressing a tender kiss to Nikki's deliciously tanned neck.

Nikki groaned. 'That's not helpful,' she said, with a chuckle. She was finding it hard to adjust to the shift between them, wanting to believe Ariana was in love with her, yet expecting to wake up from some horrid trick of her imagination. She chastised herself for the insecurity that had her defences raised, her heart competing with her innate desire to protect herself.

Ariana continued to kiss up her neck, lingering, taking in the flowery-spicy scent, nipping at her ear, groaning, 'Mmm.'

Nikki pulled back with a wild look in her eyes and a tired smile. 'We've got work to do,' she said with a broken voice, taking Ariana by the hand and leading her through to the kitchen. She stopped, turned Ariana towards her, and caressed her cheek. 'We'll talk about the house when Manos gets back,' she confirmed.

Ariana glanced around the bar and then across the beach to the water. She hadn't noticed the vacant spot at the jetty when she'd walked from the house. 'Where is he?' she asked suddenly distracted.

'He's fetching some wood and bits,' she said, indicating with her eyes to the workshop.

'I need to speak to him,' Ariana said in a hushed voice, as if to herself.

Nikki nodded. 'Later,' she whispered, coaxing Ariana into the kitchen.

18.

Ariana sat on the wooden slats, her feet dangling in the warm sea at the end of the jetty. Looking into the clear water, she marvelled at the vast shoals of tiny sandy-silver coloured fish, darting this way and that, holding formation as they navigated the rocks on the seabed. Her toes tickled the water; the fish reacted; Ariana smiled. She didn't need to look up to know the ferry was larger than it had been a moment ago, the jangling nerves in her stomach told her so. She tried to breathe through the tightness in her chest, but the pounding of her heart was making it impossible.

She had insisted to Nikki that she wait for Manos alone. Nikki had simply nodded, and taken herself into the workshop after lunch. Ariana had wandered along the beach for a while going over what she wanted to say to him, but now all that was redundant.

Her mouth dry, her lips refusing to move, she stood and stared at the approaching boat, her body trembling. She watched as the whirring and grinding of the engines, and the white foam spurting at the rear of the boat brought the ferry to a stop next to the jetty. 'Aye,' Manos shouted, with a broad grin, throwing a rope from the deck onto the wooden slats.

Ariana instinctively grabbed the rope and wound it around a metal post. She stood, speechless, time slowing, observing Manos step off the deck and secure the ferry firmly to the jetty. Two local men followed him off the boat and ambled up the beach towards the bar.

Manos stretched, studied Ariana's intense silence, and smiled warmly. 'Everything okay?' he asked.

'Are you my father?' Ariana said, the words coming out with more calmness than she felt.

His eyes shifted from her for a moment, his lips pinched, and he sucked through his teeth. When he looked back at her, the sincerity in his gaze was unquestionable. 'Yes,' he said, his voice quiet, his head nodding, almost imperceptibly. A coy smile teased at his lips, pride danced in his eyes, but he remained respectfully reserved.

Ariana's eyes fell to the wooden slats under her feet and then her restless hands by her side. 'Oh!' she replied. It wasn't one of the well-rehearsed lines, and she didn't know where it came from. She hadn't known how she might respond to facing Manos and directly confronting the truth. She hadn't expected the anxiety that had plagued her to disappear in an instant, or the tenderness of affection she felt as she held his loving eyes. There was warmth spreading from her chest, releasing the tension from her muscles, and a soft chuckle bubbling up inside. She looked up. His gaze held concern and reassurance, and a smile slowly emerged on her face. The urgency, the questions she wanted to ask, had diffused. They needed to talk, but that could wait. He stepped towards her with arms open, and when they folded around her, she melted against his chest, the subtle smell of diesel-oil triggering something recognisable, something intangible yet genuine. Home.

Manos kissed the top of Ariana's head and released her from his grip, his chest bursting with pride, and love. He hadn't believed Sophia at first, though he had wanted to, when she had assured him repeatedly that Ariana would return. 'You want to give me a hand?' he asked, indicating to the planks of wood and other items lying on the deck and stepping onto the boat.

Ariana nodded. 'Why didn't you tell me?' she asked, unable to contain the question that had been burning on her lips since the penny had dropped.

He stopped and held her inquisitive gaze. 'I promised your mother,' he said, a solemnness overcoming his eyes as he spoke. He studied his daughter as she processed the words, an unfamiliar surge of adrenaline reminding him he was totally unprepared for the discussion he knew he needed to have. 'Let's get a drink,' he said, the unloading of the ferry could wait. Nikki would have questions too, and he owed it to them both to provide the answers he had.

Ariana nodded and followed him up the beach.

'What would you like?' he asked, approaching the bar and urging her to sit at table number 5.

'Beer, please.'

Ariana sat, her breathing relaxed and an unexpected feeling of calm occupying the muscles in her body. The taverna was empty but for the two men who had just disembarked the boat, who leaned on the bar chatting happily, as they probably did after every trip.

'I'll get Nikki,' he said, heading through the back of the bar.

He approached with two bottles of beer and a clear glass filled to the brim. Placing them on the table, he sat at the head of the table, to Ariana's right. The aniseed aroma drifted into her awareness, warming and unexpectedly comforting. She watched his eyes studying her and welcomed the interruption when Nikki approached, with tiny wood shavings stuck to her arm and forehead. Ariana smiled. Nikki sat opposite her, closing the triangle around the table, reached for the beer and gulped down the cold liquid with ease. She had turned her attention to Manos, her eyes seeking answers. She looked tired, drained. Ariana's smile oozed the love that she felt.

Manos cleared his throat, picked up his drink and took a long slow sip. He placed the glass delicately on the table, rotating it on the spot. 'Teresa and I were engaged to be married,' he started.

Nikki flinched.

'I loved her more than life,' he said, a soft twinkle in his eye. His demeanour shifted in the same moment. 'But, she

202

never loved me back, not really,' he said, with genuine remorse. 'I think, in honesty, she agreed to marry me because the prospect of anyone else coming along was slim and she couldn't leave the island, not without someone to take care of her. At that point, the estate was financially struggling, and she didn't have the funds to be able to leave on her own. She never wanted to stay here though; she had grown to hate it.'

Ariana frowned, hating her mother more by the second.

'When Aaron Carter arrived, we had been engaged for about eighteen months, but Teresa had been putting off setting a date for the wedding, and.' He paused, reached his glass to his lips and sipped. 'She married him within two months of knowing him,' he continued, his tone flat, a thin sheen forming on his dark eyes. 'I didn't know for sure when you were born, but the timings gave me cause to suspect. Teresa vehemently denied that I was your father and invested all her time ensuring you kept away from me, and this place,' he said, his eyes wandering fondly around the taverna. 'I think she hated me by then, too. Especially being stuck here for so many years before Aaron made his fortune,' he added philosophically, his eyebrows rising. 'I'm sorry, I didn't have the heart to challenge your mother,' he said, glancing at Ariana. 'It would have ruined her life and her marriage, and I couldn't do that to the woman I loved. I wouldn't have wanted her living here with me and resenting every moment of it. And, out of respect for Sophia, I couldn't bring disgrace to her family either. And, at that point, I still wasn't completely sure. Lord knows I've questioned whether I should have done things differently every day since,' he said, his hand shaking as it made its way uneasily to his lips. 'I got lucky,' he said, a half-smile forming with his thoughts. He looked from Ariana to Nikki and back again, both women poised, waiting on his words. 'I assumed Teresa would leave the island at the earliest opportunity and as luck would have it for me, that turned out to be fifteen-years later than she would have liked.'

He chuckled. 'I had the privilege of having you in my life, even if at a short distance.' He held Ariana's gaze. 'It was only after Teresa took you away from here that Sophia and I talked.' He stopped, waited.

Nikki sat up in her seat and her eyes rested longingly on Ariana.

Tears flowed down Ariana's cheeks. 'Sophia knew,' she said, her voice broken.

'Yes. Sophia had suspected from the start too, but by the time she found out the truth you had settled in the UK. She never trusted Aaron, but Teresa was a strong woman and adept at getting her own way,' Manos said, sucking through his teeth.

Ariana swiped at the tears with one hand, Nikki reached across the table and held the other.

'I'm sorry, Ariana. I feel I've let you down. I didn't think about the impact on you.' He wiped at his damp cheeks.

Ariana released a long breath, reached out and squeezed his arm. Reminded of the many times he had entertained her and Nikki on the beach as a child, cooked for them and hidden them in the face of Teresa's wrath, she smiled warmly. She didn't understand her mother, she never would, and she didn't plan to try. Teresa was dead to her. She wiped at her cheeks, a confident smile directed at Nikki before looking back to Manos with a sense of having been reborn.

'You have a granddaughter,' she said, a slight chuckle bursting through the tears.

'I do,' he said, his cheeks glistening, the stubble curling on his dimpled cheeks. He glanced across to Nikki. 'I'm sorry, I couldn't say anything to you,' he said, reaching out and squeezing her hand.

Nikki nodded. She couldn't feel more vulnerable than she did right now, her insides still trembling from the events of the last few hours, but she understood his dilemma. 'What about the house?' she asked.

Manos blinked. 'What about it?' he asked.

'I sold the house,' Ariana said, her voice quiet, her eyes focused on the table.

Manos looked confused. He stayed silent until Ariana's eyes lifted and addressed him. 'How can you sell the house?' he asked, his tone matter-of-fact.

'I signed the contract before I came here,' Ariana started, stopping as Manos lifted his hand up, his palm facing her.

Manos sucked through his teeth and sipped at his drink. 'You cannot sell something you don't own,' he said, with utmost sincerity.

Ariana's head was shaking back and forth of its own volition, as she processed his statement. 'What do you mean?' she asked.

'I am aware of the conditions that Sophia applied to your inheritance,' he said.

Nikki looked from Manos to Ariana, feeling entirely out of the loop. 'Conditions!' she said her tone questioning.

'The refurbishment of the house, living here unassisted for the time it takes to do the work, and the specific instructions for Sophia's ashes,' he said. 'Until you've met the conditions, you do not own the house. The trust holds it, and it goes without saying that if you do not own the house, then you cannot sign any contract to sell the house,' he said. 'Anything you signed before wouldn't be worth the paper it's written on,' he added. 'And, of course, if you do not meet the conditions Sophia set out, the estate will remain in trust. She always believed you would choose to stay,' he said, with a wry smile, gazing towards the rose garden with a sparkle in his eyes.

Ariana slumped back in the seat, her initial irritation at the fact Manos had known all along about the conditions and not said anything swiftly replaced by the ecstatic feeling of being able to negate the sale. 'Really!' she exclaimed, allowing the hint of a smile to form, an overwhelming sense of relief flooding her.

Manos nodded, sipped at his drink and smiled.

A frown started to form on Ariana's forehead, a question poised on her lips. 'Why did you help me with the decorating?' she asked, curious as to why he would help her if it meant she would leave the island earlier as a result.

Manos inhaled deeply, gazed toward the rose garden and released a breath, slowly, aware that Nikki was also seeking answers. 'I wanted to get to know you again,' he started. 'And, I thought that helping you might get you to see that you are loved and that there is a home for you here,' he continued. 'And, I suppose the selfish side of me wanted to spend time with you in case you did choose to leave in the end.' He shrugged, brushed at his damp cheeks and sucked through his teeth.

Nikki's stunned expression lifted, her eyes lighting up as the information settled. 'The house isn't sold?' she asked, for clarification.

Manos nodded his head. 'Not possible,' he said, with certainty.

'Hey look,' Soph shouted, stepping up the beach sporting a broad grin, a net resting over her shoulder.

Ariana's eyes locked onto Nikki's momentarily, something intangible passing between them, before turning her attention to her excited daughter. 'Hey,' she said with a genuinely enthusiastic smile. 'What did you catch?'

'Seven mullet,' Soph said, struggling to hold up her pole with two hands, dumping it on the sand by the table. She looked elated, her hair scruffier than usual, tiny streaks of salt sitting in the fine smile-lines on her tanned cheeks.

Gianna approached with a second net and an equally satisfied grin. 'They're huge,' she added.

'Best I get the fire going,' Manos said, rising from the table. 'Mullet for dinner,' he said with a chuckle, his cheeks shining at the family that surrounded him.

'Yeah!' Soph cheered, her voice raised, her enthusiasm infectious.

Ariana laughed.

Nikki chuckled, warmed by the absence of tension and stress in Ariana. She looked radiant, glowing, her eyes projecting deep affection.

'Bring them through; I'll show you how to gut them,' Manos said.

Soph baulked; Gianna laughed.

'Come on. We'll do it together,' Gianna said, dragging a protesting Soph through the bar to the kitchen.

Ariana held Nikki's weary gaze, her heart aching at the dark rings under her hazel eyes. 'I love you,' she said.

Nikki nodded. She was exhausted, drained, thrilled, excited, and confused all at once. 'I love you too,' she said, the ripple of a smile making its way through to the surface. 'It's just...' she started, averting her gaze.

'It's been a shit start,' Ariana finished for her. 'Can we start us again?' she asked, reaching across the table and taking Nikki's hand. She rubbed her thumb across the tanned skin, the warmth of the touch closing the distance between them.

Nikki drew in a deep breath and released it slowly. 'I'd like that,' she said, the soft smile going some way to revitalising her light-hazel eyes.

Musical notes started to fill the bar. Soph was perched on a stool, guitar in hand, and starting to sing.

Nikki and Ariana looked at each other and chuckled.

'Gutting fish didn't last long,' Nikki said.

'She's squeamish,' Ariana said with adoration.

'Another drink?' Nikki asked, standing from the table.

'Sure,' Ariana said, standing with her. 'I'll be over there,' she said, indicating towards the driftwood bench.

Nikki's eyes responded.

Ariana eased onto the bench, fractured fragments settling inside her, blending, forming a renewed sense of fullness that warmed and softened her. The airy sensation; the lightness, the peace and inner tranquillity painted a different kind of smile on her face: a smile that resonated with confidence, assurance, and a sense of belonging. She breathed in deeply, enjoying the expansion that flowed through her chest, sighed out slowly and eased back in the seat resting her head back on the rock.

Nikki approached from the bar, sat next to her and handed over a bottle of beer. 'I don't understand,' she started to say.

Ariana sat up and turned to face her. 'Sshhh!' she said, pressing a finger to Nikki's lips and resting it there. 'There's a lot I don't understand too, but what I do know is that I love you and I am not leaving, and I'd like to spend the next few days enjoying that feeling.' She closed the space between them until their lips touched, tenderly, lovingly... unhurriedly.

The kiss came to a natural end, and Nikki pulled Ariana into her shoulder. 'I love you, and I'm glad you've chosen to stay,' she said, gazing out across the beach, the silky-sweet sound of the guitar and Soph's voice drowning out the chirping crickets, her eyes drawn to the glow above the rose garden. She sighed, smiled, and pulled Ariana closer. 'Do you fancy a swim later, when it's dark?' she asked.

A mischievous grin appeared on Ariana's face. 'I'd like that,' she said, snuggling into Nikki, the flowery, spicy, warmth, igniting her senses. Her eyes closed, a low groan falling from her lips.

19.

Manos eased back on the lounger with a deep sigh, Soph and Gianna still singing as they meandered across the beach towards the white house, Nikki and Ariana strolling hand-in-hand in the other direction, to the rocks at the western edge of the cove. He raised his glass to the silver-white haze, lighting up the rose garden and chuckled. 'You old coot,' he whispered, sipping at the drink, savouring the warmth that suffused him. Ariana had decided to stay on Sakros. He would inform the solicitors in the morning, and as soon as they nullified the sale, he would arrange for the transfer of the estate to Ariana. He tipped the glass, swallowed the burning contents, rested his head back and closed his eyes, enjoying the soft hush of the waves and the chirping and buzzing noises that surrounded him. Today was another good day. The hair curled on his cheeks, contentment softening the lines on his aged skin. He wouldn't wait up for Nikki tonight.

*

Ariana interlocked her fingers through Nikki's, her thumb finding Nikki's and dancing across its surface, her feet moving in sync with Nikki's, the same length of stride, breathing in the same balmy, salty, night-air. 'It's so beautiful here,' she said, with a sense of awe.

Nikki squeezed the soft hand in hers, the truth beginning to settle in the tingling that filtered through her fingers and up her arm. 'It is,' she said, her eyes studying Ariana's profile with a sense of giddy disbelief and love.

Ariana turned, locked onto the hazel gaze that had stolen her heart.

Nikki's heart skipped a beat at the smile directed at her; the intimate connection between them that even the twenty-year separation hadn't been able to destroy. Her eyes narrowed, and a mischievous grin slipped onto her face. 'Race you to the rocks,' she said, dropping Ariana's hand, and running towards the water, stopping at the shoreline to throw off her t-shirt.

Ariana dropped her top as she ran past Nikki laughing loudly, shouting forfeit, and then dived into the water. She was still chuckling when she surfaced.

Nikki chased after her, reached the rocks first and pulled herself up effortlessly. She held out a hand and tugged Ariana out of the water. She could feel Ariana's breath against her skin, her dark-eyes smiling, and her lips tantalisingly close. The trembling that had exposed her sense of helplessness since earlier in the day was slowly taking on a different quality. The vibrations were lighter and caused the hairs on the back of her neck to rise, and a wave of excitement was building and filtering down her spine.

Ariana gasped, the heat of Nikki's bare skin and the light sheen of water sparkling, Nikki's flesh pressing against her, Nikki's eyes wild, asking something of her. Her lips quivered, and Nikki looked as if she might pounce. Ariana wanted her to. Instead, Nikki was studying her, penetrating deeper into her inner world, and causing her to shudder with the intensity behind the hazel eyes.

Nikki watched the water trickling from the hair around Ariana's face, the shift in her complexion, the slight flutter of her fair eyelashes and the darkening of her eyes, knowing full well the impact she was having on the woman in her arms. She couldn't help the wicked grin widening, with her thoughts. 'You lost,' she said, her voice gravelly, sincere, passionate.

Ariana bit down on her lip, her gaze firmly fixed on the seductive smile and fiery hazel eyes assessing her. The ache in her chest told her how much she loved Nikki; how much she wanted Nikki, but her voice got lost and the silence between them and the heavy weight of expectation. 'What's the forfeit?' she said, her voice shaky, barely audible above the hush of the sea against the rocks.

Nikki narrowed her gaze in thought, her mind scanning for the right punishment, reminded of the few times they had spent as teenagers playing on these same rocks and Ariana's resistance to jumping from the ledges. She leaned closer, her voice at a whisper, 'You have to jump from the bottom ledge,' she said, easing away, studying Ariana carefully. She frowned, confused, at her broad smile and enthusiastic acceptance of the challenge.

Ariana released herself from the embrace and started to climb the rock face with enthusiasm. Passing the lower ledge, and the middle shelf she had jumped from a few days ago, she kept climbing.

The smile dropped from Nikki's face, a wave of concern niggling her conscience, and then a grin reappeared as Ariana stood on the top ledge, turned and chuckled.

'You thought I wouldn't do it,' Ariana shouted, and before Nikki could deny the truth, she jumped letting out a delighted squeal as she dropped and a whooping sound as she resurfaced.

Nikki's competitive sense roused by Ariana's confidence, she started to climb. By the time she reached the top Ariana was out of the water and scaling the cliff again. Nikki screamed out a much-needed release as she jumped.

Ariana reached the top and jumped again, resurfacing quickly, her grinning face within inches of the hazel eyes gazing at her, the exhilaration stirring other sensations in her body as she fought to keep her head out of the water.

Nikki could feel Ariana's presence; so close, the thrill sending shivers down her spine and making it hard for her to tread water. She splashed away, creating a distance between them, and turned to face Ariana. 'Race you to the shore,' she said, 'double or quits.'

Ariana chuckled, leaned forward in the water and started the chase, knowing full well she hadn't got a hope of catching Nikki. She followed her out and around the rocky outcrop and back towards the west-cove beach, puffing, her heart racing with anticipation, as she waded through the shallow waves to the shore. 'Guess I lost, again,' she said with a sultry smile, her eyes fixed firmly on Nikki.

Nikki, t-shirt over her shoulder, smiling, held out a hand and Ariana took it. She directed the hand around her back, drawing them to the point of Ariana's warm breath on her face. Closing the short space, salt on her lips, Ariana's body pressed to the length of her own, she released a soft groan.

Ariana's eyes closed with the touch of Nikki's mouth, soft, tender, gently taking her hungry lips. She reached up, her fingers tracing Nikki's neck, massaging her head, pulling her closer, and deeper into the kiss. The feel of Nikki's arms around her waist and the tingling touch of the fingers sliding up her back drew a long moan that etched Nikki into every cell in her body.

Nikki shuddered at the goosebumps forming under the trail of her fingertips, the desire coursing through her veins and heat flaming her skin, driving her on. Ariana's tongue was exploring her, stimulating the pulsing through her body, connecting them for eternity, opening her heart and loving her with everything she had. She still wanted more, wanted to feel the soft bare skin against her own, the throbbing heat reacting to her sensual touch, and driving Ariana over the edge. She wanted it all, and she wanted it never to end. Easing slowly out of the kiss, silently taking Ariana's hand, holding her dark, penetrating gaze, she led her up the beach.

Ariana's heart raced with the sense of expectation and her fingers intertwined with Nikki's. Light vibrations intensifying in her stomach with every pace, Nikki's spicy scent causing her to feel quite giddy, spellbound. How many times had she dreamed of the things Nikki could do to her? She felt the reassuring squeeze of Nikki's hand in hers, studied the soft lines on the caring face, the compassionate eyes that caressed her and the intensity and desire that shone from them. The butterflies in her stomach were beginning to dance; only this dance was an unfamiliar one.

They walked past the empty lounger, through the back of the bar, the silence broken by the buzzing and chirping noises emanating from the foliage surrounding the beach, and the unspoken messages that hung between them. They stopped outside the apartment front door.

Ariana was trembling; her heart beating at a pace she thought would cause it to burst, her stomach throwing somersaults. She licked her tongue around her dry mouth, her lips tingling. 'I'm scared,' she whispered.

Nikki nodded, the shuddering in her stomach telling her that she felt it too. The fear of never wanting to lose Ariana again, merging with the excitement of the moment she had longed for. 'Me too,' she said, softly. Saying the words helped to shift the tension, through a gentle breath and a deep smile.

Ariana could feel the surge of adrenaline take over her body and absent her of thought, just a moment before she pounced, the force of the kiss throwing Nikki hard against the door.

Nikki opened to the soft lips pressing firmly against her, the taste of Ariana in her mouth, the tongue teasing her, her breath stalling. Easing out of the kiss, her hazel-irises darkening, enquiring, she opened the door and led Ariana into the room. She stood, the urgency in Ariana's eyes causing her to struggle to breathe.

Ariana took the t-shirt and dropped it to the floor, her gaze lingering on the tanned skin of Nikki's shoulder and then down to the rise of her breasts, fascinated by the shivering wave that rippled across the soft flesh in the wake of her touch. Ariana's fingers traced around Nikki's back, released the bikini-top and slipped it to the floor; her focus unwavering, holding those dark-hazel eyes, she could feel her skin tingling with the vulnerability passing between them. 'I'm in love with you and I'm not leaving,' she whispered, her voice broken, her tone certain.

Nikki stood, feeling exposed, her pert breasts begging to be touched, her dark nipples alive with the expectation, heat flaming through her. She watched, transfixed as Ariana released her own top and allowed it to fall. Her tongue wetted her mouth and she swallowed, studying the beautiful pale skin, and the small, pink buds that had swelled with their release, the pulsing in her core intensifying with the desire to touch.

Ariana stepped closer. She reached up and tucked a loose strand of hair behind Nikki's ear, her hands unsteady, clumsy. She toyed tenderly with the soft lobe before trailing her fingertips down Nikki's neck and tracing the line to her breast, her gaze never faltering from the darkening eyes. The sense of the dark-brown nipples hardening at her delicate touch, the heat emanating from the burning skin at her fingertips, the mumbled gasp from the trembling lips, so close to hers, caused her hands to tremor and her heart to pound through her chest. Ariana bit down on her lip, stalling, her desire building until the urgency claimed her. 'Make love to me,' she whispered. She couldn't be sure who moved first because the point at which she blinked their teeth clashed, and Nikki had cupped her head, and their breasts were touching, Nikki's hand was on her, and she was being pulled into the kiss. Lost in the moment, her ability to think stripped from her, she followed Nikki's lead.

Nikki released a groan at the warm salty taste on her lips, the soft bud puckering at her fingertips, her hand caressing the full breast pressed to her own, and the feel of Ariana's warm skin that was causing her own to burn. She could sense the urgency rising within her through the swelling in her heart and wanted to bathe in the moment for eternity. She eased out of the kiss, her hands silently, tenderly, continuing to explore the curves her eyes feasted on, the soft skin prickling, down to Ariana's stomach, slipping the button on her shorts, releasing the clothing and easing it to the floor. She moaned with a sensual smile, Ariana's sweet-musky scent drifting, taking her breath with it, and challenging her patience. Nikki stripped naked and claimed the space that had separated them.

Ariana's breath hitched, leaving her body quivering at the proximity of Nikki's naked warmth. The searing heat and the tenderness of the touch piquing her arousal, she pressed closer, connecting their bodies along their length.

Nikki moaned at the erotic sensations coursing through her body. She could feel Ariana's sex against her, Ariana's hand cupping her breast, the thumb dragging mercilessly across her nipple causing her to tense, and bolts of fire to shoot through her body and ignite the nerves along their path. She groaned out, loudly. Her eyes widening, filled with passion, her mouth crashing against Ariana's, she led her across the room, through the bedroom, clumsily hitting the bed and falling into the firm mattress.

Deepening the kiss, she moved on top of Ariana, re-connecting them and then pinning Ariana's hands at the side of her head against the bed. She slowly withdrew from the kiss, stopping time, studied the intensely dark eyes and the tender smile that gazed up at her, a reflection of the love she felt towards the woman beneath her. 'I never stopped loving you, Ariana,' she said, in a whisper. She released a hand and traced Ariana's face with tenderness, as if sensing her for the first time, the touch light, sensual, curious, her fingers discovering something far deeper, far more dangerous in the intimacy they shared. Ariana's eyes were darker than she had ever seen them, and the fine-lines emanating from them seemed softer. The dimple in her cheek sat deeper too, her lips full, swollen with lust. The fingers entwined in hers were stronger and more assured. The sensation of the nipples rubbing against hers, and their bodies beginning to ebb and flow effortlessly in tune, their hips starting to rock together, felt so good. The sound of Ariana's short gasps, her lips quivering, her eyelashes fluttering, begging for more. She watched lovingly, Ariana losing herself in the slow, sensual movements, taking her deeper, her own eyes closing involuntarily with the arousal steadily building in her core.

Ariana released a soft throaty cry as Nikki's nipples teased against her own, sending sparks through to her centre. The firm hand that restricted her movement, controlling her, steadying her, increasing her desire to be taken; the fingertips brushing tenderly against her soft skin, erotically, caressing her, adoring her. With the sensations pulsing from her nipples through her body, leaving her desperate for Nikki's touch and to feel Nikki inside her, she cried out. Overwhelmed by the surge of passion, she wriggled her hand free and reached hungrily for the muscular thigh, squeezing, pulling the leg up towards her, spreading Nikki wider, pressing her own leg tighter against the wet heat. She groaned at the warmth of the breath and the tenderness of the lips against her skin. The tingling sensation in her clit beginning to throb, she groaned out again. The words, I want you, whispered on Nikki's breath, she eased her hand between them. Enjoying the feel of Nikki on her fingers, she teased the warm, silky spot, sliding tenderly and parting her, and then circling the swollen bundle of nerves that were swelling and hardening.

Nikki released a guttural moan, her hips bucking at the precision of the fingers that seemed to be on her everywhere between her legs and driving her to the edge. Rising above Ariana and opening herself to the touch, she crashed her mouth down, retaking the rigid nipple, sucking, biting, licking and flicking, enjoying the exquisite sensation on her tongue and Ariana's fingers, causing the tremors to increase and a low, long moan of approval to release.

Compelled by the electric fire coursing from her nipple to her crotch Ariana entered Nikki with urgency. The move eliciting another guttural groan, stronger, more rooted than the last, and taking them to a place they had never shared before, to a life that had only ever existed as a dream, a desire that had remained unfulfilled for so many years.

Nikki screamed out, wave after wave of shocks causing her body to vibrate, her heart to swell and tears to form. Burying her head against Ariana's chest, tempted by the salty-sweet taste and musky scent, she traced tender kisses down her body, the gentle hum between her own legs continuing to sing.

Ariana shuddered as Nikki's tongue swept across her lower belly, down the inside line of her leg and settled on the engorged, silky-soft point between her legs, circling, teasing, pulling and twisting her. Then, she could feel Nikki inside her, penetrating her, slowly, and deeply. The glow in her lower belly transformed into a buzz, which then shifted to a tremor, that started to build, taking her mind with it, and then a bolt of lightning shot up her back and into her neck, causing her body to arch and her hips to buck uncontrollably. Her screams were drowned out by Nikki's mouth, and she could taste herself on the salty lips that caressed her, loved her. When she opened her eyes Nikki was smiling, mischievously, seductively. Ariana reached up, her gaze hazy, and cupped Nikki's tanned, flushed cheeks, 'I love you,' she said, her voice a croaky whisper.

Nikki placed a tender kiss to Ariana's lips, eased onto the bed next to her, and pulled her into the crook of her arm, squeezing her tightly. 'I love you,' she said in a contented sigh, with a smile that promised so much more.

'So, this is your place,' Ariana said after a while, with a chuckle on her lips, staring up at the bedroom ceiling, her body ringing from the orgasm that had just invigorated her senses and cast her back into life with a renewed sense of purpose.

Nikki laughed. 'Yes,' she replied, her eyes mapping out the small space in her mind's eye. 'It's not like your place,' she said, 'but it's home.'

'I love it,' Ariana defended.

'You haven't even seen it,' Nikki said.

'I've seen enough,' Ariana said, with a soft tone, snuggling closer.

Nikki chuckled, aware of the pounding of her heart against Ariana's naked flesh, and Ariana's chest, thumping against her warm skin.

'We need to tell Soph,' she said in a more serious tone.

Ariana pulled up from Nikki's chest and gazed at her.

'About the house sale,' Nikki confirmed. 'I think she already gets this bit,' she added, her finger wagging between herself and Ariana.

'I need to let Nikos know too,' Ariana said, reminded of the practicalities, with a more settled feeling than she had ever experienced. The realisation resulted in a deep sigh, and she pressed a soft kiss to Nikki's soft lips. This was home. She was home.

Nikki eased out of the kiss and swept the hair from Ariana's eyes, tenderly pinning it around her ear. 'I went to Athens to get a loan to buy the house,' she said, holding Ariana's gaze, watching for a shift in her demeanour. She smiled weakly, watching the lips purse as the words landed.

'Oh! I...' Ariana didn't know what to say. The time Nikki had been away, trying to secure the property; the time she had missed her dreadfully, worried about her, when she had only been trying to create a future for them both. 'I...' she started again.

Nikki pressed her finger to Ariana's lips. 'It doesn't matter now,' she said. 'I just wanted to explain,' she added, her finger already stimulated by the contact and distracting her from the past.

Ariana kissed the finger exploring her lips, her tongue flicking at the tip, her senses aroused by the texture and scent that distracted her from any further thoughts. She released a sensual moan, taking the fingers deeper into her mouth.

Nikki drew Ariana closer, her lips joining in the dance, deepening the kiss that stirred her and rendered her powerless. As she groaned, Ariana groaned, and a flash of fire flamed deep inside her. It was going to be a long night.

20.

The strong aroma of coffee and baked bread drifted into Ariana's awareness, her body pleasantly awakening to the warm skin pressed against hers, and the arm around her waist.

'Morning!'

Nikki's sexy, sleepy voice thrust Ariana's eyelids apart, and the loving smile directed at her brought a rush of heat to her cheeks. 'Hey,' she said, her voice groggy from the absence of sleep. She moved in the bed and groaned with pleasure at the sensual ache between her legs.

'Mmm,' Nikki responded, arousal painted in her dark-hazel eyes, and raised eyebrows. Instantly, she closed the gap, connecting their lips briefly, and then eased back, running her fingers through Ariana's wild hair. 'You look gorgeous,' she said, with a contented grin.

Ariana reached for Nikki's hand, pulled it to her mouth and kissed the palm. 'You are beautiful,' she said, pressing the hand to her cheek, taking in the tantalising scent of their earlier lovemaking. She would never tire of Nikki's touch or the delicious scent and taste of her.

'Breakfast!' Nikki said.

The room was still reasonably dark, the shutters doing a better job than at the windows on the white house, but a slither of light crept around the closed door.

Ariana had no idea what the time was, or for how long they had slept. She nodded as she spoke. 'I think I worked up an appetite,' she said, with a wide grin.

Nikki jumped out of bed and opened the shutters, revealing her toned, tanned body, and a surge of heat filled the room, bathing them in sunlight.

Ariana swallowed hard, debating whether breakfast could wait, but within seconds, Nikki had stepped from the bedroom and into the en-suite shower.

Ariana followed her.

*

'Have you seen mum?' Soph asked, her eyes scanning the taverna.

'She's with Nikki, working on the shutters,' Manos said, his eyes sparkling, the toothpick shifting in his mouth.

Soph headed around the bar and into the workshop. 'Hey,' she said, spotting the two women, paintbrushes in hand.

'Hey Soph,' Nikki said, putting the brush down and making a move. 'I'll get some drinks,' she said, leaving Soph and Ariana alone.

Soph watched Nikki with an approving gaze. 'So, are you two an item then?' she asked, a coy smile darting across her face.

Ariana stood, put the brush down and stepped closer, her head tilting as she pondered the question. 'Yes,' she said, her cheeks flushed, her eyes studying Soph's response.

'She's hot, and cool, and great fun,' Soph said, with a shrug.

Ariana's cheeks darkened, and her mouth felt suddenly dry. It was an odd conversation to be having with her daughter, and yet it was the most sincere she had ever had with her. 'Everything okay?' she asked, suddenly aware of Soph's mild agitation.

Soph shrugged.

'Is Gianna okay?' Ariana asked with more than a hint of concern.

'Yeah, she's good. It's just.' Soph stalled.

'What is it?' Ariana stepped up to her with open arms.

Soph accepted the embrace and leaned into her mother. 'If she leaves, I'll go with her,' Soph said, her body limp in Ariana's arms.

Ariana eased her out of the hug, leaving a comforting hand resting on Soph's shoulders as she held her gaze with a compassionate smile. 'I understand,' she said, her heart fracturing at the idea of her daughter leaving the island. 'I need to talk to you,' she said, brushing a stray hair from Soph's face, holding her dark-blue eyes and leading her out of the workshop. She poured two cups of coffee and walked towards the driftwood bench. Sitting, she handed a cup to Soph.

'Thanks,' Soph said, with a deep sigh.

'You're in love with Gianna,' she stated.

Soph nodded, turned to face her mother, her eyes watery. 'Yes,' she said, her voice breaking. 'I don't want to lose her,' she added. She sipped at the coffee, her hands trembling.

'You won't Soph,' Ariana said, with absolute certainty.

Soph studied her mother quizzically. How could she be so sure?

Ariana sighed. 'I made a mistake once,' she started, staring out to sea, finding the memories that seemed like a past lifetime ago. 'I left this place against my will and my better judgement. I didn't feel I had a choice back then. I was in love with Nikki when I was a bit younger than you,' she continued, her voice faltering a wry smile appearing. 'When I sold the house before we arrived here, I was doing it for you, and me,' she said.

Soph's mouth moved as if to speak, elicited a soft grunting sound, but Ariana continued as if she hadn't even tried to talk.

'I had convinced myself that we could create a better life somewhere else, that you could get the music training you've always wanted and that we would be happy, away from... my mother,' she said. 'I didn't know that Nikki would still be here, and naively I hadn't given it any thought before we arrived.

Seeing her, and spending time together has made me realise, I've always loved Nikki.' She turned to Soph with a warm smile, cupped her cheek, and tenderly rubbed her thumbs under the damp blue eyes. 'It doesn't change how much I love you, and I have no regrets about having you or even the life I had to endure to get to this point.' She sighed, pressed a kiss to Soph's forehead. 'The important point is that I wasn't thinking straight before. I thought we needed the money, needed to sell, needed to create a new life when the reality is that that new life is here, for me, and I think for you too.'

Soph's eyes shifted, lightened, her face softened, and a smile started to appear.

'We don't need to sell, Soph. Manos needs to speak to the solicitors,' she added, 'to sort out the legalities, but we don't need to leave here, and I'm not selling the house.'

Soph stared in bewilderment.

Ariana gazed at her lovingly. 'That means Nikos can stay working at the estate if he wants to. I need to speak to him, to let him know,' she said, registering the fact that she needed to talk to him sooner rather than later and would head up to the house as soon as she had finished explaining things to Soph.

Soph's eyes sparkled, and she moved to jump up, almost spilling the drink in her hand.

'Wait,' Ariana said. 'There's something else.'

She settled back down.

'I found out some other things I didn't know before,' Ariana said.

Soph shook her head back and forth; her lips pinched, the comment not making any sense to her. She shrugged as if to say, so what?

'I didn't know that Manos and Teresa were engaged, once,' she said.

The additional detail didn't make any more sense to Soph, though the fact did bring a faint smile to her face. The idea of her grandmother and Manos ever being together was a bit odd, but then they were both ancient, so it must have been a long time ago.

Ariana breathed in deeply, her eyes cutting to the sea. She hadn't been aware that her hands had started shaking. She eased the cup to her lips, hoping the strong bitter liquid would distract her concerns. 'To cut a long story short, Manos is my father, your grandfather.' She turned to face Soph as she delivered the sentence, observing her daughter's response closely.

Soph's mouth dropped, her eyes widened and she gulped around like a fish just pulled from the sea, as she tried to reconcile the words her mother had just spoken. Stunned, silent, she sat, staring open-mouthed.

'I didn't believe it at first, either,' Ariana said, filling the uncomfortable quiet. 'I found some photographs of them, the dates matched, and then there was the way Manos treated me when I was growing up here, how he is now with me, and with you, and it started to dawn on me, so I asked him, and he confirmed,' she continued to ramble.

Soph's mouth had closed, but her eyes appeared vacant to the outside world. *Her grandfather, Aaron Carter, wasn't her grandfather.* The thought didn't elicit an emotional response; he had never shown her any interest, and she hadn't much cared for him either. Manos had been different though. She had just thought of it as his way, the Islander's way maybe, and it had been nice and made her feel at home. The warmth that infused her chest told her she liked the idea of him as a grandfather, and a smile grew across her face.

Ariana breathed a sigh of relief. 'I'm sorry, I only found out yesterday, and, well.' Her voice faded, and her eyes lowered to the cup in her hand, a wave of heat passing over her with images of the evening's supper after the girls had returned from their fishing trip, and the events of the night with Nikki.

Soph's grin widened, and her eyes sparkled. 'So, I have a girlfriend and a grandfather,' she said, with a chuckle.

Ariana started to laugh with her. 'Yes, you do,' she said, enjoying the sense of release that had calmed her hands and racing heart. 'I need to go and speak to Nikos,' Ariana said, rising from the seat. 'Do you want to go and say hi to your grandfather?' she asked, with an encouraging smile.

Soph's lip curled a fraction as she processed the awkwardness that hadn't existed before. 'Sure,' she said, standing and rubbing her clammy hands down her shorts, acutely aware of the fizzing in her stomach.

Ariana pressed a kiss to Soph's cheek and started across the beach. She couldn't think of any reason why Nikos might refuse to stay on at the estate, now that she wasn't selling, but until he confirmed the uncertainty sat uneasily. By the time she reached the top of the slope, the familiar disconcerting feeling she had lived with for so long had taken up residence in her stomach. She strode out through the grove, heading for the office attached to the manufacturing plant. The sound of raised voices shifted her direction, and she dodged between the olive trees, across the rows, until Nikos was in sight. Gianna spotted her, her glare fierce, turned away from her father and started to run.

'Ariana,' Nikos said, his tone flat. He looked flustered, his eyes hunting down his disappearing daughter.

Ariana wanted to ask him if everything was okay, but nothing could be until she had updated him. Only then could they have a sensible discussion and put the recent past behind them. 'I'm sorry, I need to tell you, Nikos, I'm not selling the house,' she blurted. Her eyes averted his gaze, unable to face the possibility of the reprieve being too late.

The tension in Nikos' posture softened instantly, and his hand rubbed at his worried eyes. He tried to stand taller, but his

225

shaking shoulders stopped him. He pulled his hands from his face. 'You're not selling,' he said as if waking from a deep sleep.

Ariana smiled warmly and shook her head. 'No, I'm not selling the estate, Nikos. I'm so sorry for all the...' She hadn't finished the sentence before Nikos had launched himself at her, pulled her into a firm embrace, the vice-grip squeezing the air from her lungs.

Eventually releasing her, Nikos wiped his eyes, allowing the smile to grow on his face. 'Thank you, thank you!' he said. He paused as if asking the question.

Ariana rubbed at her crushed chest, recovering her breath, feeling a strong sense of relief that tickled her. 'I'd like you to stay,' she said, answering his plea, a beaming grin on her face.

'Of course, of course,' he said, unsure of where to put his hands. 'Thank you, thank you,' he said again.

'Is Gianna okay?' Ariana asked, her tone serious.

Nikos nodded. 'She tells me she's in love with Soph and was threatening to stay on the island if we left,' he said with a wry smile, his shoulders rising and falling with his words. 'I was trying to explain that might not be possible, but she wasn't having any of it,' he added, with a shrug.

'Ah!' Ariana nodded. 'Soph would have gone with Gianna too,' she said, a swell of pride filling her smile. Gianna and her daughter were well suited, and in love. And, nothing felt better than that.

Nikos blushed. 'I remember when you were younger,' he said, with a remorseful smile. 'Before your mother took you away. You had the same look in your eyes as Gianna does for Soph,' he said, with sincerity. 'It hasn't gone away,' he added, studying her dark-eyes.

Ariana glowed. 'No it hasn't,' she agreed.

Nikos nodded contentedly. 'I'm happy you've decided to stay,' he said, with genuine fondness.

'I'm pleased too,' Ariana said with a warm smile. 'We can talk later, I just needed to let you know, and to be sure you wanted to stay,' she said.

'I'm sure Soph will tell Gianna before I see her again,' he said, his eyes scanning the path down which she had scampered, his head shaking to and fro, a compassionate smile starting across his face.

Ariana turned to leave, then turned back again and reached for his arm. 'Nikos!' she said, her fingers squeezing tenderly.

'Yes,' he replied.

'It's Soph's 18th birthday a week on Sunday. I'm not sure where the party will be, but I'd like you all to come,' she said.

Nikos nodded. 'Of course,' he said, his eyes retrieving the sparkle that had been present in them when she had arrived.

Ariana turned away and wandered back towards the house. She hadn't thought about Soph's birthday party, but now it was at the top of the to-do-list. In fact, it was the only thing on the list! An excited smile pinned to her lips, she continued past the house, down the slope and across the beach to the taverna.

21.

'Looking good,' Manos said, leaning against the frame of the open workshop, flicking the toothpick across his mouth then sipping at the glass in his hand, holding out a beer in his other hand.

Nikki stood, stretched her back and rubbed her hand across the Mediterranean-blue painted wood on the lower bow of the fishing boat. 'She does, doesn't she,' she said, nodding her affirmation. She traced the letters on the side of the boat. 'Do you think she'll like it?' she asked.

Manos' shiny cheeks, the curling hair at his dimples and his sparkling eyes answered the question for her. He tried to speak, choked by the emotion caught in his throat and sipped at his glass instead.

Nikki pulled the cover back over the boat, put the polishing cloth down, and took the bottle from his hand. She took a long slug and grinned. 'Come on Pops; we've got a party to prep for,' she said. 'We can get her to the water later,' she added.

'Kitchen's ready,' he said, sucking through his teeth.

Manos had started preparing the food long before the sun had risen, and the volleyball net was up before Nikki had stepped out of her apartment that morning. Gianna and Soph had been practising already and had disappeared over to the rocks on the west coast, no doubt jumping from the ledges of the cliff, and Soph snorkelling around the rocky outcrop with the new mask and flippers Gianna had given her for her birthday. She smiled at Manos' flustered state, excitement warring with worry deepening the wrinkles on his weathered skin. He wasn't going to fail his granddaughter on her 18th birthday. Today would be a good day. But, then again, it always was.

'Hey,' Ariana said, interrupting the moment passing between her father and Nikki. She flushed, the warmth filtering to her chest.

'Hey,' they responded in unison, both wearing a broad smile, their eyes darting, unsettled.

Ariana flitted from one to the other. They were up to something. She grinned. 'What?' she asked.

'Nothing,' they said, too quickly.

'You ready to go?' Nikki asked.

Ariana nodded, squinted at the pair suspiciously and turned into the bar.

Nikki ruffled Manos' cheeks. 'We'll be back in a couple of hours,' she said.

'Aye,' he said, heading into the bar.

Nikki picked up the fishing gear and walked out to the beach. 'Twenty Euros a fish,' she said, holding out her hand to shake on the deal.

'Deal,' Ariana said with a nod of her head, knowing she had always won the fishing bets they had agreed, even though there was no doubt in her mind that Nikki was both more adept and better practised at fishing.

'You got enough money to pay your debts?' Nikki teased with a laugh.

'I'll pay in kind,' Ariana replied, unable to avoid the croak appearing in her voice.

Nikki laughed loudly. 'Make that two hundred a fish then,' she said.

'Deal,' Ariana responded, her eyes firmly fixed on Nikki's backside as she strode out towards the motorboat. As Nikki leaned over the boat to drop the gear, Ariana's hand slid underneath the outside leg of her shorts.

The hand elicited the wet heat between Nikki's legs, and had her buckling over the side of the boat. 'Seriously,' she said, in mock disbelief, the fire bursting through her making it hard to breathe let alone move.

Ariana stepped casually past her and into the water, and started dragging the boat out to sea, leaving Nikki, groaning and hanging onto the side as if her life depended on it. 'Take me,' Ariana said, with a seductive glint in her eye.

Nikki gulped, righting herself, pushing the boat into the deeper water.

'Fishing,' Ariana added, laughing.

Nikki cursed under her breath, the smile on her lips sending the message that this game was far from over. She held the boat steady, with a beaming grin, indicating with her eyes for Ariana to climb in, watching her intently as she did, her heart melting, her pulse racing. 'Let's fish,' she said, jumping into the boat and firing up the motor. Within a moment they were bouncing out to sea.

*

Manos observed his daughter from a distance, through squinted eyes. He'd never seen her look as happy as she did now, with Nikki, here on the island. He'd never seen Nikki so content, either. He could feel his heart singing. He looked at the envelope in his hand through the soft sheen that made his eyes glisten and blurred his focus. He had been under strict instruction from Sophia not to give Ariana the letter until she had decided to stay. He placed the note with Ariana's name on it on the side of the bar, next to the envelope with Soph's name, a sense of pride bursting in his chest. He sucked through his teeth, poured a small glass of ouzo and sat on the lounger on the beach, yawning, the early start and the excitement of the day already catching up with him, and it wasn't past 10am. People wouldn't start arriving for the party for at least a couple of hours; there was nothing to hurry for; everything would work out just fine. His eyes closed of their own volition and within a short time the rumble through his nose carried across the west-cove, competing more than adequately with the low hush of the waves lapping at the shore.

*

Soph pulled herself up onto the rocks and lifted the mask from her face, her eyes alight, her smile all-consuming. 'Did you see that there must have been thousands of fish,' she babbled.

Gianna gazed affectionately, in spite of the slight exaggeration. She didn't care. Soph was enjoying her birthday, and she was enjoying Soph. She closed the gap, her lips redirecting Soph's thrill to the sensual touch.

Soph could feel the sense of urgency rising within her, the tingling on her lips, Gianna's breath, her body touching. She traced her fingers the length of Gianna's strong back, eliciting a moan that enticed her to kiss her harder and love her more completely.

Gianna pulled back, her breath stilled, her legs floundering under the profound passion that challenged her balance. She gazed into the deep-blue eyes, the diamond piercing in the nose; ruffled her fingers through Soph's wet, mousy-brown hair, her thumb tracing the line of her tanned cheeks and across her shapely rouged lips. 'Happy birthday,' she said with all the love in her heart. She pulled Soph into her arms and held her tightly, fighting the tears that threatened to expose the fear that lurked beneath. The intensity was too strong and the bittersweet tears fell onto her cheek, in spite of her efforts to hold them back, sliding and finding the broad smile that lit up her cheeks.

'Hey,' Soph said, pressing soft kisses to her damp cheeks. 'What's up?'

'I love you so much,' Gianna said.

'Hey,' Soph repeated, pulling her into a warm hug. 'I love you too,' she whispered, her lips tickling Gianna's ear to reinforce the message. 'I'm here to stay, I promise,' she whispered.

Gianna sniffed, the hot breath sensitising her skin. 'I know,' she said.

Soph fixed her gaze on the dark, shiny eyes and smiled reassuringly. Moving closer, she sealed her promise with a tender kiss, enjoying the mutual sense of openness that bound them in the moment. Slowly easing out of the kiss, 'Want to jump?' she asked, with a crafty smile.

Gianna's lips curled. 'As long as you're not going to freak out again,' she replied, her eyes smiling excitely.

Soph chuckled and started to climb, Gianna right behind her. Standing on the bottom ledge together, Gianna counted to three, and they jumped, their delighted squeals lost on the hush of the waves against the rocks.

*

Nikki lay back in the boat, not caring whether the fish bit or not, watching Ariana intently. The way Ariana studied her hands as she hooked the bait, the way she carefully cast the line, the subtle shift in the tightening of the thigh muscles as she moved, the look of concentration that narrowed her eyes a fraction and had her biting down on her lip. The heart-warming smile on Nikki's face wouldn't budge, tickling her chest until she released a chuckle.

'What?' Ariana asked, suddenly aware Nikki had been staring at her.

'Nothing,' Nikki responded, sitting up, the boat rocking gently with the easy movement. She gave a cursory glance towards the float bobbing on the water, before fixing her gaze back on Ariana. She couldn't prevent another chuckle, at the intensity of concentration on Ariana's face as she studied the water. She reached across, swept Ariana's hair behind her ear, determined to distract her.

Ariana flicked her head away at the touch, a smile creeping onto her face. 'I'm fishing,' she said, mocking seriousness, trying to ignore the tingling sensation that the touch elicited.

Nikki shifted closer, abandoning her rod to the boat, ignoring the float at the end of the line that continued to dance in the shimmering water. Leaning towards Ariana's exposed neck, her mouth poised, Ariana's sweet scent teasing her senses, she could feel the small hairs against the surface of her lips. Her eyes closed, losing her to the subtle sensation, her hunger increasing with every second passing.

Ariana gasped.

Nikki groaned as her lips made full contact with the warm skin, Ariana leaning her neck into the kiss. She shifted to Ariana's earlobe, nipped, her warm whispers coaxing Ariana away from the float, the sea, the boat.

Ariana shivered, arousal drawing her in. She turned into Nikki's hazel eyes, the specks of dark-brown entrancing her, causing her mouth to dry. Nikki's mouth was on hers before she could release the gasp on the tip of her tongue and she fell back into the boat, Nikki pressed heavily on top of her. She had never known such hunger, such desire, or a need so compelling. She caressed tenderly, her tongue brushing lightly across Nikki's top lip, eliciting a groan from them both, and she could feel Nikki shudder at the delicate touch.

Nikki eased back, gazed at Ariana with a beaming smile, her eyes conveying the deep love she felt, a question held in the space between them. Her mouth opened as if she were about to voice that question, stopped by the whizzing, whistling sound of the reel on the fishing rod unwinding at a pace. She leapt up, grabbed at the rod. 'Ahhh!' she shouted, taking control of the reel, and starting to bring the fish closer to the boat.

Ariana jumped up, grabbed at the long pole and leaned over the boat, watching the water, positioning the net beneath the glistening silver fish squirming below the surface. Effortlessly, she lifted the large mullet into the boat, her eyes locking with Nikki's, beaming smiles on their faces. 'Damn,' she said with a sly grin, 'looks like I'm losing.'

Nikki laughed, unhooked the fish and threw it back into the water. 'No chance,' she said.

'What? That was tea,' Ariana complained, through the laughter, her admonishment lacking conviction.

'In kind, remember,' Nikki reminded Ariana, mischief written across her face. This was one bet she was determined to lose.

Ariana pulled Nikki swiftly into her arms, their mouths clashing clumsily with the fierce embrace, on the moving surface.

Nikki groaned, the subtle taste of iron blending with the salty sweet taste of Ariana on her lips. She eased back, her index finger seeking out the tiny bloody mark on Ariana's lip and tenderly kissing it better. Holding Ariana's gaze, her heart skipped a beat, and her throat tightened. The question on her tongue, hovering, the butterflies dancing in her stomach, hopeful, anxious.

'What?' Ariana said, her voice broken.

'I was wondering,' Nikki started, aware that her hands were now shaking and the words wouldn't come.

'What?' Ariana repeated, the sense that she was missing something bringing with it a wave of uncertainty.

'We've got fish in the freezer,' Nikki said, diverting her thoughts with a shrug, kicking herself for not speaking her mind and then regaining her composure. 'I could think of better ways to spend the morning,' she added, the tip of her tongue tracing her lips seductively.

'Take me home,' Ariana said.

Nikki pulled the rods into the boat and turned the engine. They sat in relative silence, bouncing across the water, gazing intently into each other's eyes, grinning, a light chuckle coming to the surface now and then.

22.

'Hey Nikki,' Soph shouted, diving for the ball and directing it over the net, as Nikki approached from the white house.

'Hey Soph, we'll be up for the next match,' Nikki said, beaming a smile at Gianna as she hit the ball back, high over the net, only to have Soph smash it to the ground.

'One, nil,' Soph said, with a sly grin.

'We're practising,' Gianna bleated, through uncontrollable laughter.

Nikki laughed with them. 'You got drinks?' she asked.

'Yep,' Soph said, diving for a smash Gianna had thrown at her, her body hitting the sand after the ball.

'One, one,' Gianna said, turning towards the service line with a seductive wiggle of her body.

Soph's eyes sparkled as she watched the woman she loved taking her position at the service line.

'Here,' Manos said, handing Nikki a beer, heading for the fire pit. 'I'll get this on the go,' he said, appearing a little more hurried than usual.

'Sure,' Nikki said, taking the bottle and heading for her apartment. 'A quick shower and I'll be back,' she said, not that anyone responded.

'She's in the water,' Manos added, his eyes directing Nikki's smiling gaze at the fishing boat glistening, moored behind the ferry.

'Thanks Pops,' she said.

By the time Nikki returned, Nikos and Maria stood chatting to Manos, and a couple of other locals at the bar and Ariana sat drinking a glass of wine on the driftwood bench. Nikki swallowed hard; Ariana looked stunning, even though she was only wearing white cotton shorts and t-shirt. Nikki approached the seat. 'I've got something for you,' she said, drawing Ariana's eyes.

Ariana's eyebrows rose, widening her eyes just a fraction, just enough to cause Nikki's pulse to race again.

'Come,' Nikki said, holding out her hand.

Ariana stood, took the offered hand and allowed Nikki to lead down to the water's edge. She stopped dead half-way up the jetty, her heart skipping a beat. Her eyes studied carefully from one point to the other, the Mediterranean-blue, so distinctive set against the white, and the word ARIANA, handwritten on the front of its bow. She clasped her hand to her mouth, her eyes filling as her mind registered the old fishing boat. 'This was,' she started, tears stopping the words.

'The original Sophia,' Nikki said, grinning broadly, a sheen forming on her own eyes.

'The boat we went out on as kids,' Ariana continued.

Nikki nodded, pride lighting up her eyes.

Ariana stepped closer, her shaking hand carefully tracing the letters of the name on the boat. 'You renamed it,' she said.

Nikki cleared her throat. 'It's yours,' she said, her voice still struggling, standing behind Ariana and observing her appreciation with pride. Ariana turned and stepped up to her, her breath warm against her face, her eyes revealing vulnerability, and love. Nikki swallowed hard.

Ariana stood facing the woman she loved, her words stolen by the strength of her emotions.

Nikki kissed away the tears from Ariana's cheeks and smiled. 'I'm glad you like it,' she said, her voice broken.

Ariana gazed, mouth slightly agape, pulled Nikki into her arms and held her there for what seemed like an eternity. 'I am so in love with you,' she whispered. She eased out of the embrace and smiled.

237

'We've got a match to play,' Nikki said with a warm smile, taking Ariana's hand and starting back towards the taverna.

Ariana squeezed the hand in hers before releasing it, adjusting to the sensations heating up her chest and exposing her deepest vulnerability, breathing deeply and enjoying the excitement that emerged. Her eyes scanned the court as they approached. 'Right birthday girl,' she announced, with a beaming grin aimed at her daughter. 'You ready for a beating?' she asked.

Soph rolled her eyes to Gianna and laughed. 'What do you reckon?' she asked her girlfriend.

'No chance,' Gianna said, her grin turning into a determined glare as she stood her ground on the volleyball court, facing Nikki on the other side of the net.

'Game on,' Nikki said, sticking out her tongue at Gianna, causing her concentration to falter as Ariana served the ball.

Gianna was slow, moving to receive, and the ball came up short over the net, Nikki putting it away effortlessly. 'That's cheating,' Gianna complained.

Nikki shrugged. 'Kefalas rules,' she said, holding back the hysterics that were bubbling in her chest, picking up the ball and passing it to Ariana.

With a glint in her eye, Ariana served again, launching the ball high into the sky.

Manos chuckled, one eye on the game, turning the meat on the spit over the fire pit, the crackling of fat and the spicy aroma filling the air around him. He wandered back into the bar and sipped at his drink, before collecting the marinated fish from the kitchen.

A loud cheer went up, Ariana and Nikki skipping in each other's arms around their side of the court, Soph bent double, her head shaking and Gianna complaining through the tears of laughter.

'Good game,' Nikki said, approaching the net, holding out her hand.

Soph shook it, and then her mum's. 'Brilliant,' she said. 'The best birthday ever,' she added, throwing her arms around Gianna and kissing her firmly, before leaving the court and falling into a heap on the sand.

Nikki disappeared.

Ariana lounged on the driftwood seat, enjoying the light breeze and the aroma emanating from the fire.

Nikki returned, lugging a wrapped box and plonked it on the sand next to Soph. 'Happy birthday,' she said, returning to the bar to collect the drinks.

Soph sat up, and studied the box with curiosity, ripped enthusiastically at the paper and revealed its contents. 'Wow!' she exclaimed. 'Proper diving gear.'

Gianna wrapped an arm around Soph's shoulder and squeezed. 'That's awesome,' she said. 'We can go diving.'

Soph tensed.

'Fish can't bite through that,' Gianna said, with a chuckle.

Soph relaxed her shoulders, opened the box and pulled out the wetsuit, and then studied the breathing apparatus with mute fascination.

Nikki sat next to Ariana and handed her glass of wine.

'That's very kind of you,' Ariana said, her eyes on her daughter.

Nikki shrugged. 'Gianna will enjoy teaching her to dive; she's good,' Nikki said, reassuringly.

Ariana cleared her throat. 'Good,' she said, settling back in the seat, sipping at the glass in her hand.

Manos wandered back from the bar, envelopes in hand. 'This is for you,' he said, handing the letter to Ariana. 'And this, young lady, is for you. Happy birthday,' he said, taking a pace to Soph and handing her the gift.

Ariana studied the envelope. Sophia's handwriting. Tentatively, she opened the seal and pulled out the letter.

Welcome home Ariana.

I am so happy you decided to stay here. I never doubted you would do anything else of course. I am truly sorry I had to include the conditions for your inheritance, but I needed to ensure you had sufficient time to reconnect with yourself and this beautiful place. I hope it didn't take too long! The decorating and fending for yourself rather than relying on Maria, I knew would give you that time. Laying my ashes under the roses was a little self-indulgent on my part, but I wanted you to see the beauty here, as I saw it. I am so proud of you my darling.

You need to know that I always believed in you Ariana, but I couldn't pressurise you into coming back here. If I had, I would have been doing to you what your mother, and I'm guessing your husband, have done to you over the years. I would have been removing from you the power of choice and forcing your hand, and that would never have worked in the long term. Maybe, I should have stepped in sooner with your mother, and if you believe that is so, I can only apologise. I fear if I had interfered though, it would have been for my own gains more than yours. I want you to know that I always loved you so dearly and I missed you until the day I passed from this world. But, you are here now, and here of your own volition, and that is what matters.

Nikki is a beautiful woman, and I know you will both be happy together. She may never tell you, but I can now. She has waited all these years for you. She never stopped loving you. She has a strong heart and has been of great support to me over the years. I have loved her like a granddaughter too. I will never be able to repay her for her kindness, but you have done that for me because I know you will never leave her. Not now, not ever again. She has always been as much a part of you as is this island. You all belong together.

Your mother was wrong Ariana. In so many ways, she has been wrong, but sadly, my hands were tied, and her yearning for money was far greater than her loyalty to her real family. She married for money and money will most likely kill her in the end. I feel sorry for her, but I could never change her. Money may have cost me my daughter, but it didn't cost me my granddaughter, and for that, I will rest in peace.

If you have not worked this out already, and I can safely assume that Teresa has never had the courage to tell you, then I should confirm that Manos is your father. I wanted you to know the truth, but your mother disagreed, and Manos was too in love with Teresa to go against her wishes, and too kind a gentleman to bring disgrace to our family. He loves you very much and always has done. I am sure you will have much to discuss over the coming years.

I am sorry to have never met Sophie, but I know she too will feel at home here. I feel it in my heart, and my heart has never let me down before. Of course, it will soon, and when it does my body will return to the earth, in the rose garden, but know that I will be watching over you all.

Your loving grandma, Sophia

With trembling hands, Ariana folded the letter and placed it back in the envelope, swallowing past the lump in her throat, her eyes wandering to the rose garden. She drew in a long breath and released it slowly.

'Everything okay?' Nikki asked, aware of the shift in Ariana's demeanour.

Ariana turned, her fingers reaching, tenderly stroking the line of Nikki's face, down to her chin, across her lips. 'Everything is just perfect,' she said, leaning towards her and planting a confirming kiss.

'Wow!' The exclamation claimed Nikki and Ariana's attention. Soph was reading the letter in her hand, one hand over her mouth, her eyes popping from her head. 'You can't be serious,' she said, her gaze shifting to her grandfather.

'Aye,' Manos responded, his cheeks glowing, his dimples showing even more than normal, and revealing more teeth than anyone realised he had. 'It's yours now,' he said.

Soph read and re-read the letter, Gianna glancing over her shoulder at the paper in her hand. Ariana shrugged, Nikki shrugged, neither having any idea what Pops had done.

Gianna squealed, as the information registered. Soph now owned Manos' share of the Kefalas business.

'I can't take this,' Soph insisted, holding out the piece of paper, trying to get Manos to retract the offer.

'Deal's done,' Manos said, casually. 'Of course, it's on the premise that I have a job for life,' he said, with a light-hearted shrug of his shoulders. 'Though there's no telling how long that might be,' he added.

Nikki groaned and rolled her eyes. Not that little chestnut again. 'You aren't going anywhere for a long time, Pops,' she said, with an admonishing smile.

Manos chuckled. 'Time to party then,' he said, raising his glass. 'Happy birthday to you,' he started to sing, much to Soph's embarrassment.

Voices from the bar joined in the song, ending in a resounding cheer.

'Food's nearly ready,' Manos said.

Soph stepped up to the fire-pit. 'Thank you,' she said, pulling Manos into her arms.

Manos held her tightly, allowing the tears to trickle freely onto his white stubbly face. Every day was a good day, but today was definitely the best day.

Ariana reached for Nikki's hand and squeezed, leaned into her arm, and watched her daughter. 'Want to go fishing?' she whispered, releasing the arm, her eyes shifting from the silver-white sheen lingering over the rose garden to the rocks below the white house and then to The Ariana moored to the jetty.

Nikki followed Ariana's gaze and smiled. She drew her eyes back to the woman by her side, sensing the energy shift inside her with the thought that needed to be voiced. She could feel the tension reaching her throat, the anxiety starting to churn in her stomach. Her eyes must have reflected her hesitation because Ariana was looking at her with a puzzled expression. 'I...' she started.

Ariana shrugged, with an encouraging and slightly quizzical smile.

Nikki could feel the weight of the words on her tongue stopping her mouth from moving. Ariana looked so gorgeous, so enticing; so perfect. She was smiling so sweetly, so earnestly. Blowing out a deep breath, she committed to speak, unaware of at what point her eyes had closed as the words flowed. She had to go through with it. 'Will you marry me?' she almost blurted, her eyes full of concern as she waited for Ariana's response.

Ariana froze, faltered, and then released a deep breath.

'I'm sorry, I shouldn't...' Nikki started to babble, to backtrack, her heart racing, her eyes flitting. She'd got it wrong.

Ariana pressed a finger to Nikki's lips to quiet her, studied her skittish eyes until they settled on hers again, and when they did the smile on her lips answered the question before the word appeared. 'Yes,' she said.

Nikki stood, staring, momentarily stunned, needing to adjust, the excitement inside her slowly building from a trickle into a torrent. Her eyes widened, shining brightly with the broad grin that appeared. 'Yessssss,' she screamed, thumping a fist into the air, drawing pairs of eyes.

Ariana laughed at the animated response, reached across and cupped Nikki's happy face. 'I love you,' she said, pulling her close and drowning her in soft kisses.

'I love you,' Nikki responded.

'Fishing?' Ariana asked.

'Double or quits?' Nikki responded, with a tantalising grin.

'Deal.' Ariana chuckled.

About Emma Nichols

Emma Nichols lives in Buckinghamshire with her partner and two children. She served for 12 years in the British Army, studied Psychology, and published several non-fiction books under another name, before dipping her toes into the world of lesbian fiction.

You can contact Emma through her website and social media:

www.emmanicholsauthor.com
www.facebook.com/EmmaNicholsAuthor
www.twitter.com/ENichols_Author

And do please leave a review if you enjoyed this book. Reviews really help independent authors to promote their work. Thank you.

Other Books by Emma Nichols

Visit **getbook.at/TheVincentiSeries** to discover The Vincenti Series: Finding You, Remember Us and The Hangover.

Visit **getbook.at/ForbiddenBook** to start reading **Forbidden**.

Thanks for reading and supporting!

28799051R00143

Printed in Poland
by Amazon Fulfillment
Poland Sp. z o.o., Wrocław